“Sabine ar

although h ... t overly confident.

She opted not to share the details of her morning lest he be worried about them more.

“Just keep your head down, please.” Marcel took a step toward her, closing the gap between them until they were standing toe to toe.

The two stood eyeing each other intently. Alexis smiled. “You be careful, please,” she said, her voice a low whisper.

Marcel took a deep breath and held it. He stared, his eyes skating back and forth across her face. He looked deep into her eyes and held the gaze, wishing things were different for them. He slowly eased an arm around her waist, inching himself closer to her. When she didn’t resist, he drew her against him, feeling her body settle warmly against his own. His eyes danced along the line of her profile and then he felt his heart sync with hers. It skipped one beat and then a second, and then every muscle in his body tightened as he captured her lips beneath his own.

Dear Reader,

The Martins of Louisiana are back with another adventure! The daughters of Claudia and Josiah Martin love to keep you on the edge of your seat! Book two of the series is daughter Alexis's story. Alexis is a hard cookie to crack, and no one knows that better than FBI special agent Marcel Broussard.

Alexis and Marcel have history and Marcel didn't leave their relationship on good terms. In fact, when he disappeared from her life, he didn't bother to say goodbye or explain himself. So, when he comes crawling back to make amends, Alexis isn't interested in being bothered.

But Marcel needs Alexis. He has secrets and only she can help him solve his case and bring down the head of a criminal operation who has mastered hiding behind his religion to get his own way. Will Alexis have enough faith in Marcel to help him? You'll have to read the book to find out!

As the story came together, I was reminded how much I adore the Martin family. They have been one of my favorite families to ever write. Getting to know them and the bonds they share has been a thrill. I'm excited to share their story with you and hope you'll enjoy them as much as I do!

Thank you so much for your support. I am always humbled by all the love you keep showing me, my characters and our stories. I know that none of this would be possible without you.

Until the next time, please take care and may God's blessings be with you always.

With much love,

Deborah Fletcher Mello

www.deborahmello.blogspot.com

AN INNOCENT HOSTAGE

DEBORAH FLETCHER MELLO

Recycling programs for this product may not exist in your area.

ISBN-13: 978-1-335-47162-8

An Innocent Hostage

For questions and comments about the quality of this book, please contact us at CustomerService@Harlequin.com.

Harlequin Enterprises ULC
22 Adelaide St. West, 41st Floor
Toronto, Ontario M5H 4E3, Canada
www.Harlequin.com

Printed in Lithuania

A true Renaissance woman, **Deborah Fletcher Mello** finds joy in crafting unique storylines and memorable characters. She's received accolades from several publications, including *Publishers Weekly*, *Library Journal* and *RT Book Reviews*. Born and raised in Connecticut, Deborah now considers home to be wherever the moment moves her.

Books by Deborah Fletcher Mello

Harlequin Romantic Suspense

The Sorority Detectives

Playing with Danger
An Innocent Hostage

The Coltons of Colorado

Colton's Secret Sabotage

The Coltons of New York

Chasing a Colton Killer

The Coltons of Owl Creek

Colton's Blizzard Hideout

To Serve and Seduce

Seduced by the Badge
Tempted by the Badge
Reunited by the Badge
Stalked by Secrets
In the Arms of the Law

Visit the Author Profile page at Harlequin.com for more titles.

To Micaela's Papa,

I miss you, Daddy!

Chapter 1

The noise was loud, vibrating from one end of the street to the other. *POP! POP! POP! BOOM!* What sounded like gunfire sent Alexis Martin ducking for cover. She had just left the Walgreens Pharmacy, crossing the street at the corner of St. Claude and Elysian Fields avenues. She had been standing outside the Baldwin and Company bookstore when the harsh bang sounded sharply, startling her out of her Stuart Weitzman stiletto heels. She tripped, falling headfirst through the bookstore's doorway. From the corner of her eye, she caught a quick glimpse of an old Ford Crown Vic driving past. She landed with a loud thud on the hardwood floor as the front door slammed closed behind her. The noise pulled the attention of the other patrons inside, everyone seeming to turn to stare.

Alexis cursed; the words muttered softly so not to be heard. She pulled herself upright, brushing her hands across her knees and down the length of her denim jeans. She took a deep breath to calm her nerves. A salesclerk suddenly came from behind the counter and hurried to her side.

"Are you okay?" he asked. "Did you hurt yourself?"

Alexis turned to meet the concerned gaze. He was young. Still more boy than man and he had a warm umber complexion that was as clear as polished glass. His lengthy lashes flattered his dark eyes. The subtle hint of a sensual, musky body spray wafted off his dark skin and Alexis was suddenly aware of his large hand pressed gently against the small of her spine, meant to help her steady herself.

Not fond of being touched, Alexis took a sidestep away from him, moving out of his reach. She pretended to brush more dirt from her pants and top. She nodded her head, no words easing past her thin lips. Her pride was more bruised than her body. She took another deep breath.

The young man continued rambling, seemingly oblivious to the embarrassment that had shaded Alexis's cheeks a deep red. "That kid really needs to get that muffler fixed. It sounds like a machine gun every time he drives by. Scared me to death the other day when I was locking up the store. Thought I was about to be a statistic in a drive-by shooting." His hand settled down against his side, his eyes narrowing ever so slightly. "Are you sure you're okay, Ms. Martin?"

Alexis cringed. Being recognized only served to raise her blood pressure ten degrees. She knew that most of her family would know what had happened before she made it back to her office. She hated the notoriety that had followed her and her siblings since birth. Being the offspring of Claudia and Josiah Martin had shone a spotlight on them for as long as she could remember. "I'm fine. Really," she muttered. "Thank you for your concern."

"Did you break your heel?" he questioned, staring down to her shoes. "Maybe you should consider wearing flats. My grandmother had to give up her high heels after she broke her hip falling. I'd hate for you to break something."

Alexis took a deep breath. "Nothing's broken. I assure you, I really am just fine."

"I could get you some water," he said.

His persistence was beginning to wear on her already-fragile nerves. Alexis was past ready for the attention to be turned toward someone or something else. "That's not necessary," she said. "I just need to pick up my book order and be on my way. I have a meeting in a few minutes that I need to get to."

The young man smiled. "Yes, ma'am. It's all ready for you." He moved back to the counter.

Ma'am. Now, not only did she feel clumsy, but he had somehow managed to add *old* to her emotional checklist without blinking an eye. Between falling on her face, his comment about giving up her heels for his grandmother's flats, and calling her *ma'am*, he had aged her fifty years in a few short minutes, and she was beginning to feel some kind of way.

She tossed a quick glance around the room, noting that most patrons had already gone back to their own business and weren't paying her an ounce of attention. Alexis bent back down to adjust the strap on her shoe. She stood upright, lifted her chin and pulled her shoulders back. Minutes later, with a shopping bag of newly purchased books in hand, Alexis headed out the door and back to her car.

As she opened the driver's-side door, that old Crown Vic passed again, headed in the opposite direction. This time when the muffler backfired, the driver gunning the engine as he took off from the light, she only jumped slightly. Admittedly, she was skittish and more so than most. Childhood trauma had done that to her; the official diagnosis,

PTSD—post traumatic stress disorder. She rarely thought about that time in her life, determined to leave the past in the past. But every so often something would trigger a flashback and leave her dropping to the floor.

She took another deep breath. It was then that she saw a man across the street staring at her. He was staring so intently that she paused to stare back. He seemed familiar to her, but recognition was slow to come. Between the oversized hoody he wore, the blue medical mask and his ill-fitting clothes, he could have been anyone she'd passed by in her daily travels. But there was something about him that suddenly had her heart racing. Something she couldn't put into words, but it frightened her.

She quickly realized it was not her first time seeing that man. Nor was it the first time that he had been so near to her. It dawned on her that, days earlier, he'd brushed against her at the grocery store as he'd hurried past. His head had been down, that same hoody hiding his face. He hadn't bothered to look back at her, let alone apologize. She'd dismissed the encounter, thinking it an accident and him rude. And now he was there, watching her as she watched him.

With one hand holding her car door and the other wrapped tightly around the grip of the SIG Sauer P238 micro pistol in her purse, she was prepared if the stranger decided to play stupid. But he turned instead, hurrying swiftly down the street and around the corner.

Alexis hadn't realized she was holding her breath until she exhaled an audible sigh of relief. She was also shaking, her muscles quivering of their own accord. She inhaled again, sucking air deep into her lungs to stall the wave of anxiety that painted her expression a dark shade of unhappy. Sliding into the driver's seat of her Tesla, she engaged the car's door locks then started the engine. She had questions; starting with who that man was and why was he following her. Or was she making something out of nothing, their chance encounters simple happenstance? His stare had felt personal, but was it? Or was her imagination working overtime for no reason? With no real answers, Alexis inhaled deeply, determined to shake the thoughts from her mind.

She stole a quick glance at the digital clock on the dashboard. She was late getting back to the office and knew she would hear it from her mother the minute she walked through the door. Not because she was late, but because she hadn't bothered to call to check in and let them know her whereabouts.

Alexis was the third child in the family. Like her sisters, she'd been coddled and spoiled since her birth. As an adolescent, there had been some trouble. Trouble she still struggled daily to forget. That bad business had changed the entire trajectory of her life. Of all their lives, even if her family tried to pretend otherwise. Since then, her daily existence had become a prison of sorts. More times than not she was fearful of her own shadow. She continually second-guessed herself. And most men petrified her.

She'd been made to grow up too fast. The coddling and spoiling were mere memories replaced by stifling fear. She was forever looking over her shoulder and waiting for the shoe to drop, kicking her straight back into hell. Now, if she made it through a day without a meltdown, things were good. Working kept her standing. Working closely with people she trusted had been life-changing. Working for family definitely had its perks and privileges, but it also came with its own unique brand of challenges.

A private investigator for a local detective agency, Alexis worked for her mother, Claudia Martin. Hands down, working for Claudia was its *own* unique challenge, and Alexis, along with her three sisters, Lenore, Celeste and Sophie, had been working for their mother since the inception of the business. From the start, it had been a learning experience, each case its own lesson. As the boss of her business, Claudia Martin was not a woman to be played with, and Alexis knew her mother would not be happy with her. She swore under her breath again and pulled out of the parking lot into a line of traffic. But even as she headed toward the offices of the Sorority Row Detective Agency, memories of that man in the hoodie were still haunting her.

Marcel Broussard sprinted around the corner, panting as if he'd just run a marathon. His heart was racing and it took him a moment to finally slow his pace and not look like he was being chased by something. He hadn't been prepared and everything about that wasn't sitting well with his spirit. What would he have done if Alexis had recognized him? If she had called out his name while rushing in his direction? He sighed, gasping for air to catch his breath. Truth be told, he had wanted her to discover his identity, to rush forward to wrap him in a hug, or maybe even slap his face. He would have deserved that slap, the two not parting on good terms the last time they'd seen each other. But he missed her, and he hadn't realized just how much until that moment when Alexis stood across the street staring at him.

Marcel released another heavy sigh, slowly moving in

the direction of his parked car. He was short on borrowed time and he still had a lengthy list of things to do. Trailing after Alexis Martin had been a side trip of his own making; a necessary diversion as he tried to figure out his next steps. If he'd been discovered, years of work would have been thrown away and the lives of those he loved most would have been at risk. But he believed Alexis could be the answer to the prayers he whispered daily.

Marcel could feel his heart pounding in his chest. He was running out of time. He knew he couldn't keep following Alexis without announcing his return. Each random encounter put him, and her, at risk. But how could he just insert himself back into her life? How would he explain all that had happened since he'd disappeared and hope that she would want to trust him again?

But for the grace of God, he thought. Because his faith in a higher power was all that kept him fighting for what was right and standing on the foundation of everything he had ever believed. He leaned his forehead against the steering wheel, closing his eyes. Whispering a prayer skyward, he asked for guidance, hopeful that God would soon show him a sign. Praying that God would put Alexis on the path to forgive him.

He and Alexis had dated for almost three years, their relationship feeling like everything a man could have ever wanted. He'd been fully invested and believed what they'd shared would last them a lifetime. Alexis had been fragile at first, sensitive to anything that didn't fit into the comfort of the walls she'd built around herself. When she'd allowed him past those locked thresholds, shining a spotlight on her vulnerability, he hadn't taken that lightly. She'd given him her heart, trusting him to cherish it with everything he held near and dear. And then…well…then he'd broken it. Shattering her heart, and his own.

There was no walking that back. No apology that could make things well again. No explanation that would ever make what he'd done okay. He deserved to have his face slapped. He would understand if she unleashed a tirade of hurt against him. He couldn't blame her if she wanted nothing to do with him ever again. But he needed her. He needed Alexis to allow him back into her life. He needed her help. His need for her was one of sheer desperation. Desperation because his daughter's life depended on her.

Chapter 2

"I'm sorry," Alexis said as she hurried into the conference room of the Sorority offices.

The Martin women were all seated around the table, halting their conversation as Alexis had rushed into the room. Heads turned as everyone's gaze settled on her.

Alexis cut an eye toward her mother before resting her stare on Lenore, the eldest of the four sisters. The two siblings locked eyes, seeming to have a silent conversation that only they were privy to.

"What took you so long?" Lenore finally said, a wide smile pulling across her face. Lenore nudged Sophie. "Getting yourself some afternoon delight?"

"Wouldn't you like to know?" Alexis muttered as she dropped into the cushioned executive's chair.

"I would!" Sophie said. "I'm not getting any lately. I've got to live vicariously through the rest of you. Even Mom's getting more that I am!"

"Stay out of my sex life," Claudia snapped, the slightest smirk on her face. Her eyes narrowed on Alexis as she studied her daughter intently. "Is everything okay, Alexis?"

"Everything's fine," Alexis said softly. "I stopped by the bookstore to pick up some books and got stuck in traffic. I apologize if I held up the meeting."

Claudia continued to stare. She finally sat back in her seat and spoke. "You didn't. We start on time around here. With or without you." The matriarch nodded her head at her second-born child. "Celeste, continue, please."

Celeste tossed Alexis an easy smile then turned back to the stack of files in front of her. "We closed out six cases last week. Sophie, I think you're scheduled to meet with a perspective client later this week?"

"I am," Sophie said. "The client is being recruited by the New Orleans Rogues. He thinks he's being blackmailed, which could jeopardize his chance to be their next quarterback."

"Football! Interesting," Lenore muttered.

Claudia slanted a glance in her direction, annoyance seeping from her eyes. She shifted her gaze back to Sophie. "He thinks? He's not sure?" Claudia questioned.

Sophie shrugged. "That's all I got from his agent. I'll know more when I meet with him."

Claudia shook her head as she gestured for Celeste to continue.

Celeste shuffled through her files, shifting a stack off to the side of the table. "Correct me if I'm wrong," she said, "but I believe Lenore has cleared her caseload so she can go on vacation with that man of hers for a few days."

Lenore nodded. "That would be correct. I only have one open case and Alexis is taking that over for me. It shouldn't take long. The wife suspects her husband is cheating. He's the pastor of some church and spends most of his time ministering to his female congregation. Her attorney hired us. They want proof before she files the paperwork for their divorce."

Alexis could feel her mother's eyes boring into her. Sorority Row Detective Agency had been born out of community need. Claudia, a former cotillion debutante and fashion model turned wife and mother, had constantly navigated unknown territory to help family and friends resolve their problems. Problems that always seemed to drop in her lap by way of their father, her ex-husband, Josiah Martin.

Having been married to a known drug kingpin in the streets of New Orleans had put the matriarch in a unique position to seek out answers where others feared to tread. It had also afforded her the opportunity to keep eyes on her husband, his philandering ways eventually leading to their separation and divorce. Many of their clients had history with the family that didn't need to be explained when they came calling. It was why their mother was so invested in quick resolutions and happy clients. Most thought her mother angelic. She was highly regarded in the community, but she could also be vicious. People bent over backward to stay on her good side. Most especially her daughters.

Alexis took a deep breath. "I've reviewed the file, but I haven't put a team on him yet."

"What are you waiting for?" Claudia questioned.

"Nothing," Alexis quipped. "I'm on it."

A blanket of silence seemed to swell full and thick around them. There was no missing the angst in Alexis's tone. Her voice had cracked and a wave of perspiration suddenly beaded across her skin. Her lashes fluttered, batting back tears that had risen with a vengeance.

"Clearly," the matriarch said softly, "you're not okay. Something's wrong. You're not focused, your duties are slacking, and you look miserable. Tell me how we can help."

Alexis took a deep breath before answering. "I'm fine. And my duties are not slacking. I can tell you that Reverend Marshall spends two nights per week down at the rec center watching the boys play hockey. His attention is usually focused on one young man in particular. The boy's name is Maxim and Maxim is twelve years old. There is a very strong resemblance between the two. I need to do a little more digging for information, but just watching, I think Maxim might be Reverend Marshall's son. Thus far, though, all he does is watch and then he leaves. He's never approached the child or spoken to him. That may be what he's hiding."

"How long have he and his wife been married?" Celeste questioned.

"Ten years and they have no children. The First Lady hasn't been able to conceive," Alexis answered.

"Sounds like this is going to get messy," Lenore muttered. "It may not be as cut-and-dry as I initially thought."

Alexis shrugged. She folded her arms over her chest and leaned back in her chair. "Either way, I should be able to close the case by next week. Cash is doing some digging for me on the kid," she said, referring to Cash Davies, the agency's resident tech guru and a close family friend. A vital part of the agency, there was nothing Cash couldn't find if they needed it. Even if it was sometimes illegal for her to do so.

Claudia nodded. "Update me before you finish your report. We may have to handle how we tell the wife a bit differently."

"We're assuming she doesn't already know," Celeste

said. "Is it possible it's more about his relationship with the boy's mother and not the boy?"

"I've never seen his mother at practice," Alexis said. "There's an older gentleman who brings him and picks him up. I think he might be the grandfather. But from everything I know thus far, I don't think the First Lady has any idea her husband might have a child."

Claudia rose from her seat. "Keep me posted. Celeste, come see me before you leave for the day please." She paused, her gaze narrowing on her daughter. "Find me if you want to talk, Alexis."

"I'm fine, Mom. Really. Everything is okay."

Claudia took a deep breath. As she hesitated, the room seemed to fill with a wave of unbridled discord painting the walls a dark shade of unhappy. No one spoke; the women waiting for their mother to respond or Alexis to break. Alexis cleared her throat but said nothing more. Claudia headed for the door. "It's your lie, baby girl. Tell it any way you need to," she said as she moved out of the room.

When the door was closed, the air shifted, an electrical current of concern detonating like fireworks on the Fourth of July.

"So, now tell us what's going on," Lenore said. She was the eldest daughter, more maternal than sisterly when necessary. Rising from her seat, she stepped over to the glass wall that looked out into the office reception area. She shuttered the blinds before returning to her seat."

"How'd you hurt your hand?" Sophie questioned, pointing to the black-and-blue bruise that had risen along the outer edge of Alexis's right appendage.

"And there's a tear in your jeans," Celeste added. Her gaze narrowed. "And they look a lot like *my* jeans."

Alexis shook her head. "I tripped and fell. It was an accident."

"You just tripped and fell?" Lenore eyed her with a raised brow, concern furrowing her brow.

"Yes, I just tripped and fell. Don't make it something it's not," Alexis said softly.

"Okay, I won't."

"But I will," Sophie said. The youngest of the four girls, Sophie was not known to bite her tongue and hold back her opinions. She was notorious for causing scenes and spilling tea when it wasn't expected. She could be brash and unfiltered, and their mother was constantly admonishing her to distinguish when to speak and when to listen. "You can lie to Mom and anyone else, but we tell each other the truth. So, spill it!"

Alexis sighed. Settling back against her seat, she recounted the events of the morning. Her sisters listened, no one saying anything until she mentioned the stranger who had left her unsettled.

"Did he approach you?"

Alexis shook her head as her sisters began to pepper her with questions.

"But you've seen him before?" Lenore asked.

Alexis nodded. "Once that I'm certain of. Another time that's questionable. I thought someone was there but then they weren't."

"We need to pull the footage on your dash cam," Celeste started. She tapped a message into her cell phone and pushed the send button. Almost immediately, it beeped in response. "Cash is on it," she said.

"Do *not* tell Mom," Alexis implored. "I don't need a security detail following me everywhere I go, and you know she'll have them posted outside my door."

"It might not be a bad idea," Lenore noted, her eyes darting back and forth. "At least until we're certain there's no threat we need to be concerned about."

"I don't think there's any threat," Alexis said.

"But this person made you nervous," Celeste countered.

"And it looks like he might be stalking you," Sophie added.

"A security detail is starting to sound pretty reasonable," Lenore concluded.

"Because they won't be following you," Alexis muttered. She shot each of the trio an icy glare.

Sophie giggled. "Do you really want us to believe that you wouldn't feel better having someone there just in case?"

"Have I ever cared about what you believe?" Alexis snapped.

"Oh, you care, but for some reason you've decided to not be a team player all of a sudden."

Alexis threw up her hands. "Does anyone else find it weird that we're all supposed to be some warm and fuzzy musketeer gang?"

Lenore shook her head. "We're sisters and we do warm and fuzzy because Mom says we do."

"It is kind of weird," Celeste said, nodding in agreement.

"I like us," Sophie said. "What's wrong with warm and fuzzy?"

They all laughed, even Alexis, despite the angst that

seemingly plagued her. She took a deep breath. "I was scared. Really scared," she said finally. "I don't like feeling scared all the time."

"Has it gotten worse lately?" Celeste questioned.

Alexis shrugged. "I've just been feeling off kilter and I don't know why."

"When's the last time you spoke to Dr. Mayfield?" Lenore asked. Dr. Mariah Mayfield was the psychiatrist their parents kept on call if ever the women needed to vent.

"I'm still seeing her weekly," Alexis whispered, feeling embarrassed. Color had risen to her cheeks, her face heated.

Celeste shrugged. "Well, that makes two of us."

"Three of us," Lenore said.

"Brilliant minds think alike," Sophie said. "Sounds like we're four for four."

They all laughed again.

"What do you want us to tell Mom when she asks?" Lenore queried.

Alexis shook her head from side to side. "Whatever you do, please don't tell her the truth. I'll never hear the end of it."

"Only if you let us call Daddy and get one of his guys to keep an eye on you. Just to be safe."

Alexis hesitated. There was a calmness in her tone when she finally spoke. "Even if I say no, you're going to do it anyway, aren't you?"

Lenore smiled.

"See, there's the warm and fuzzy!" Sophie chimed. "This is what we Martin women do best!"

"Because clearly you do not work!" Claudia bellowed

as she came back into the room. "Is there a holiday no one told me about? Have all our cases been cleared?"

Her daughters jumped, their laughter like a warm breeze billowing through the air. As they walked out of the conference room toward their offices, Claudia pressed a dry kiss to each of their cheeks. When Alexis reached her mother's side, Claudia wrapped her arms tightly around her child's shoulders and held her close.

He was tall. Alexis reasoned that if she stood beside him, the top of her head might come to his shoulder. And only if she were wearing heels. A paper mask covered his face and dark shades hid his eyes from view. She had spotted him parked outside the restaurant where she'd gone for lunch. Although she suspected he'd probably been following her since she'd left her apartment, she was only certain that he'd pulled his van behind her Tesla after she'd stopped for lunch at Chef D'z Café on Basin Street.

Chef D'z was one of her favorite haunts. It was one place Alexis still frequented like clockwork, never changing her routine despite promising herself that she would. And she always ordered the same meal: the cheese-stuffed ravioli tossed with a pesto cream seafood sauce of shrimp, crawfish, crabmeat and lobster. The dish was then topped with fried catfish and a soft-shell crab. It was a whole other level of comfort food that Alexis often craved.

From the Basin Street location, Alexis headed to the T.J. Maxx department store on South Claiborne Avenue. It was a quick six-minute drive and the white-paneled van had followed, the driver not even trying to go unnoticed. Inside the department store she'd kept an eye on the entrance, noting when the man exited his vehicle and followed her. He wore the same clothes he'd been in the day before and the day before that. His hood was again pulled up over his head and he wore a mask and those dark sunshades. He'd stood tall, slowly assessing the landscape. Shifting the shades off his face, his eyes darted back and forth until he'd spied her in the shoe aisle, then he pushed the lens back up over his nose. Now he loitered near the entrance, his gaze still following her.

She moved slowly through the store and pretended to look through a rack of summer dresses, considering her options. Her sisters didn't have anyone tailing her yet, so there was no security standing nearby. Since he had never approached her, or made like he meant to do her harm, she could ignore him. Or she could put an end to this once and for all and confront him in a very public place, demanding that he explain himself. Deciding on the latter, Alexis checked for the sidearm beneath her suit jacket and headed in the man's direction.

Marcel had thought himself prepared for this moment but as Alexis headed toward him, resolve hardening her expression, he found his confidence wavering. He really didn't know what to expect and suddenly he felt as if he might vomit from the anxiety.

As she got closer, Marcel could see the determination in her eyes. He took a deep breath, inhaling swiftly until his lungs were full. His head dropped slightly as he slid his sunshades from his eyes and lowered the paper mask that covered his face. Sliding the hoodie off his head, he pulled himself up straight and tall. He fixed his gaze on her face and held it. As he did, Alexis came to an abrupt halt. Her eyes widened and she began to shake like a tidal wave had flooded through her.

Marcel smiled sheepishly. He greeted her warmly, his voice a loud whisper. "Hello, Alexis."

Alexis stood still, staring as if she'd seen a ghost. He watched as she tried to whisper his name, but no sound escaped past her lips. She blinked, still seeming uncertain she was seeing him clearly, and then she whispered his name a second time. "Marcel?"

"I didn't mean to frighten you," he said. "I just needed to talk. I need your help." His words came fast; his speech so hurried that the words seemed to run together. "If we could go somewhere to talk, I promise not to take up too much of your time."

"You *promise*?" Alexis spat the question with venom, her cheeks turning a deep shade of red. Heat washed over her expression.

Marcel reached his hand out as if to touch her and she recoiled, taking a step back to widen the distance between them.

"I need to apologize and explain…" he started. "It's not what you think…"

But before he could finish his comment, Alexis brushed past him and out the door.

Chapter 3

Marcel swore, loudly, and with such fury, it drew the attention of strangers who eyed him warily. He was a man who rarely resorted to profanity to express himself, but it seemed fitting at the moment. Racing after Alexis, he knew he'd made a huge mistake and there might not be any way for him to come back from it.

She hadn't been happy to see him. In fact, the look she'd given him was on a level of hostility that he couldn't begin to comprehend. Rage had carried her past him and out the door and, as she'd jumped into her car, speeding out of the parking lot, that rage had lingered heavily in the warm air. It was unsettling and now he stood foolishly staring after her, wishing he'd had more time to think things through. But time was not his friend and he was quickly running out of the little scraps he had left. Still uncertain about what his next steps should be, he sighed then hurried off to his own vehicle.

One traffic light and two quick turns put Alexis in front of the Sorority Detective Agency building on Dorgenois Street. She pulled her car into her assigned parking space and shut down the engine. She leaned forward, pressing her forehead against the steering wheel. Her eyes were closed tightly as she struggled not to cry.

Marcel Broussard.

Beautiful, sexy, Marcel Broussard. He was still as handsome as when they'd first met. Not quite as polished or dressed as pretty, but there was no missing his good looks. Marcel had been blessed with skin the color of a shiny new copper penny and natural blond, sun-kissed hair twisted in lengthy dreadlocks that he'd pulled into a ponytail down his back. Since she'd last seen him, he'd grown facial hair; a goatee and the hint of a mustache. He actually looked like the naturalist, living an organic lifestyle, that he'd always professed himself to be. Tall and lean, Marcel's rugged good looks belied his thirty-five years. And those piercing bright blue eyes that had always left her wanting still managed to have an effect on her.

Alexis hadn't believed it possible to love anyone as much as she had loved Marcel Broussard. They'd met by chance at one of her mother's philanthropic extravaganzas. She'd gone reluctantly, ordered there by the matriarch. Adorned from head to toe in Alexander McQueen, the heel on her strappy harness sandal had rolled like a marble. Marcel had been standing close enough to reach out and stop her from falling to the floor. Clutching her elbow, he'd held on to her for most of the night, blessing her with the brightest smile and his quick wit. And she hadn't been repulsed by his touch.

Despite thinking the night would be tortuous, Marcel's presence had made it the best night of her life. They'd followed the black-tie event with a late-night meal of cheese omelets and turkey bacon. They had been inseparable from that moment forward. For three years, he'd been the lifeline to possibilities she had never imagined for herself.

And Marcel had loved her back. Or so she'd thought. She'd believed him when he'd whispered the words against the arch of her neck, sealing them with his kisses. She'd grown to trust him with her secrets. She couldn't have imagined any man becoming as important to her. And her entire family had adored him. Even her father had found him worthy. Alexis had thought them and their relationship perfect before Marcel had betrayed her and broken her heart.

It had been the third of September, three years ago, when he'd walked out of her home and disappeared. He hadn't said goodbye, just kissed her on the cheek and whispered *See you later* into her ear. *Later* had come and gone, and it was as if he'd vanished off the face of the earth. His apartment had been emptied out and there had been no paper trail to lead her to him. Alexis had used every resource at her disposal. She'd even deferred to her father, Josiah Martin, asking for his help.

Like her mother, Josiah was legendary in the New Orleans community. He had controlled every illegal operation in the city from drugs to prostitution. While he'd done that, her mother'd had them hobnobbing with the city's elite, running in all the right circles. Alexis knew that her father had three, maybe even four, former presidents on speed dial. But he was also as cutthroat as they came, and in the city's streets, he was still the law. With her father's help, Alexis had called in every favor she could to help find Marcel, hitting one dead end and then another and another.

She'd finally had to give up the search. Marcel hadn't

wanted to be found and she didn't know why. But giving up didn't stop her from holding out hope that she'd find him alive and well. Or that when he was found, he would still love her and she could go back to loving him. Until the day came when Alexis had finally let hope go, too.

Now, Alexis couldn't fathom what Marcel being back could mean. He'd returned like he hadn't just up and disappeared from her life without so much as a goodbye. Like he hadn't professed his love and adoration before ghosting her. After promising her forever. She couldn't begin to process why now and not before, or even why at all. And why had he been following her? Why was his appearance so disheveled, practically making him unrecognizable? What game was he playing? And after breaking her heart, why would he want to bring her any more hurt?

It had begun to sprinkle, the hint of an afternoon rain bearing down on the day. Dark clouds were rolling slowly across the sky. The humidity had grown thicker, the air feeling like clotted pudding. A sense of foreboding swept through Alexis's spirit and all she wanted was to head home to hide under the covers on her bed. But the nervous energy that knotted her stomach would never let her rest. She took a deep breath and then a second and third. Then she let the tears fall, crying as if it had been Marcel's dead body that had been returned to her.

The Martin sisters were packed into Alexis's office. No one spoke, her pronouncement about seeing Marcel Broussard slow to register. Alexis's tears had finally stopped flowing and she sat, looking as if the weight of the world had dropped onto her shoulders.

Lenore spoke first. "He's alive?"

Alexis nodded.

"And you spoke to him?" Celeste questioned.

"No. He spoke to me. I had nothing to say to him."

"You didn't ask where he's been or what happened to him?" Sophie's expression was incredulous. Her eyes were wide with confusion. "How could you not ask him where the hell he's been all this time? I would have asked!"

Celeste rolled her eyes skyward. "You don't know what you would have done."

"I would have asked, too," Lenore quipped.

"Me three, but that's just us," Celeste said with a shrug. "I was trying to be sensitive to her feelings."

"I really don't need all this sisterly bonding right now," Alexis snapped. Her head shook slowly from side to side.

"What's going on?" Claudia questioned, the matriarch suddenly standing in the doorway. Her hands rested along the curve of her hips. She looked from one daughter to another.

Sophie answered. "Alexis saw Marcel Broussard."

"He's been stalking her," Celeste added.

Claudia took a quick step forward. "Stalking her? Why am I just now hearing about this?"

All eyes turned to stare at Alexis. She dropped her face into the palms of her hands and groaned. "There was nothing to tell," Alexis said finally, lifting her eyes to meet her mother's stare.

"What did he say?" Claudia asked. "Where's he been?"

Alexis shrugged her narrow shoulders. "He said he wanted to talk to me. But I left before he could say anything else."

"And how long has he been following you?" Claudia asked with a deep frown.

"For a few days, I think. But I didn't know it was him until I approached him in the store and he unmasked."

"Unmasked?"

"He's been wearing a medical pandemic mask. And dark shades. He didn't want me to recognize him."

"I think I need to call your father," Claudia said. "We need to get to the bottom of this."

Alexis suddenly wanted to scream. It was difficult enough trying to process her own feelings, but she suddenly felt responsible for what everyone else was feeling as well. Her tears started flowing again and her body shook with frustration.

Cash suddenly ran into the space, closing the door behind her. They all turned to stare. "There are two men in the lobby wanting to speak with Alexis. Marcel Broussard and an agent named Waters."

"Agent? What kind of agent?" Claudia asked, shifting into mother bear mode.

"FBI," Cash said, her brow lifted for emphasis.

Claudia turned and pushed past the woman. "I'll escort Mr. Broussard and his agent friend into the conference room personally," she said.

"Mom, please," Alexis said, her voice pleading.

Claudia walked through the entrance, tossing her last comment over her shoulder. "Everyone in the conference room. Now!"

The man Marcel stood with looked like he was fearful of being jumped. All eyes were on them and even he wasn't sure what to expect. He took a deep inhale of breath. The agency offices were impressive. They had redecorated the reception area since the last time Marcel had been there. The space was minimalistic; a contemporary love seat, two cushioned chairs, a coffee table with issues of *Architectural Digest* laid neatly atop and someone's original painting hanging on the wall. The room colors were muted, soft shades of gray interspersed with pink and ivory. The painting adding a juxtaposition of vibrant greens and purples that danced off the wall. The setting was tasteful and refined.

Agent Matthew Waters tossed him a look, his morbid expression belying any confidence he might have had. "This could go very wrong," he said, his voice dropping to a loud whisper. "You could be upending all the work you invested these past few years."

"You've said that before," Marcel whispered back. "But I haven't been left with any other options."

"Yeah, but why this woman?" Waters questioned.

Before Marcel could answer, Claudia Martin swooped toward them like a firestorm determined to do damage. The thought that maybe Waters could be right slapped him almost as hard as Alexis's mother did.

"How dare you, Marcel!" Claudia hissed between clenched teeth. "You have some nerve! How dare you stalk Alexis after what she's been through."

"Mrs. Martin, I can explain—" Marcel started before she interrupted him.

"You damn well will explain," she snapped. She flashed her glare toward the agent, looking him up and then down then up again. "Who are you?"

"Agent Matthew Waters, ma'am. I'm with the FBI."

"And why is the FBI escorting Mr. Broussard into my business?"

Waters answered. "If there's some place more private where we can go to talk, I'll be glad to explain."

She shifted her eyes back to Marcel. He was rubbing the side of his face, contrition furrowing his brow. She said, "I've called Alexis's father. If I were you, I'd make sure my lies were straight before he gets here." Then she turned, gesturing with her head for them to follow.

Knowing that Josiah would soon be joining them put Marcel on edge even more. The Martin family history was extensive. No one said it out loud, but they ran the city. People trusted them. Their philanthropic endeavors were legendary. There was a generation in the community that would call on them before they called on the police—and only because many of the locals had worked for Josiah and Claudia. Some kept his secrets, and hers, and loyalty earned them protection and perks for their families. That adage about the apple not falling far from the tree aptly described the Martin sisters. How people treated their parents dictated how they were seen and how they were able to move through these New Orleans streets. Agent Waters would soon learn that if the two of them made it out of these offices to see another day, it would only be by the grace of God and the benevolence of Josiah Martin. He shot the man one last glance as the two followed Claudia.

There wasn't a hole big enough for Alexis to crawl into and disappear. She'd felt as if the air had been sucked out of her when her mother had stormed from her office to the reception area. Alexis couldn't begin to imagine that she would ever see Marcel again when Claudia was done with him. And truth be told, she wanted to see him again. To ask him what they all wanted to know and to hear his answer.

She blew a heavy sigh and could feel her sisters all turn to stare at her. They had moved into the conference room as ordered and now sat on one side of the oversized table. Lenore was sitting beside her and had reached for her hand, squeezing her fingers. It was taking all Alexis had not to cry, and she wanted to scream at them to leave her alone, but her family would never just leave her floundering if they even *thought* she needed their support.

When her mother returned, Marcel followed. His own discomfort was etched across his face. He looked like he might be sick and, despite her own frustration, Alexis actually felt bad for him. And then she didn't, thinking he was getting everything he deserved and then some. Lenore squeezed her fingers a second time as Alexis steeled herself for the storm she could feel coming.

Chapter 4

Marcel would have given anything to wrap Alexis in his arms. She was even more stunning than he remembered. She was a natural redhead, with curls that cascaded down to the middle of her back. Her crystal complexion was a warm sienna with a spattering of chocolate-chip freckles dotting her skin. She had always had a bohemian spirit, living a relaxed, laidback lifestyle. Not one to conform to anyone else's standard, she'd been a sensitive soul and empathetic to the plight of others. He sensed that she was more disappointed with him than angry, and her being present in the moment meant she was at least willing to hear him out.

She sat staring at him, her head held high. Her eyes followed him from the door to the seat across from her, where he eased into the chair. Their eyes locked, their emotions holding hands as a silent conversation that only they were privy to played in their heads. Neither noticed when Josiah entered just a few minutes after they had all settled in their seats.

Standing at the end of the conference table, Josiah called her name, pulling Alexis from the trance she'd fallen into. She immediately snatched her eyes from Marcel as she turned her attention toward her father. Josiah had been huddled in conversation with her mother and the duo had paused to glare at Marcel. Alexis suddenly felt the room begin to spin. She felt like she'd entered a hollow tunnel, the noise only a dull echo in her ears. She took a deep breath and held it, fearful that she might pass out.

It was taking everything in him not to vomit, Marcel thought. Only Alexis seemed to comprehend the magnitude of their situation, both riding an emotional roller coaster. He wanted the conversation to be between the two of them, without all the outside opinions chiming in, but he also knew her family was overly protective and would gladly wage war against him to protect her. Before he could even think to ask for her help, he would have to appease them first. And they were angry. So angry, that they were all mired down in their collective rage, the feeling akin to drowning in quicksand.

Everyone's attention was focused on Josiah, the man standing at the head of the table. He called Alexis's name a second time.

His voice was a deep baritone, his tone authoritative and firm. "Baby girl, I didn't like hearing from your mother that some man was stalking you and that you didn't tell us. You know the safety of all you girls is paramount where we're concerned." His eyes skated around the table and rested on the other girls. "And you all knew?" he questioned.

Lenore shot her sisters a quick glance. "We just found out."

"And that's when your mother and I should have been told. Don't make that mistake again."

The Martin sisters chimed in unison. "Yes, sir, Daddy."

Josiah shifted his stare toward Marcel. "Mr. Broussard. This is quite a shock for us all. Why were you following my child?"

There was a moment of pause before Marcel answered. He cleared his throat and then spoke. "I didn't mean to frighten Alexis. I need her help and I just wanted to speak with her."

"Well, that sure takes balls!" Sophie muttered. She crossed her arms over her chest and glared in Marcel's direction.

Alexis sighed. She sat straight in her seat, her eyes leveled on Marcel a second time. "My sister is right. You disappear out of my life without any warning and then suddenly reappear wanting me to *help* you? I'd say that takes *brass* balls!" she quipped.

"I am so sorry, Alexis. I never intended to hurt you. I just…" Marcel suddenly looked dejected.

Alexis interrupted him. "You just what? Needed a break? Were you kidnapped and not able to call? What, Marcel?"

The man at Marcel's side shifted in his seat, abruptly interjecting himself into the conversation. "You could definitely call it kidnapped, and no he wasn't able to call," Agent Waters said.

"And who the hell are you?" Alexis snapped.

"Agent Matthew Waters. I'm with the FBI and, for lack of a better explanation, I'm Mr. Broussard's handler."

"Handler?" Alexis frowned. "Why does Marcel need a handler?"

The man hesitated. "I'm not comfortable…"

"We have no secrets here, Agent Waters," Claudia said.

"But I can assure you whatever is said here in this office will not go any further; if that's your concern."

Marcel gave his friend a nod of his head.

Despite the reluctance that creased his brow, Waters continued. "Marcel has been undercover, working on a case for the Bureau for the past three years. He was able to infiltrate one of the largest religious cults on the east coast and maneuver his way up the hierarchy. We were set to take down its leaders for a laundry list of crimes when the situation took a turn."

"What kind of turn?" Alexis asked.

Marcel picked up the story where Waters left off. "They suspected someone was feeding information to the police after one of their warehouses was raided and a shipment of contraband was confiscated. They kidnapped the families of those who knew what was going down. I was on that suspect list. The others have since disappeared without a trace. I'm the only one left and they're holding my daughter hostage. She's innocent in all this and I need your help to get her back."

Alexis's eyes widened. "Daughter! Since when do you have a daughter?" she asked, her voice sounding shrill in her own ears.

Marcel took a deep breath. "Her name is Sabine and she's only eight months old. I know where she is, but they won't let me near her. If I continue to do what they need me to do, they say she'll be safe, but I'm running out of time."

"Well, looks like you've been busy since you ghosted our sister," Lenore said snidely. "A whole baby!"

Alexis shot her sister a look. "As opposed to *half* a baby? Really, Lenore?" The sarcasm in her tone was as thick as her Southern drawl. She shifted her attention back to Marcel. "Who's this baby's mother?"

"It's not what you think," Marcel said, a gust of air blowing past his full lips.

"Then what is it?" Alexis questioned.

"It's complicated and I promise to tell you everything, but I need to get back to the compound before they start to question where I am. And I need you to go with me."

Alexis bristled. "Excuse me?"

"Sabine is being held by the Saints of the Moral Order. Alexis, you know better than anyone what they're capable of and you understand how they operate. I'm praying you'll help me get my daughter back."

"And just how is *my* daughter supposed to do that?" Claudia quizzed.

"I need her to go with me as my wife," Marcel said matter-of-factly. "We need to pretend we're married."

If silencing a room had been an art form, then Marcel would have been a master of the craft, Alexis thought. It had gotten so quiet, so quickly, that she fathomed you could hear an ant pee if you listened hard enough. The incredulous expressions around the room more than matched her own, she thought, every one of them caught off guard by his comment.

Marcel's words had summoned memories of a time in her life that Alexis had tried hard to forget. They came rushing forward, seemingly desperate for her attention. Alexis stared into Marcel's eyes, reflecting on all that she had shared with him when she had been fearful that the baggage she carried would be more than he could handle. She's been scared that he would think her tainted and he would no longer find her desirable. But Marcel hadn't turned from her, instead, wrapping her in his arms and clutching her tightly as if afraid to let her go. He had promised to never cause her hurt or to leave her side. He'd broken that promise. He had also promised to never let her past, or his, come between them, and now here he was bringing back memories that had the potential to leave her broken.

As children, the Martin girls had been sheltered and protected from the bad things in the world. Their parents had gone to great lengths to give them a perfect childhood. But that perfection had sometimes been fractured; the intrusion of other people's crap upsetting the balance Claudia and Josiah worked hard for.

Alexis had been thirteen, still more child than woman, despite her efforts to pretend otherwise. Her sister Lenore had just celebrated her sixteenth birthday. Celeste had been fourteen, maybe fifteen, and Sophie had barely been eight years old. They'd been running around on Decatur Street while their father finished up a meeting at Café Du Monde. No one had given any concern for them running around the building and jetting across the roadway to steal glimpses of the great Mississippi. They were the children of Josiah Martin, and there were protective eyes around them wherever they went. Lenore had also been in mama bear mode since Claudia had declined the invitation to join them. With Lenore's full focus on Sophie, it had afforded Alexis and Celeste an opportunity to explore the market square on their own.

Disappearing as they played an impromptu game of hide-and-seek, they hadn't been prepared for the handsome stranger the two girls had run into. He'd been charismatic and charming and prettier than any picture. As he'd engaged them in conversation, he hadn't been prepared for the bodyguards that often jumped out and walked up on them when least expected. Men her father paid handsomely to keep them safe were always lurking around every corner. Intimidating figures who'd have you contemplating all your life choices or peeing in your pants.

He'd been a beautiful specimen of male prowess. Tall and slender with ocean-blue eyes and an Elvis Presley haircut in a cool shade of corn-silk blond. His porcelain complexion had made him seem angelic. So much so that Alexis had completely missed the hauntingly demonic stare in his eyes. She had been instantly enamored with his soft-spoken persona. And enraptured by all the attention he'd been showing her. Not Claudia, or Lenore, but her. As if she were the only beautiful girl in the whole wide world. But as expected, their conversation was cut short when a hulking brute of a man called them by name, saying their father wanted them back at the café. That had been Alexis's first encounter with the religious prophet named Stefan "Symmetry" Guidry, but it had not been her last.

After that first encounter, Guidry had been the fodder of fantasy and every teenage perversion Alexis could muster. Then, days later, he had entered a classroom at Academy of the Sacred Heart, the private Roman Catholic girls' school the Martin sisters attended. Discovering he was the new math teacher had been Christmas come early for Alexis.

Guidry had soon become a popular figure at Sacred Heart, building a cult following of sorts. Staff and students had loved him. By the time anyone had realized what was going on, it had been too late, the harm already done. Guidry had mastered preying on children, the destruction he'd left behind damaging multiple families.

During this time, Alexis had honed her own skills, lying and sneaking off to follow after the charismatic instructor. She'd even taught Lenore and Celeste a thing or two about shaking their parents' security team. Most had seen her antics as normal teenage behavior, sometimes mischievous and most times not.

All hell had broken loose the day Alexis disappeared, running away from home to be with Mr. Guidry. She had honestly believed that it was love. Guidry had made promises, too. His betrayal had culminated in a tattoo being branded on her hand, labeling her as one of the prophet's chosen.

Alexis had later learned her parents had been manic, Josiah calling in every favor ever owed to him to find her. She'd been on the run for months until the day she'd gotten away long enough to call home, begging her parents to come get her.

To this day, no one had ever spoken about everything that had happened to Alexis. Her sisters had been shielded from the details of her trauma, but it wasn't hard to piece most of it together. The man who called himself Prophet Symmetry had eventually been arrested. His charges had run the gamut from child pornography and prostitution to sex trafficking. His victims had been easy to identify, each of them marked with the same damn tattoo. The same tattoo still imprinted on her middle finger. The tattoo of the Saints of the Moral Order. Alexis had only shared the intimate details of her experiences with two people. Her therapist and Marcel.

Years of therapy had helped Alexis to smile again, her life seeming as close to normal as possible. After she'd returned home, she'd been homeschooled, and rarely, if ever, let out of their parents' sight for any length of time. It had been a difficult time for the entire family. Her parents had eventually divorced, and Alexis still blamed herself for everyone's unhappiness.

Moving swiftly, Alexis jumped from her chair and rounded the conference table. She gestured for Marcel to follow as she launched herself through the door and out the room. He rose from his seat just as quickly, close on her heels. Behind them, the comments echoed off the walls.

"He has lost his mind!"

"I hope she punches him in his face."

"This doesn't make any sense."

"How brazen do you have to be to ask for help with someone else's baby after breaking her heart?"

Her father's voice was the last she heard as the door slammed shut behind them. "I'm going to kill him! I swear to God, Claudia, I am going to kill that boy!"

Pausing at the reception desk, Alexis jotted two lines across a notepad and handed it to Cash. Amusement danced across the woman's face as she read what Alexis had written.

Cash nodded. "I'll get right on this," she replied, waving the little blue Post-it note in her hand.

"Thank you," Alexis said, striding toward the front door. "I'll be back."

Cash shot Marcel a quick glance. "What about him? Is he coming back, too?"

Alexis whispered something that only the other woman could hear. When Cash laughed, Marcel visibly tense. His own eyes locked with Alexis's one last time. Saying nothing, she retreated out the exit, and like an obedient puppy, Marcel followed.

Chapter 5

Alexis was careening through the backroads as if she were competing in the famous Le Mans high-speed street race in France. She still hadn't spoken to Marcel, and truth be told, he was a lot uncomfortable about initiating the conversation. Although anxious to tell her everything, he wasn't confident that it would be received well. Neither was he sure that she was ready for his explanation. But he did understand she might need time and, in that moment, he didn't have much left to give to her. He took a breath, determined to let her set the pace. He couldn't risk rushing her, nor could he let things drag along indefinitely. Thankfully, it didn't take long before she finally spoke.

"How in hell did you get tangled up with the Saints of the Moral Order again?" Alexis suddenly questioned as she took a sharp curve, her tires grazing the edge of swampland.

Marcel exhaled a soft sigh. He wasn't sure where to start, the beginnings of his association with the religious cult seeming like eons ago. Did he go back to when he was six, when his parents had initially joined the fledgling religious group? Back then, they'd been known as the Moral Order, a gathering of hardworking individuals who'd only wanted to live a life of moral fortitude while giving meaningful service to the deity they'd worshipped. They'd been a community that had turned from mainstream ways to live a quiet, communal existence. The commune had been a safe space and his childhood almost idyllic. But Alexis knew that history.

Perhaps, he thought, he should revisit the day he and his father had fled the fanaticism of its new leadership. When they had left his mother and baby sister Camille behind. The matriarch had refused to follow, proclaiming her husband and son insolent for turning against their church and betraying their brotherhood. But leaving had been necessary for their survival and, despite tearing their family apart, his father had had no regrets with his decision. But Alexis knew that as well. So, he started with what she didn't know.

Alexis would never have imagined that Marcel had always kept one foot in the door in case his mom or sister might one day need to be saved. Believing that he could be their knight in shining armor, if they called. But his beloved mother had died before he could rescue her and his sister had been left with no one to watch over her. The day Camille had reached out in dire straits, believing she had nowhere to turn, Marcel had dropped everything to reach her.

"Camille was being trafficked," Marcel said softly. "I knew I had to get her out, but I needed help. I reached out to my old friend Felix Humphries. You might remember him."

Alexis knew Felix, the *New York Times* journalist who'd been researching the legitimacy of these new religious movements. She had shared her thoughts with him a time or two, vaguely answering questions about her own experience. She nodded.

"Felix put me in touch with a friend of his at the FBI."

"So, you just went undercover to help them?"

"My police training made it easy. But I had to spend time at Quantico for additional intensive training. While that happened, they were looking for Camille."

"Where is she now?" Alexis questioned.

Marcel turned to stare out the passenger's-side window. There was a deep pause that hung like a heavy shroud between them. "I didn't get to her in time. She took her own life. After that, I couldn't just walk away and not do something. I owed that to her."

Marcel suddenly felt Alexis's hand press over his own. She squeezed his fingers tightly. "I'm so sorry," she said softly. Tears rained down her cheek. She pulled her hand from his, her fingers clutched into a tight fist.

Marcel continued. "The FBI had already been investigating them. They needed someone to help take down the church leaders and gather evidence of their illegal operations. I took the assignment and was able to infiltrate the apostolic hierarchy. Everything was going well and then I made a mistake."

Alexis had pulled off the road, parking the car in a convenience store parking lot to listen intently to his story. "What did you do?" she asked.

"I showed too much concern for my daughter. It raised a red flag."

"Your daughter." Alexis's jaw tightened as her eyes darted back and forth. "You have a daughter. I'm still shocked by that, Marcel."

Marcel nodded. "Sabine is a beautiful baby, Alexis." He gushed, joy dancing over his words as he whispered them loudly.

"Who is Sabine's mother?" There was a hint of animosity in Alexis's tone. Marcel had left her and found favor with another woman who had birthed his child. For the briefest moment, that anguish washed over her face, Alexis unable to hide the hurt of it.

"I don't know," Marcel said, turning back to look Alexis in the eye.

Confusion washed over her expression. "How could you not know, Marcel? That makes no sense."

"One of the tenets of this new Moral Order is the disconnection of family associations. All the children belong to the Prophet and to insure there are no familial connections, most of the women are artificially inseminated and the children taken from them right after birth. Before I ascended to leadership status, I was required to donate sperm. It was only one time and was necessary to prove my loyalty to the Order's mission."

"So how do you even know she's yours?"

"I knew the minute I laid eyes on her. You will, too. But to be certain, I was able to get Agent Waters to do a DNA test. Sabine is my biological child."

"But what about her mother? Someone gave birth to her."

"The mothers are shipped out to one of the other communes before they can form any kind of attachment to their babies. I don't know who she is, where she is, or if we'll ever be able to find her. No one will tell me, and I can't just ask."

"But now you're able to have a wife?"

"I'm able to have many wives, but only to fulfill the Prophet's plan for his kingdom. Intimate relationships are solely for procreation. Emotional connections aren't encouraged. We are to love the Prophet and the Prophet only."

"I don't understand, Marcel. You marry to have children, but the family unit is defunct?"

"That's correct. The children are taken because they are the offspring of the Prophet. If we were actually married and had a child, it would belong to the Prophet and we would not be allowed to raise it."

"And women are inseminated to have children as well. Why don't they just marry the fathers?"

"The Prophet is the only father, and only the church hierarchy are allowed to marry. But that's just to keep the illusion that marital bliss is attainable for those who remain true to the Prophet."

Alexis shook her head. "That's completely crazy, Marcel."

"I didn't say it made sense, Alexis. When has any of it ever made sense?"

Questions were racing through Alexis's mind, the absurdity of it all feeling amiss. Marcel could see it on her face, her eyes narrowed ever so slightly, a frown dipping toward her chin. "So, how do I fit into this? Why me? Why not just partner with another FBI agent?"

He reached for her fist and took her hand in his, lengthening her fingers. He drew the pad of his index finger across the tattoo that marred the skin of her middle finger. "Because you already know what they expect and how to carry yourself. I don't have time to train another agent. I've already lost my mother and sister. I can't risk my daughter's life, too."

A pregnant pause swelled full and thick between them. Marcel's anxiety was palpable. So much so that he feared Alexis might choke on it as she considered his plea. He knew what he was asking of her and, more importantly, that he had no right to ask anything of her at all.

Alexis pulled her hand from his, the warmth of his touch disconcerting. A chilly shiver ran the length of her spine. She didn't want to feel anything but feared her body was betraying her head and her heart.

Marcel continued. "You'll be able to access areas of the commune that men are forbidden to enter. The birthing rooms. The nursery. The girls' school. Your cover story is that you have been wanting to return to the fold. We met, became friends, and were in a relationship when I decided to return to the church. We stayed in touch and you, too, saw this as an opportunity to return to the covenant with favor."

"But why the urgency? If she's there, then you know she's being cared for, right?"

"The congregation doesn't know, but the Prophet is selling the babies on the black market. As far as he's concerned, it's all about money. I recently discovered he's planning to ship children born in the last year overseas, and I don't know where they're going. If they put Sabine on that boat, I'm afraid I will never see her again."

Silence filled the space one more time. Marcel could see Alexis reflecting on his statement, his words billowing through her thoughts. His comments were matter-of-fact. He didn't want to scare her. But the situation was dire.

No one in the religious order was safe; most especially, the children. But Alexis knew that. From her own experiences with the religious order, she knew it better than anyone else.

Alexis took a deep breath. "Did you think about me at all?" she asked. Her voice was low, the faintest quiver rippling over her vocal cords. "When you left, did you even consider what that would do to me, Marcel?"

"I thought about you every day, Alexis," he answered, his own voice a low whisper. "I hated what I did, and I hated why I did it even more. But I knew that if I was going to make this work, that I had to stay focused. Once I got in and realized the depth of deceit and depravity I was dealing with, I couldn't put you at risk. You have always been my Achilles' heel and I would not have been able to play this role knowing I might be putting you in harm's way."

"But you're okay with putting me in harm's way now?"

Marcel shook his head vehemently. "I would never let anything happen to you, Alexis. I swear! And I would never ask this of you if there was any other way. I trust you. I trust you with my child's life. Once you find Sabine, we are all out of there."

"You've broken every promise you ever made to me, Marcel. I don't have any reason to believe you now." There was an edge to her words, bitterness floating like stagnant water across her tone.

Marcel cringed, regret pulling at the lines in his face. "And again, I'm sorry for hurting you. God knows I am. If there had been any other way..." He paused, unable to find the words to make things better between them.

"Why didn't you just tell me?"

"Would you have let me go, knowing that you couldn't ever contact me?"

Alexis hesitated before answering. "I don't know, but you didn't give me that choice. You didn't trust me."

"I didn't trust *me*, Alexis. And, at the time, my decision felt like the best choice for all of us. I knew your family would be there for you and that they would help you get over me."

She shook her head, not bothering to respond.

Marcel apologized one more time. "I'm so sorry that I hurt you. I can't apologize enough, but I'll do it every day for the rest of my life if I need to. I haven't been able to forgive myself for what I did, so I don't expect that you can forgive me."

The two sat in silence for what seemed like an eternity. When Alexis suddenly restarted the car and pulled the vehicle back onto the roadway, he knew that she had made her decision. He desperately wanted to ask her what she had decided, but he knew better. He knew that Alexis would tell him what she wanted him to know, when she was ready. She had always been a woman who thought things through on her own time. She would not be rushed, coerced, prodded or pushed. She could dig her heels in like a prize bullfighter prepared to dodge oncoming trouble. And she could not be moved from whatever she had set her mind to. It was one of her many traits that had impressed him about her. She never vacillated about anything, never wavered from her decisions. It was a sign of strength even when she herself might have felt less confident.

They drove back to her office in silence. Marcel prepared himself to say goodbye, knowing that this could be the last time he'd see her. He had officially run out of time, and options, and he had no one to blame but himself.

As Alexis parked her car, they both noted the security team her father had already put in place. Marcel shot her a quick glance as she shook her head in annoyance.

"I'm sorry," he said, knowing how much she hated the hulking men sometimes enlisted to watch and report on her every move. Josiah Martin didn't play when it came to his daughters and any man who had dated them eventually learned that the hard way.

Alexis shrugged. "They just worry, and they definitely are not going to be happy about me doing this."

Marcel felt his nerves twitch, a ripple of energy gone awry. He shifted his gaze to eye her anxiously. "You going to do it?"

"How could I not, Marcel? I could never forgive myself if something happened to your daughter and I didn't do anything to help." Alexis shook her head, her eyes rolling skyward. "What time do you have to be back on site?"

"Sundown, but definitely no later than nine o'clock, and it's a good hour's ride from here."

"It should take me an hour, maybe two, to get ready and put some things in place."

"Thank you, Alexis. This means everything to me."

"I'm not doing it for you, Marcel. Make sure you understand that."

"I'm still grateful."

Alexis disengaged the door locks on her car. "They've probably put a tracker on your van. If you think the Order might look for it, I'll tell my father to remove it. Otherwise, it might be a good idea to leave it in place. Just in case."

Marcel gave a nod. "I agree."

"Be at my place in an hour," Alexis said. "We'll leave from there."

Marcel opened the car door and moved to make his exit. He turned to give Alexis one last glance. "Thank you," he said as he held her gaze, her eyes dancing like small fireworks across his face. And then he stood back and watched as she pulled her car out of the lot and back into traffic, an unmarked security car following behind her.

Chapter 6

"You're not going!" Claudia snapped, she and Alexis exchanging glares. "I mean it, Alexis. I will not allow you to put yourself in danger."

Alexis shook her head slowly. She sighed and sat down on her queen-sized bed. Minutes earlier, most of her wardrobe had been scattered across the carpeted floor, the recliner in the corner and the dresser. Dirty dishes lingered in the kitchen sink and the master bath had needed a good scrubbing. Alexis had come home with a plan that had been easier to execute once her mother and sisters had come banging at her front door, the extra hands knocking out the chores in record time.

Her family had moved their meeting from the office conference room to Alexis's bedroom. The only person missing was her father and Alexis imagined he was somewhere bullying Marcel for information or carting his dead body off to Neverland.

"Mom, I understand your concerns, but I must do this. A child's life is at risk. Not to mention all the other women and girls who might be in trouble."

"We're concerned about you, Alexis," Lenore said as she placed a knit sweater on a padded hanger and hung it in the closet. "From what Agent Waters told us, the FBI has already put plans in place to get those other women out and shut down that commune. They had only been waiting for Marcel to give them the go-ahead."

Alexis nodded. "And Marcel is not going to do that if his daughter is in harm's way. Mom and Dad would do the same thing to protect one of us."

"Yes, we would," Claudia acquiesced. "But that baby not being *your* responsibility is why you need to distance yourself from this. Risking your safety with that crowd is bad enough, but why risk your peace of mind, too? It took you a long time to get over what happened, Alexis, and I don't want you to lose your sanity going back to the scene of those horrid memories."

Alexis turned her body to face her mother. "I'll never get over what happened, Mom. Every horrific detail is engraved in my brain and on my heart like this tattoo is on my finger. I've learned how to ignore it, to hide and run from it, even how to pretend it didn't happen. But I'll never truly be able to let it go. If I do, then I'm as bad as the monsters who are still out there preying on innocent lives. Because I wasn't the first, or the last, and definitely not the only one. If I can save even one little girl or another woman from the abuse I endured, then I need to do that. I need to do *this*. And I need to do it for me. No one else."

A round of heavy sighs bounced off the room's four walls. There was moment of reflection as they all contemplated Alexis's decision, wanting to offer advice on her next steps.

Sophie spoke first. "Is this all you're packing?" She

shifted the few pieces of clothing Alexis had tossed into a backpack.

"I won't get to keep those. They will take my things when I get there and put me in appropriate attire." She raised her hands and made an air quote sign when she said the word *appropriate*.

"This doesn't feel right," Claudia muttered. She pulled off the rubber gloves she'd been wearing, dropping them into the hamper with a cleaning rag.

"Please, don't worry about me," Alexis said, knowing the comment was falling on deaf ears. No one and nothing was going to stop Claudia Martin from worrying about her daughters.

Lenore smiled. "We will take care of Mom while you're gone.

Claudia rolled her eyes skyward. "*Mom* doesn't need you to take care of her. *Mom* has been taking care of herself since before you four were even a fleeting thought between me and your father."

The women laughed nervously, each exchanging gazes as they noted the anxiety that seemed to wash over their mother's spirit, her shoulders rolling forward and hot tears pressing against her eyelashes.

Alexis rose from where she was sitting to wrap the matriarch in a tight hug. They clung to each other until Claudia let her go, pushing her away gently. She swiped at her eyes with the backs of her hands. "You just stay close to Marcel, and he better take damn good care of you or we are all coming for his testicles. And you can tell him I said so."

"I know that's right!" Sophie interjected.

Alexis grinned as she sat back down. "I'll be fine. I

promise. And Mom doesn't need anyone to take care of her," she said to her sisters, echoing their mother's words. "So, don't you all be harassing my mommy while I'm gone!"

"Not *your* mother!" Celeste said with a giggle.

Claudia did not look amused as her daughters all burst into laughter.

"I just want to know if you get conjugal privileges," Sophie asked, amusement dancing in her tone. "Because Marcel is still *foine* as hell! Since you two will be pretend married, does that mean you can get you some if you want?"

"Sophie!" Claudia snapped.

"What?" Sophie snapped back. "It's a valid question. They do need to make the marriage look real, right?"

"I swear," Celeste said. "Your mind is always in the gutter."

"Like you all weren't thinking it," Sophie scoffed.

Lenore laughed. "We might have been thinking it, but you weren't supposed to say it out loud."

"I ask what I want to know. My mother taught me that. Isn't that right, Claudia?"

Claudia tapped her youngest child in the back of her head. "Call me by my first name again and see if I don't hurt you."

"Ouch!" Sophie quipped, still smiling as she rubbed at the back of her skull. "It was a joke!" She crawled onto her sister's bed, leaning her back against Alexis.

"Clearly, you are not a comedian," Alexis giggled.

Lenore changed the subject, shifting the conversation back to serious. "If you can find a way to call, you call."

"And the minute things feel off kilter, you get out," Celeste added.

Alexis nodded her head. All her sisters dropped beside her on the bed. Lenore wrapped her arm around Alexis's shoulders, hugging her tightly.

"One call and we will be there," Sophie said. "You won't be alone."

Their mother leaned to press a kiss to Alexis's forehead.

"I'll be okay," Alexis repeated.

Claudia gently pressed the palm of her hand to her daughter's cheek, looking her evenly in the eye. Neither spoke. And Alexis sensed her mother didn't believe her words any more than she had when she'd uttered them.

Marcel had not been prepared when Josiah suddenly charged at him. He put his hands up as if surrendering, calling out just a quick minute before the patriarch grabbed him by the collar of his shirt. Josiah was so close, Marcel could feel the rage that radiated out of the man's pores.

"Hear me out, please!" Marcel said, his eyes wide. "Please!"

Marcel had been standing in the parking lot of the detective agency in conversation with Agent Waters, who'd suddenly shifted his hand to his service weapon. As Josiah had snatched Marcel, Waters had been ready to pull it from his holster but then felt the barrel of a revolver pressed tightly to the back of his head.

"It's okay," Marcel said, shooting his friend a quick look. The pitch of his voice was a tad higher than normal, not inspiring an ounce of confidence in his friend.

The men pointing their weapons were ready for a fight, only awaiting a command from Josiah.

Waters slowly lifted his hands and pushed his arms up and over his head. "You do know you're aiming your weapons at two federal agents, don't you?"

The look Josiah Martin gave the man was chilling.

Marcel shook his head. "It's fine, Waters. Just relax, please. I'm trying to keep us from being two dead agents whose bodies are never found."

Josiah suddenly let him go, shoving him harshly. "I thought I told you not to come back?"

"I know. And I would have stayed away, but this was necessary."

"Necessary?"

"Just like you, sir, I need to make sure my daughter is safe. You, of all people, have to understand that."

"What I understand is that you have no right dragging my child into your mess. You know her history. You knew how fragile she was. You broke her heart and when I caught up with you, I promised to let you live as long as you stayed away from her."

Marcel's look was pleading. "I'm sorry. I couldn't keep that promise. Alexis knows their operation. She can predict how they might react when I can't. If anyone can help me get my daughter, I knew it would be Alexis. She was my only hope!"

Confusion washed over Waters's face. "Wait! He knew where you were?" His frown shifted toward Josiah. "You've known all this time?"

Josiah glared. "No one hurts a child of mine and walks

away unscathed. No…one…" he snarled, his words falling like bricks against concrete.

"Mr. Martin, although I can appreciate your passion, you are still bound by state and federal laws. I'd be derelict in my duties if I stood by and did nothing while you tried to harm Agent Broussard."

Josiah's eyes narrowed, the look he gave the other agent cutting. "The only laws I'm bound by, Agent Waters, are the laws I make. And if I wanted this fool hurt, he wouldn't still be standing here. And neither would you."

There was an awkward silence as the two other men reflected on Josiah's words. Both were acutely aware of the men standing in a protective circle around their benefactor, their guns still pointed at Waters's head. It was a standoff of sorts, but neither Marcel nor Agent Waters was standing on a level playing field. Josiah Martin had the upper hand and he clearly had no intentions of letting it go.

Marcel had great respect for Alexis's father. Marcel had known him by reputation even before he and Alexis had started dating. Josiah was suspected of a long list of crimes, but the New Orleans police department and the FBI had never been able to tie him to any of them. He was like a ghost that could not be trapped.

He and Alexis had dated for almost a year before she'd taken him home to meet her parents. They had been serious about their relationship and meeting her father had given him a whole other perspective on the man. Marcel quickly discovered that in every decision Josiah Martin made, he considered Alexis, Lenore, Celeste, Sophie and his wife first. His children were everything to him and he would have sacrificed his own life before letting anything happen to any of them.

The two men had become friends and Josiah hadn't had many of those. His inner circle was small and sweet. Josiah had embraced him with open arms, welcoming him into their family. He had treated Marcel like the son he'd never had and had afforded him the same protections and perks as the rest of his kin. The only thing he'd expected in return was that Marcel treat Alexis with respect and kindness. When Marcel had disappeared from her life, Josiah had hunted him down. After discovering the why of Marcel's disappearance and Alexis's heartbreak, Josiah had shown him grace, and mercy, and had made Marcel swear to never risk Alexis's heart again by returning.

Now standing toe to toe with the patriarch, Marcel knew he was asking for a lot from the man. He also knew the stories told about Josiah and the rumors of his crimes weren't far from the truth. Marcel had never allowed his police work to cross paths with whatever Josiah was into. They had made it work and Marcel believed that if Josiah gave him half a chance, it could work for them all a second time.

His final comment was stoic and determined, his words uttered with finality and purpose. His tone was low and deep. His chest was pushed forward and his head held high. "Respectfully, Josiah, I did exactly what you would do. I couldn't save my sister, but I can make the people who hurt her pay for what they did, and I will do everything I can to protect my daughter. Just like you would. But not only will I protect my daughter—I will move heaven and earth to protect *your* daughter, too. Because I still love Alexis. I never stopped loving Alexis. Let me prove it to you, sir, and to her. Please!"

* * *

Marcel was parked in front of the Richmond Place property that he had once shared with Alexis. The Craftsman-style house had been gifted to Alexis by her parents the same year the two had met. It was located on one of the prettiest tree-lined streets in the middle of the Uptown/Audubon Park area of the city. Alexis had fallen in love with the wraparound porches and the array of period-style woodwork and moldings.

He and Alexis had invested in a lavish renovation that included a new kitchen with quartzite counters, stainless-steel appliances, polished hardwood floors throughout the entire space, and a whole-house generator. Alexis had also splurged on custom gas lanterns, French doors, and a meticulously crafted garden to add a romantic ambience to the space. They'd managed to preserve its original charm while adding modern benefits. Together, they had made that beautiful cottage their home, filling it with love and laughter and hopes for a bright future together.

Eyeing the new landscape and abundant plantings, Marcel felt a lot melancholy, thinking about what could have been for them both if only he'd been dealt a different hand. Remembering some of their sweetest moments together broke his heart just a little more. He had honestly believed that together, he and Alexis could conquer the world. And he often questioned if the decision he had made had been the biggest mistake of his life.

Shaking himself from the reverie he'd fallen into, he looked up to see Alexis hugging her sisters goodbye. The Martin quartet was lined up on the front porch eyeing him intently. Her mother stood in the doorway, her arms folded across her chest, her jaw tight. Clearly, none of them was happy with him and there was very little he could do about that.

As Alexis headed down the walkway, he exited his van and rounded the front of the vehicle to open the passenger's-side door. He gave her the slightest smile before seeing the tears that misted her eyes. He suddenly wanted to kick himself for making her cry yet again.

"You're late," Alexis said, masking the emotion in her tone.

"I'm sorry. I ran into a roadblock."

Alexis suddenly laughed. "I've heard my father called a lot of things, but roadblock is a new one."

Marcel smiled. "They're all worried about you. Scared that I'm going to screw things up. Again."

"I don't have a lot of confidence in you, either, but then, you haven't earned it."

Marcel winced. "I deserve that," he said before closing the van door. He hurried back to the driver's side and jumped in. "Do you need to stop for anything?" he questioned as he started the vehicle's engine.

Alexis shook her head. "No. I just need you to tell me everything you can about what I'm walking into," she said.

Chapter 7

Before pulling the van onto the roadway, Marcel lowered his head and whispered a prayer for safe travels. He had reached for Alexis's hand, entwining his fingers with hers. She would have snatched it away but the memories of him practicing his faith flooded through her. They had never traveled anywhere together without Marcel asking for safe passage along the journey. There was something about the words he whispered that felt comforting. Something she had missed without even knowing it.

Alexis's own faith walk had always been a tumultuous journey beset with one obstacle after another. She had been a good Catholic girl until *good* had become metaphorical. Then she'd stopped trusting in God altogether, thinking that the Holy Father had failed her. Her faith had gone into a hibernation of sorts; there, but stagnant. Until Marcel had come into her life.

Marcel's own faith had been evident in every aspect of his existence. He lived it as easily as he breathed. It nourished him, kept him standing, and rarely did he waver from his beliefs. Because it was so natural for him, he never came across as being preachy or fanatical. His dedication to his faith was just how Marcel maneuvered on a daily basis.

Because Marcel prayed, believing in the totality of its power, Alexis had found her way back to her own belief system. They had prayed together regularly. Marcel had prayed for her often. Together they had forged a relationship grounded in faith that gave praise and honor to a higher power.

Alexis felt a wave of warmth drop against her shoulders like a warm blanket. It was a déjà vu moment and revived memories of all the good times the two had once shared. With a heavy sigh, Alexis turned to stare out the window, proffering one last wave of her hand as her family turned to head back inside her home.

The first fifteen minutes of the ride were silent. Alexis had withdrawn into herself and Marcel knew she was knee-deep in thought, her mind racing to make sense of it all. Alexis had always been pragmatic, things very black and white with no shades of gray. She didn't take change well and the occasional speed bump life sometimes threw could easily devastate her. Him tossing an entire mountain of problems at her head wasn't doing her any favors.

She was the first to speak, breaking the silence with a sledgehammer.

"I really want to hate you, Marcel Broussard. I really do!" she snapped suddenly.

He took a deep breath and held it for a quick minute. "I'm sorry."

"And stop saying you're sorry because I don't believe it. You hurt me and you did it on purpose."

"Hurting you was the last thing I wanted to do, Alexis. But I had to walk away to help my sister! I didn't have any other choice. I wasn't expecting it to completely upend our lives. Then, after Camille died, and I agreed to continue working with the FBI...well...time seemed to take over until nothing made sense. I just knew I had to keep up the façade to take the Moral Order down. By then, I figured you'd gone on with your life and were better off without me."

"All you had to do was make one call. Just one call, and I would have supported you."

Marcel suddenly hit the brakes, the van coming to an abrupt stop. "Was it easy for you to make that one call, Alexis? How long did it take before you could make that one call to your parents for help? How long?"

Alexis bristled, once again thrown back into a time that she'd been lucky to survive. She bit down against her bottom lip, eyeing him through forest-thick lashes.

"Exactly!" Marcel exclaimed, his voice rising an octave. "You, of all people, know what I was up against. Trying to make that one call makes you vulnerable. Vulnerability makes you weak. Weakness makes you and anyone you love a target. I was trying to save my sister's life; not put her, you, me, or anyone else at risk. And I failed! I failed Camille and I failed us! And I have to live with that for the rest of my life."

Tears suddenly rained down Marcel's cheeks as he continued his rant. "Every single day I had to think about my decisions and the consequences of my actions. And every day, knowing that I hurt you, devastated me. So, you could never hate me as much as I hate myself. Never!"

He took a breath and held it. Alexis was staring at him, waves of uncertainty billowing through the air. "I can live with you hating me, Alexis," he said, no longer shouting at her. "And you can be as angry as you need to be. But if this is going to work, we'll need to get past it before we drive through those gates. Because when we next step out of this van, they can't see an ounce of animosity between us. And if you can't do that, tell me now, because my daughter's life depends on it. And I can't fail Sabine. I can't."

Alexis was still staring at him. Something shifted in her disposition, the rage that had been in her eyes wavering. She blinked and turned to stare out the passenger window. "Drive," she muttered, nothing else needing to be said.

Marcel nodded, restarted the engine then slowly pulled back into traffic.

Alexis sat with her eyes closed, suddenly uncertain about how she felt. She wasn't angry and the hurt she'd been holding on to had finally begun to assuage. It was like bubbles rising and popping, something like clarity flooding through her. But she still wasn't happy and nothing she imagined was ever going to make that sadness go away.

She really didn't despise Marcel and even though she'd said she *wanted* to hate him, she also knew that would never happen. If she were honest, Marcel still had a claim on her heart. But that piece of her heart had yet to thaw, still frozen like a small chunk of ice trapped in the deep freezer. Confusion came because Alexis felt like she was on emotional overload, everything she was feeling spiraling out of control. And Alexis was determined to not lose control.

"What do I need to know?" she prompted, turning her attention to focus on the mission she was tasked with.

"Not much has changed. Women are still expected to

be subservient to the men and we all bow down to the Prophet."

"Who is the sovereign elder now?" she asked.

"A man named Amos Lee is the Prophet. He took the reins from Prophet Isaiah."

"Isaiah was second in command when Prophet Symmetry was in charge. I remember him. He was a vicious man!" Her voice cracked ever so slightly and Alexis felt herself tense at the memories.

Marcel shot her a quick look, then shifted his gaze back to the road. "He's no longer with the brotherhood. But, unfortunately, many of his more damning practices still remain."

"Did he walk away from the ministry?"

"Cancer took him, and Prophet Amos stepped right into his shoes before his body was cold. Amos is bad news with all capital letters. He has a criminal past that would make the FBI's Ten Most Wanted offenders look like choirboys. He initiated that damn breeding program. He craves attention and is desperate for adoration. He's the false idol from the Ten Commandments that God warned Moses of in Exodus."

Alexis nodded her head slowly. "Who's his First Wife? And how many does he have? Because the wives are probably my fastest way into the inner circle."

"There is only one. Her name is Belinda, but you'll want to befriend Brother Harris; if that's even possible. He and Amos have a *special* relationship." Marcel's eyebrow quirked to emphasize the insinuation.

"The Prophet is gay?"

Marcel nodded. "Or bisexual. But you know it's against

the teachings of the Moral Order. They hide their relationship, but a few in the congregation suspect something. No one will challenge either of them, though. You'll need to be especially careful around the two of them. They don't particularly like women. In fact, with the brutality they've displayed, I'd say they genuinely despise them."

Alexis took a deep breath. "So, how do I fit into all this? Do they even suspect you might be involved with someone that you'd just run off and marry?"

"They know you, so there's nothing you'll need to lie about or try to hide; other than our being married. And they're aware of our previous relationship. They also know that you were handpicked by Prophet Symmetry. Use that to your advantage. Had you stayed, you would no doubt be First Wife to the Prophet and Moral Mother to the flock. I would leverage your PI license to offer an added measure of security to the congregate. Prophet Amos is all about increasing and protecting the revenue in his more lascivious endeavors. He likes money. And he's flashy with it even when he pretends to be humble about the growing profits. The man is the personification of greed and at least five of the other seven deadly sins."

"Do the others not see it? Why do they support him?"

"He's a master manipulator and he's used fear and intimidation to control everyone."

"What if this doesn't work, Marcel? What then?" Concern painted Alexis's expression. Her own reservations wafted between them.

There was an awkward pause as Marcel reflected on her question. It had begun to rain, a steady drizzle falling from a darkening sky. The humidity was thick and rancid, seeming to foreshadow what they might soon face.

Marcel answered. "It must work, Alexis. You and I need to make sure it works."

Her head bobbed against her thin neck as she absorbed his response, his anguish seeming to flood through her body. *Only by the grace and mercy of God*, Alexis thought to herself. *Because way too much could go the wrong way too fast.*

Marcel was lost in thought when they turned off the main roadway and onto the muddy dirt road that would lead them past acres of swampland to the makeshift community of the Moral Order. They'd been driving for over an hour, heading toward the Atchafalaya Basin. Once a thriving center for logging, hunting, trapping and fishing, flooding had degraded the area, burying it underneath at least twelve feet of silt. It was now filled with bayous, bald cypress swamps and marshes. Few residents inhabited the area; the others encouraged to seek higher ground to make their homes along the fringes of the basin in towns like New Iberia, St. Martinville and Breaux Bridge. The Moral Order had settled in the area because of its proximity to neighboring towns and the seclusion it offered from meddling outsiders.

Marcel was suddenly having second thoughts about dragging Alexis into his problems. And even more concerned that she would be isolated from her family and friends as she willingly followed him into harm's way. Admittedly, he was more frightened than he was willing to acknowledge.

He had gone through every imaginable scenario in his head. There wasn't anything Marcel hadn't considered. But the adage about only being able to control one's self played on a continuous loop in his head. He couldn't control what anyone else did or how they might react. He could only control himself. That lesson had hit home when his sister had died. Despite all his efforts, Camille hadn't been able, or willing, to hold on until he'd gotten there. She hadn't trusted him, or herself, and so she'd let go, giving up hope that he would save her. He understood there was nothing he could have done once she'd made her choice, but he still questioned if he could have helped her make a different choice.

Now, his sister Camille was gone, a narcissistic demagogue threatened his daughter's security, and the woman he loved didn't trust or even like him anymore. Control was the very last thing he had, and despite all his efforts to hide that fact, he knew that Alexis could see the truth.

Chapter 8

Despite her best efforts to remember each turn, Alexis didn't have a clue where she was or how to find her way out. The Saints of the Moral Order had situated themselves back in deep swampland, surrounded by darkness and scary swamp things. One could easily get turned around and lost, left to perish in the elements.

There was a method to their madness and Alexis found herself thinking about the pit of hell she herself had been trapped in years before. Prophet Symmetry had taken her to the Midwest compound, a farming community, miles from civilization. The torture had started almost immediately, Symmetry proclaiming her unworthy and in need of orientation. An infraction could have been as simple as not dropping her eyes in the presence of an elder or speaking out of turn. She still wore the scars on her back from the multitailed whip he'd used to administer punishment. But those lashings had been easier than the solitary confinement in the hotbox. The hotbox had broken her; leaving little resemblance to the little girl who'd arrived wide-eyed and starstruck, completely infatuated with the man who'd proclaimed himself her savior.

The hotbox had been a small cage that sat in a field,

miles from the main house. Confinement to the hotbox was extreme torture, leaving its victims in excessive heat or severe cold. Naked and alone, they would suffer dehydration, exhaustion and sometimes death. Alexis had often prayed for death, believing it easier than the abuse she'd been made to handle. She had quickly learned to be an obedient subject, eventually garnering the Prophet's trust. When he'd granted her a trip to town to gather supplies, Alexis had made her escape, running to the local sheriff's office to call home. Prophet Symmetry had been furious. He had considered her a prized possession and her outwitting him had made him look weak. He had vowed revenge and then, like a magician's magic trick, he had disappeared. Alexis didn't have to be told that her parents had somehow been responsible, the two promising he would never cross her path again. Just knowing he was gone had been enough for her. She hadn't needed the details.

"When do the lights go out?" she asked. She and Marcel still sat in the van, both staring toward the front of the commune's main building. Bathing them in darkness at the end of the day was standard practice for the Order, no matter where they were. Mostly, it was due to there being no electricity in the remote areas they always chose. A system of generators kept the place going during the day but would be shut down at night to conserve the fuel. It had often been referred to as the bewitching hour.

"Nine o'clock," he answered.

She took a deep breath. "Do not let them put me in the box," she whispered, changing the subject. "I don't care what I do, or why they think I deserve it, please don't let them do that to me."

The panic in her tone was cutting, every word pulling at Marcel's heartstrings.

Marcel nodded. "Never," he answered. "I won't let anyone here hurt you. I promise you that, Alexis."

She took a second large inhale of air deep into her lungs and then another, wanting desperately to believe him.

A small welcoming committee had gathered on the front porch, appearing out of nowhere like a horror movie apparition. Alexis instinctively knew the Prophet, a short, balding man draped in a white silk robe. The man beside him was similarly dressed, his robe a deep shade of forest-green velvet. Marcel confirmed that he was Brother Harris, the Prophet's special friend. Both men wore leather Jesus sandals on their feet. Three women stood two steps behind them, their heads bowed and eyes lowered. They wore long-sleeved tunics and loose slacks in shades of dingy gray. Beside the two men, their clothes appeared tattered and unflattering, and only one wore shoes, a sturdy slip-on with a thick sole. The other two were barefoot.

Marcel reached for her hand and squeezed her fingers. "Are you ready?" he whispered softly.

"No," Alexis whispered back. She pulled her hand from his, closing it into a tight fist in her lap. "I'll never be ready."

Marcel had been welcomed back with open arms. It was evident that he had been missed by many, his departure somewhat incongruent to their expectations of him. He had attained the status of elder and was well respected. He stood beside the Prophet, having changed into his own velvet robe, the color a rich burgundy red. It flattered his tawny complexion and blond locks.

The front door had opened to a large meeting room. It was tastefully decorated and, despite the rise of humidity and heat, the space felt inviting. Alexis had been made to change clothes as well. They had confiscated her denim jeans and graphic T-shirt. Also gone was the Victoria's Secret silk tank and matching panty. She now donned a pale gray, floor-length tunic, embroidered with small eyelet flowers. Stark white cotton undergarments completed her look.

Alexis stood before the church hierarchy, the congregants at her back. No one spoke. Men were lined obediently on one side of the room, the women on the other. Her head was bowed and her hands were folded together in front of her. She stood like stone, waiting for the Prophet's approval.

Marcel spoke first when all the others had finally gathered. There was a hint of pride in his tone and Alexis wanted to look up. To see his face and stare into his eyes. But she didn't dare break her stance and risk admonishment. It would not have served her well or looked favorably on Marcel.

"Prophet Amos, I present to you my wife, Alexis Martin Broussard. Alexis is a Chosen Daughter, bearing the mark of our founding father. She willingly and joyfully desires to return to your flock. As my wife, she will be faithful to our ways and give honor to you and the Almighty."

The Prophet sauntered slowly in her direction until he stood directly in front of her. Alexis dropped to her knees as he extended his hand, but she said nothing.

Alexis grasped the appendage and pressed a dry kiss to

the backs of his fingers. “All honor to you, Prophet,” she said softly.

He grabbed her wrist, turning her fingers with his other hand until he could see the tattoo that adorned her middle finger.

“You were chosen. That means the Prophet thought you special. But you ran from our ministry. Why return now?” he questioned.

Alexis paused a moment before she answered. Her own voice was calming. “I was a child, Prophet. With childish ways. I was corrupted by the sins of Satan and other nonbelievers. I lacked the maturity to trust our faith. I’ve grown since and I have missed the sanctity of the Moral Order. I wish only to be a loyal and faithful servant, obedient to my husband, and to you, Prophet, and to the Almighty Father. I beg you to find favor with me and allow me to prove myself to you and the brethren.” Her tone was pleading, promises latching onto her words. She was very convincing and if Marcel had not known the truth, he would have believed her.

The Prophet nodded as he cupped his hand beneath her chin and lifted her eyes to stare into her face. Alexis was fighting back tears, desperate not to ugly cry. The man leaned to kiss her cheek. He smelled sour, like spoiled milk, and Alexis swallowed back the bile that threated to spew in his face. He straightened, pulling his torso upward. He continued to eye her intently. A single tear dripped past her lashes and rolled over the curvature of her cheek. The Prophet smiled.

“You give honor by being a faithful helpmate to Elder Marcel. We trust his wisdom and so I grant your request.

You have been chosen twice now. Do not fail your calling a second time. Welcome home, daughter."

The Prophet turned, stepping back to stand on the makeshift altar. Marcel eased his way to stand beside her as she straightened. He pressed his side against hers and Alexis felt herself lean into his warmth. Every ounce of anxiety she'd been feeling suddenly disappeared. She barely heard what followed, the Prophet's words going in one ear and out the other. The room felt like it was beginning to spin, and the air was stifling. In that moment, all she wanted was to be as far from them all as she could manage. She dared a quick glance toward Marcel, tears burning hot against her lashes.

When Marcel grabbed her hand in response, she gladly held tight to him, afraid that she might fall. The Prophet was still praying over them both, blessing the union. As he did, Alexis bowed her head and silently whispered her own prayer for strength and safekeeping.

Startled out of a deep sleep, Alexis sat upright in the queen-sized bed that she'd slept in. Marcel's private quarters were indicative of his position with the Moral Order. The moment Alexis had laid eyes on the space, she realized that his acceleration up the divine ladder had him in line to be the next Prophet. She also realized that if the rumors were true about Prophet Amos and his friend, a coordinated challenge could easily displace both men and see them exiled from the Saints of the Moral Order. If Marcel coveted the position even a little, it was his for the taking.

Clearly, much more had happened since she and Marcel had last been together. There was still a lot he hadn't yet shared with her, and she'd been salty about it once the marriage festivities had concluded. After the Prophet had blessed their union, there had been fresh-baked pound cake and homemade vanilla ice cream. Everyone in the congregation had gladly stepped forward to introduce themselves and wish the happy couple well. Celebrations were far and few, revelry rarely allowed. Enjoying the moment was paramount to them feeling normal again. The lights had eventually gone out on the good time they had been having and she'd been left with a lot to digest.

Alexis had wanted it to be an argument, but that hadn't been feasible. Instead, she'd given him the silent treatment, along with a pillow and a blanket to sleep on the plush green sofa that decorated the front room.

Alexis didn't realize she'd cried out in her sleep until Marcel came rushing to the bedside, concern painting his expression. He dropped down beside her on the mattress, his large hand resting atop the blanket that covered her legs.

"Are you okay?" Marcel asked.

Alexis sat upright. She shrugged her narrow shoulders. "I'm fine. It was just a bad dream," she answered.

"I'm sorry."

"What are you apologizing for?"

"Now I'm giving you bad dreams!" He tossed up his hands.

Alexis laughed despite her efforts not to. She found his expression funny and the comment amusing.

Marcel chuckled softly and the warmth in his voice made her smile. "Good morning, *Mrs.* Broussard," he said softly.

She gave him a slight nod of her head, his greeting ringing sweetly through the air. She didn't respond with the same whimsy. "Good morning, Elder," Alexis said as she lowered her eyes and clasped her hands in her lap. Her words were laced with hostility.

Marcel winced. "Ouch!"

Alexis snapped at him. "Why didn't you tell me, Marcel? You are an elder! I can only imagine what you had to do to accomplish that feat. Who you had to hurt! You should have told me!"

"First, I've never inflicted physical pain on anyone. Ever. Like you, my pedigree opened the door. I was an original brother and the only son of an elder. Our Prophets have all liked the idea of nepotism, believing this is our destiny, no matter how hard we try to fight it. I've just played the game the way I know it needed to be played."

He inhaled before continuing. "Second, I didn't think it was important, otherwise I would have told you. I apologize. I wasn't trying to hide anything from you."

Alexis sighed. "All of this is so messed up! This puts a whole other kind of spotlight on me. They know you might be the future Prophet. Now they're going to look at me differently as they try to figure out what roll I'm going to have in all of this. Not the kind of pressure I need right now."

"You'll be fine," Marcel said, trying to be nonchalant about the situation.

She shook her head. "I just want to crawl back under the covers and go to sleep," she said.

"Well, you can't. In fact, I was just about to wake you. We have a full day. We need to be down for breakfast by seven. Then Prophet wants you to get a tour of the commune. After that, he's requested a private confab with you.

I have no doubt he'll be searching for information. He'll also want to discuss your work assignment."

She changed the subject back again. "Marcel, you should have told me that you were next in line to be Prophet."

"I didn't because that's not ever going to happen."

"Have you given it any consideration?

"I've thought about it and if this was the life I wanted for myself, it would be tempting. But the Moral Order has become corrupted. It is not the community my parents had brought us to when I was a child. There's no longer any purity in their actions."

"But you could change that and put the Order back on the right track, couldn't you?"

Marcel shook his head. "The only way to fix what's broken now, is to tear it down completely and hope that those who survive unscathed can rebuild if it's genuinely important to them. Sadly, the past leadership destroyed what this community was when it started, and the current leadership has made it something I don't recognize. I don't want any part of that. Not for us, or my daughter." He reached for her hand and pulled it to his full lips, pressing a kiss into her palm. His touch was heated, and evocative, feeling like lighter fluid tossed atop hot coals.

Us. He said us, Alexis thought. Like she was more than an assignment he needed help with. She closed her hand as if to preserve the gentleness of his touch. Alexis studied him as he seemed to drift off into thought. It was then that she realized Marcel was bare-chested, wearing nothing but boxer briefs that hugged him tightly below the waist. She gasped. Loudly. Marcel was still a beautiful specimen of maleness. He was muscular and sculpted. His chest was broad and his arms taut. The nearness of him, heat rising off his pale skin, took her back to a time when things had been perfect between them. When they'd made love as easily as they'd breathed. When every new day had strengthened the bond they'd shared and held promises of a bright future. Then she blinked.

"I need to get dressed," Alexis muttered, trying to ignore the heat ignited in her feminine spirit. She reached for a pillow and held it to her chest, her arms wrapped tightly around it. Her nipples had hardened and pressed like rock candy against the cotton shift she'd worn to bed.

He nodded. "I'll give you some privacy," Marcel said. There was no missing the smug smile that crossed the man's face. He rose from where he sat and headed toward the other room. He didn't bother to hide the rise of nature that had lengthened in his shorts.

Marcel clenched his hands into tight fists. He rolled his shoulders forward and then backward, desperate to shake off the anxiety that had coursed through his body. He couldn't begin to imagine what Alexis had to be thinking about him. He hadn't wanted to draw any attention to his predicament and so he'd ignored it, hoping she would do the same.

His body had betrayed him. All his senses had responded to the sight of her. She was still the most stunning woman he had ever known. She had been angelic as she'd lain sleeping in his bed. After she had dozed off, he had stood watching her, grateful that she'd finally been able to rest and rest well. She had done a spectacular job and had made quite an impression. Many had been an awe of her as she'd moved with grace, interacting as if she had never left the Order.

He hadn't meant to stare when he'd gone in to check on her, but there had been no missing everything he found attractive about her. Her cheeks had been flushed; her tousled hair pinned in an updo. There had been the slightest pout to her lips and he'd been suddenly taken aback by the memories of everything they had shared. His heart had melted at the sight of her, and every muscle had hardened from the top of his head to the bottom of his feet.

Marcel loved Alexis with every fiber in his being and all he had wanted was to press his mouth to hers and kiss those lips again. Thoughts of touching her, of trailing his tongue across her skin, wanting to taste her, to feel her body pressed against his, had left him with a raging erection. His embarrassment had been acute, but he'd been desperate not to let it show. Acting natural, however, had been difficult at best as he'd hurried from the room, a foolish smile plastered on his face. He wouldn't have blamed her if she thought him a perverted fool with that stupid grin he'd given her.

Now, as they headed to the dining room for breakfast, things between them were awkward. He felt foolish, wishing he could wind back time and get a do-over. Alexis was stone-faced and had barely spoken two words to him since they'd gone their separate ways to get dressed.

The congregation shared all their meals together. They were a small faction of the Moral Order and were able to feed everyone in a single sitting. The other sects were larger and meals were done in shifts. This group had only been in place for a year and, despite the location, they were growing rapidly. Soon, most of the congregation would be transferred out to spread the word of the Prophet. New members would come through for induction and the process would start all over again.

Few knew that the younger girls, trained to be submissive, would be trafficked to parts unknown, purchased by lecherous, violent psychopaths. The babies and younger children were sold through private adoption, some to people who couldn't qualify to be parents through traditional methods. Young lives were being hijacked in the name of God for one individual's personal gain and no one was supposed to know. But Marcel knew. He knew and he was doing everything in his power to put an end to Prophet Amos and his demonic schemes.

Chapter 9

"You have chosen well, Elder Marcel." Brother Harris tapped Marcel on the shoulder. He stood as tall as Marcel, with a slim frame, chiseled jawline and a sunburned complexion. "Your new wife is not only beautiful but also virtuous. She will fit in well with our congregation."

"My new wife is a Chosen Daughter for a reason. She believes in the greater good," Marcel replied. "She desires to follow the ways of the Prophet and ascend to Heaven at the ordained time to honor our Savior."

Harris smiled. "We hope she will prove to be as faithful a servant as you have been. You two must be fruitful and bring forth offspring for the Prophet."

Marcel nodded. "All honor to the Prophet."

"All honor..." Harris echoed.

Marcel's gaze shifted to where Alexis stood on the other side of the room. She'd eaten quickly, a comforting meal of shrimp and grits topped with freshly grated cheese. Then she'd risen from her seat to help serve the others. She was clearing away dirty dishes and refreshing the food trays. He watched as she moved comfortably among the other women. He couldn't help but think she would indeed make a great First Wife and Moral Mother over the religious flock; if such a thing were remotely possible. But it wasn't a consideration for either of them.

He turned toward the other man. "We have a full day ahead of us. We need to get started."

Harris nodded in agreement. "Prophet needs us to coordinate the next shipment out of the Dallas compound. We may have to pay their ministry a visit. There has been some unrest there lately."

Marcel didn't bother to question what that shipment was. He knew the average age of the girls who would be trafficked from Dallas to their Midwest community for orientation was thirteen. Eventually they would be sent down to Mexico, never to be heard from again. But he also knew that a random traffic stop would derail them from making their final destination. And when that happened, he knew that he, Alexis and Sabine needed to be as far from the Saints of the Moral Order as possible.

Marcel gave Harris a quick nod. His eyes shifted to stare at Alexis one last time. Meeting his gaze, she stared back and finally blessed him with the slightest smile. He smiled, turned and headed for the exit.

Although he probably thought she was still fuming, Alexis really wasn't angry with Marcel. She was, however, embarrassed, and wished that he hadn't noticed her discomfort. Barely speaking to him and not looking him in the eye, though, spoke volumes. Had they shared another minute she would have gladly tossed aside her reservations and consummated the marriage that wasn't a real marriage. She would have gladly welcomed him back into her most intimate spaces and she wouldn't have regretted a single minute. Or she would have regretted everything. She still wasn't sure which.

Alexis hated that the two of them still hadn't found balance with each other. Even if all of this was pretend, they had been friends once. Best friends, and she genuinely missed that relationship.

She'd watched him as he had stood in conversation with Brother Harris. It didn't take rocket science to know that the other man had been talking about her, his stare blatant. Something about Marcel's stance had raised her blood pressure. He'd looked tense and irritated by the other man's presence. And so she'd smiled, wanting him to feel more at ease. When he'd smiled back, the weight that had been wearing her down began to disappear.

Watching after him as he made his way toward the exit and out of the room, she couldn't help but notice the other woman who'd also been staring in Marcel's direction. Something about the intensity of her gaze was off-putting. Marcel had barely given her a glance and that, too, seemed to disturb her even more. Alexis realized she also was staring when the Prophet's First Wife stepped beside her and whispered into her ear.

Mother Belinda had been part of the welcoming party the previous night. She'd been the woman in the heavy-duty shoes. Everything about her was heavy-duty, Alexis had thought. There was a toughness about her, something innate that no one could touch. Most especially no man, no matter what his status in the Order. Mother Belinda wasn't fearful of looking the Prophet or any of his minions in the eye and she didn't bite her tongue when it came to issues she believed the Moral Mother was responsible for. Alexis had quickly discovered that even included the punishments handed down to any of the other women. Belinda had welcomed her with open arms and, although the sentiment had felt genuine, there was still something disconcerting about it. She was close in age to Alexis's mother, maybe older, and Alexis wanted to like her despite knowing that she would probably never trust her.

"Keep your eye on that one," Belinda said with the slightest grunt. "Her name is Felicia. She hasn't been with the Order very long and there's still much she needs to learn. I've had to admonish her many times for the way she tries to throw herself at Elder Marcel. She had been hoping the elder would have chosen her to be his bride, but he had no interest in her and now we know why."

Belinda gave her a smile as she continued. "Felicia is disappointed and bitter about being passed over. What is it they say about a woman scorned and the fury of hell?" She tilted her head in the other woman's direction. "The devil stays busy! Do not turn your back on her."

"I appreciate the advice," Alexis said. "Things have really changed since I was last here. Where are all the children?"

Belinda shook her head. "The change hasn't all been for the greater good, but the Prophet says he knows best. Just be mindful of *what* you question and, more importantly, *who* you ask."

"All honor to the Prophet," Alexis mumbled under her breath. She and the other woman exchanged a knowing look.

"If you are done here," Belinda said, "I've been instructed to give you a tour before you meet with the Prophet."

Alexis gave her a slight nod. "Thank you," she said. "I appreciate your kindness."

"We all need an ally in this place," Belinda said. "Even when we think we don't."

Harris hadn't stopped talking since he and Marcel had exited the building. Marcel had no interest in the man's babbling. Whatever he was saying was going in one ear and out the other. Marcel was only thinking about Alexis, praying that she was well and that she would soon be united with his baby girl. He took a breath, realizing that Harris was shouting for his attention.

"Is that one going to be a problem for you?" Harris questioned, gesturing toward the woman who stood at the end of the pier. The annoyance in his tone was thick and rancid like clabbered milk.

Marcel turned to look where he pointed. Sister Felicia was standing anxiously, hoping to catch Marcel's attention. When she saw him looking, she raised her hand ever so slightly and gave him a wave. He shook his head, impatience rearing as he imagined what she could have wanted from him, to risk being reprimanded by one of the Elders. Felicia was the last problem he needed to contend with.

Befriending the young woman had not been his smartest move. At the time, she'd been close to one of the other elders, who'd been closer to the Prophet. She'd also had unlimited access to the babies in the nursery. She had allowed him inside to see Sabine the few times he'd been able to lay eyes on the child. He had hoped to leverage their friendship to his benefit. He hadn't realized how vulnerable, and needy, Felicia was until it was too late. She'd become obsessed with his position and what she'd hoped it might mean for her. Twice now, he'd had to save her from the harsh punishments the Prophet was famous for doling out. Twice, he'd challenged the authority, putting his own neck on the line. Since then, he had found her to be manipulative and desperate. And he knew desperation could very well make her dangerous.

He tossed Harris a quick glance. "Check that last shipment that came in. The inventory was off, and we haven't gotten an explanation for the shortage. I'll be down in a minute."

"You need to stop being so soft on these females. You show too much weakness and not enough discipline," Harris said, sneering.

Marcel didn't bother to respond, instead moving swiftly to where Felicia was standing.

"Good morning, Elder Marcel," she said softly, glancing over her shoulder to see who might be within hearing range.

"What do you want, Felicia?" Marcel asked, his tone brusque.

She pressed her fingers against the front of his tunic. The gesture was intimate and suggestive. "I missed you," she said. "I was hoping we might be able to speak for a few minutes."

"We both have work to do, and I've spoken to you multiple times before about being inappropriate."

"Most men would be happy for my attention," she answered snidely.

"I'm not most men and I will not have you disrespecting me or my wife."

Her eyes narrowed into thin slits. "I should have been your wife!" she quipped. "What do you know about this woman? You know me. You know I would do anything for you!"

"What I know is that you'll be headed to the box if you keep this up. Don't push me."

"You wouldn't dare!"

With near-perfect timing, Elder Harris appeared at his elbow. "What would Elder Marcel not dare do?" he asked.

Felicia dropped her eyes to the ground and her hands to her sides. She didn't speak, anxiety suddenly billowing in the air around her.

Harris persisted. "Do we have a problem here, Elder?"

"Nothing a day or two in the box wouldn't fix," Marcel said. He narrowed his gaze on the young woman.

"Is that your call, Elder?"

Felicia suddenly dropped to her knees. "Forgive me, Elder! Please! I meant no disrespect. Please!"

"Off to your duties," Marcel snapped.

Before either man could blink, Felicia jumped to her feet and ran in the opposite direction.

Harris laughed. "She'll be in the box by next week. That one needs to be broken. And tamed." He picked something from between his teeth and flicked it off his finger. "I look forward to giving that order," he said as he made an about-face.

If he could have punched the fool in his face, Marcel would have. He fisted his hands at his sides, fighting the urge to throw a punch. Then Marcel followed the man, adding one more problem to an already lengthy list of issues.

Knowing Marcel had been involved in building the community left Alexis with an air of pride that she had not expected. Much thought and a wealth of love had gone into planning. There were greenhouses that sat above swampland, affording them a generous bounty of fresh fruits and vegetables. The ability to be self-sufficient had been a cornerstone of the original Moral Order. Alexis understood its importance.

The main house had been built on higher ground, as had most of the living quarters. The construction was strategic, the foundations erected on stilts to raise them some three to four feet above any potential floodwaters. A series of walkways and bridges connected the living spaces to the worship center and the Prophet's residence. A row of generators powered everything that needed an electrical connection.

The landscape that surrounded it all felt almost magical, Alexis thought as she took it all in. Sunlight flickered through a canopy of tall cypress trees. A slow-moving creek ran behind the property and Alexis knew they used it to transport product in and out of the area. Belinda had warned her of the wild animals and the alligators, and Alexis understood why leaving or running would never be easy for any of them.

"This is where most of the women congregate during the day," Belinda said. "Prophet is the only man allowed through these doors." She pulled at the entrance and gestured for Alexis to step past the threshold.

Someone had nicknamed the space Moral Mother Hall. There was a warm, welcoming ambience and Alexis felt herself instantly relax.

"To answer your earlier question," Belinda said, "any children on property are confined to this area. We only keep newborns and infants here. The swamps aren't safe, and Prophet doesn't want to risk their young lives, especially since children are so curious about their surroundings. We try to send them to the larger communities before they really begin to walk. There's open space there for them to run around."

Alexis nodded. "And the mothers go with them?"

"Of course," Belinda answered. "Why wouldn't they?"

Alexis shrugged. "I'd heard rumors that mothers were being separated from their babies."

"You heard lies. The family unit is the foundation of the Moral Order. Prophet would never take a child from its mother. Never! He will often send the mothers ahead to prepare, but the children are always reunited with their moms."

There was an edge to Belinda's tone and Alexis sensed she had hit a nerve. What she couldn't figure out was whether Belinda actually believed what she was saying, was lying to protect the Order, or if she was trying to convince herself that Prophet was a decent and upstanding leader.

"That's good to know," Alexis said, smiling sweetly. "The Elder and I hope to bless the Prophet with many children to honor and praise him."

Belinda smiled. "All honor to the Prophet," she said.

They traveled slowly through the space, pausing to exchange pleasantries with the women there. Several of them were pregnant, varying stages of bulging bellies pushed forward. Alexis wanted to ask how many had been impregnated by artificial insemination and how many had gotten knocked up the old-fashioned way, but she didn't dare.

There was a full-fledged medical center with top-of-the-line equipment. The midwife, a young woman named Delilah, had been with the Order since she herself had been a child. She was bright and bubbly, and just ditzy enough to make Alexis smile. Under different circumstances, Alexis thought, the two could have been great friends.

Alexis instinctively knew the nursery would be her favorite area in the facility and, clearly, there were other women who felt the same. Fifteen babies were being hugged and cuddled and passed from one set of arms to another.

She suddenly felt Belinda staring at her, studying her, and it made her nervous. "Everyone's so happy!" Alexis chimed, feeling slightly foolish.

Belinda nodded. "It's what we want. All honor to the Prophet!"

A chorus of voices repeated what she'd said, the words echoing through the room.

"All honor to the Prophet!" Alexis said.

"There are ten more infants in the other room," Belinda said. "The young souls here are all under six months old. The other children are all over six months, but less than one year old. We don't currently have any children older than one year. Most leave us by their first birthdays."

She led the way and Alexis followed. The babies had already been put down for a midday nap and only two caregivers sat watching over them. Alexis moved from one crib to another, all of them lined neatly in a row. She paused to tap a little boy against his back as he tossed about. Another slumbered, snoring ever so slightly, and she drew her index finger along his cheek. But it was the third baby that made her stop and pause.

Marcel had been right. There was no missing his bright blue eyes staring up from the cherub face. Sabine suckled her thumb as she eyed Alexis curiously. It took everything in Alexis not to lift the small bundle from where she lay, wanting to nuzzle her nose into the folds of baby skin around Sabine's neck. There was no doubt that this was Marcel's baby, every one of his features imprinted on her small person.

Alexis suddenly looked up to see if Belinda was still watching her too closely. She stood in deep conversation with one of the women Alexis had just met. She didn't seem to be paying Alexis any attention and she was grateful, feeling like she'd been blessed with a moment of reprieve. Had Belinda been watching, Alexis knew her facial expression would have given her intentions away. She turned, forcing herself to move to the next crib and another baby who was not Marcel's.

Alexis could feel her face reddening with heat. Her heart had begun to race and she was visibly shaking. She could only imagine how Marcel had reacted the first time he'd seen her. Baby Sabine was precious, and she radiated with innocence and love. She was the most beautiful baby Alexis had ever seen.

Just as she reached the last crib, a booming voice echoed through the room. The Prophet had made a grand entrance, ensuring everyone knew he was there. One of the children started to cry and then another. As Alexis turned in his direction, she didn't miss the annoyance on Belinda's face.

The women in the room all dropped to the floor, heads bowed, palms down against the hardwood.

"All honor to the Prophet," Alexis echoed, her voice loud and crisp. She didn't move, waiting to be excused from the position.

"I see you're getting reacquainted," Prophet said. "I'm told you're fitting in nicely with the other women. That's a very good thing."

He had moved to Alexis's side and now stood in front of her. She opened her eyes, his sandaled feet directly in her face. She didn't speak, waiting for his permission. There was a moment of silence, him waiting to see what she would do. He seemed satisfied when she didn't budge. He tapped the top of her head.

"You may rise," he said as he took a step back.

Rising slowly, Alexis clasped her hands together in front of her. Her eyes were still lowered as she stared at the floor.

"You were trained well. Elder Marcel would be very proud." He trailed the back of his fingers against the profile of her face. "Eyes forward," he commanded.

Alexis held her breath as she looked up, mindful not to flinch or show an ounce of emotion. She bit back the taste of bile that burned the back of her throat. The Prophet shuffled down the line of cribs, peering into each.

"Our Father has generously blessed the Moral Order," he said. "We are honored by his blessings. Our future lies here in this room." He paused at Sabine's crib and picked up the tiny child. She cooed, the pacifier she'd been suckling dropping to the floor. Suddenly, she screeched, crying out in pain. The Prophet had pinched her chubby thigh. Hard.

From where she stood, Alexis could see the rise of a

bruise beginning to bloom a vibrant shade of red. Wailing, Sabine threw herself backward, the Prophet barely holding on to her. Belinda came to the baby's rescue, pulling Sabine from his arms.

"This one is going to wake the other babies, Husband. If that happens, I will need to pull women away from afternoon prayer to help me calm them all down."

Alexis could still feel the Prophet staring in her direction. Her expression was blank as she met his gaze with one of her own. Something deep in her spirit had risen with a vengeance. It took all she had not to scratch his eyes out for what he had done. In that moment, Alexis knew she would protect Sabine with her own life. What she assumed could only be a mother's instincts had kicked in full force. The Prophet's actions were cruel, and malicious, and had been yet another test to see how she would respond. Alexis refused to give him the satisfaction of seeing her riled. She needed to be able to come back. To be there to protect Sabine from any further cruelty.

"Let's walk, Sister Alexis," he said as he turned toward the door. And with the obedience of a well-trained pup, Alexis followed him, exchanging one last look with Belinda as the woman gently caressed the hurt out of the infant's leg and rocked Marcel's baby girl to sleep.

Chapter 10

Following the Prophet, Alexis found herself wondering if anyone had ever considered knocking him unconscious before throwing him into the swamp. With apt timing, he could be fish food for a roving alligator, she thought to herself. She had often considered ways she might send Prophet Symmetry to rot in hell, but fear had kept her from pulling the trigger. She didn't fear Amos. She detested him and everything he stood for.

Amos was no man of God and so far from being prophetic, that climbing his way out of hell would never be possible. He was narcissistic, craving power and adoration. He served no deity that she or Marcel believed in. Marcel had been right about tearing the entire Order down. Men like Amos had perverted the word of God, twisting it into oblivion. As they rounded one more corner, the pathway narrowing between a row of trees, she thought again about pushing him. And then she saw the box.

"You are quite the anomaly, Sister Alexis," Prophet said. He had slowed, sauntering slowly toward the torture chamber. As they got closer, Alexis realized someone was locked inside. The air caught in her chest and, for the first time since her arrival, she knew hiding her revulsion would be next to impossible.

She gasped. Loudly. "How is that, Prophet?" she questioned, her voice cracking ever so slightly.

"No one ever returns once they've run. You ran, and now here you are. Not only did you return willingly, but you also seem devoted to serving your new husband and the Moral Order. I would think that the ways of the former Prophet were unduly harsh. Someone who was inducted as I'm told you were, might not want to return to the fold."

"As I said before, Prophet, I was a child and I behaved childishly. Once I knew better, I was determined to do better. My training was made to prepare me to serve the greater good. I'm ready now to do that."

"And what of Prophet Symmetry? He disappeared from the Order shortly after he went searching for you. What do you know of his fate?"

Alexis slowly shook her head. She lied. "I know nothing of the Prophet. But I pray that he is well and continues to serve his God faithfully."

The Prophet turned to stare at her. Alexis lifted her chin ever so slightly and stared back. The moment felt like a battle of wills and Alexis was determined not to lose.

He finally nodded his head. "What do you see yourself doing here? How will you give to the community and show reverence to your husband?"

"I will do whatever is required of me, Prophet," she answered. Alexis sensed that if she asked for what she wanted, he would automatically deny her request. She didn't want to give him the opportunity.

He paused again. His eyes closed, he seemed to be lost

in thought. Alexis shifted her glance toward the young woman in the cage. She had lifted herself up to stare at the two of them. Tears rained down her cheeks and her naked body was covered in blisters from sunburn and bug bites. Alexis prayed that the look she gave said she would do whatever was necessary to free her. She would not leave the girl here alone. But she couldn't risk angering the Prophet. She prayed that her eyes spoke for her and that the young woman understood.

The Prophet shifted his weight, reaching for the padlock that held the cage door shut. At the same time, he searched his pocket for the key. "The Holy Word teaches obedience. Obedience has become problematic for some," the Prophet said. "Our young women are fighting the ways of our Savior, or they are choosing to leave our covenant for the sins of the outside world. You can be a shining example and help us to lead them to their true destinies. I would like to see you work with them, to help with their training. Do you think you can do that?"

"Of course, Prophet. But I have a request. Please?"

His brow lifted as he eyed her intently. He gestured for her to continue.

"Obedience requires purpose. We must give them a purpose. Something for them to aim for."

"Ascending to glory isn't purpose enough?" he snapped.

"Ascension is the ultimate reward. They require something tangible. Something that will give them immediate gratification. Something that will let them feel worthy of ascension."

"And what is this something you have in mind, Sister?"

"In the other communities, the women engage with the

children. Our nurturing instincts give us reason to want to see them ascend to glory with us. We want to be the example that will help show them the way. If we accept our true nature as defined in the good book, we will want what is best for the babies. We don't have that here."

Prophet didn't look convinced, but he hadn't said no.

Alexis continued. "Give me one week with her," she said, pointing to the young woman who was still staring at them.

"She is scheduled to leave for reorientation."

"One week and she will not need reorientation," Alexis said with conviction.

The man's silence was thundering. Around them, the sounds of wildlife chirped, hissed and squawked. There was an occasional splash of something jumping into and out of the murky waters surrounding them. And the girl had begun to hiccup as she tried not to sob outright and potentially enrage the Prophet.

Saying nothing, Prophet finally unlocked the cage and dropped the key back into his pocket. He turned to head back to the main building, calling over his shoulder, "The penalty for failure will not shine favorably on the Elder," he quipped. "Do not be a disappointment to your new husband."

"All honor to you, Prophet," Alexis said.

She was only sixteen. Her name was Christiana and Belinda was her mother. She'd survived six days in the box and only because her mother had been sneaking her bread and water when the Prophet wasn't looking. Christiana's crime had been to call the Prophet a fraud, peppering his name with colorful expletives. She'd called him everything but a child of God and he'd rewarded her with the harshest punishment imaginable.

As Alexis guided her into the women's space, Belinda had come running to help. She'd hugged her daughter tightly, but Christiana hadn't hugged her back. The girl was angry. Angry with her mother for putting them both in their current situation.

"I was seven when she became obsessed with the Saints of the Moral Order. Before that, she could have cared less. My father had died the year before, and she reconnected with a boy she'd been sweet on when she'd been a teen. It was Prophet Amos. He was an Elder then and she was completely mesmerized. He convinced her that they could have a future together if we joined. The next thing I knew, they were married, and our lives have been miserable ever since." Christiana's voice was small; a raspy whisper that made her sound even younger than her sixteen years.

"When we transferred here, Prophet made her all kinds of promises. He acts all high and mighty and she keeps his dirty little secrets. She thinks she has some power, but he gets a kick out of knocking her down when she takes it too far."

Alexis gently brushed the girl's hair. She had showered and changed and had eaten a hot meal. Belinda had come to check on her twice, saying nothing at all when Christiana had cursed her the last time.

Alexis pushed for more information. "What secrets?"

"I think he has a thing for boys and when I said something, they sent me to the box the first time."

"The first time?"

"I've been three times. This was the longest, though, and

they are never sending me back. I need to get away from here. I'd rather risk running through the swamps and taking my chances with the snakes and alligators than staying here one more day."

Alexis nodded. "I get it. I do. I ran when I was about your age, too."

"And you came back?"

"It's hard to explain, but I'm hoping to make a difference."

"You can't change anything here. The men won't let you. Not even Elder Marcel. He's not as bad as the others, but he's still one of them."

Alexis cringed. That other people believed Marcel to be cruel and evil didn't sit well with her spirit. Pretend husband or not, she still cared about him. She knew his kindness, or she believed she did. But with their history, she still wasn't certain she knew him at all.

"I want to keep you safe until we have a plan," Alexis said finally. "I just need you to trust me."

Marcel stomped back toward the main house, rage fueling each of his steps. He was not happy and had no place to direct his anger. The short time he'd been gone, Harris and the Prophet had managed to upend all the good he'd worked hard to put in place. Multiple women had been subjected to floggings and a few to that dreaded box. And not one, but two, sexual assaults had been reported to the Prophet. Two women harmed by men in the community only to be excommunicated to parts unknown in the middle of the night. The men, unpunished, had been transferred to the Midwest community to help with orientations. It was a vicious cycle perpetuated by the Prophet's greed and disregard for those who worshipped him.

Marcel snapped, lashing out at the man in front of him. His name was Roberts and he'd been with the Order for over a year. He was not a man of faith, but a con artist hoping to avoid jail time for his earlier transgressions. Roberts was dragging a thirteen-year-old to the box, offended by her rebuking his advances.

"Leave her be," Marcel bellowed.

"She is disobedient and disrespectful," the other man snapped back. He had the young girl by the arm, his vise-like grip beginning to bruise her skin. "The Prophet said..." the man started.

"She is a child!" Marcel screamed as he took a step forward, his hands folded into tight fists. "Unhand her now or I will—"

He didn't get to finish his statement before the man named Roberts pushed the child into the swampy waters beneath them. He turned and nonchalantly headed back in the other direction. Marcel reached down into the water and grabbed for the child. She was flailing about, fear like a chokehold around her.

"Take my hand!" Marcel shouted.

The girl extended her arms out toward him and when she did, he was able to grab hold of her wrist. He pulled her up onto the planked walkway.

Tears streamed down her face and she was shaking with fright.

"You're fine. It's going to be okay," he said as she wrapped herself tightly around his legs, holding on to him for dear life.

Kneeling beside her, Marcel held the little girl as she sobbed uncontrollably. When she finally settled down, he walked her to the main house and one of the women, who took her by the hand. Then he stormed off in search of the Prophet.

Marcel hadn't said much when he'd stormed out of the Prophet's private sanctuary. In fact, he hadn't spoken at all. He had stomped toward the dining room for something to eat, pausing momentarily to stand beside Alexis. The two exchanged a look, something familiar seeping out of their eyes. Without a thought, Alexis had brushed her hand against his, the two clasping their pinkies together for the briefest moment. Marcel had taken a deep breath, filling his lungs with the aroma of fresh-baked bread and then he'd moved on to take a seat, gesturing for one of the other women to bring him a plate of food.

Alexis had wanted to ask about the shouting and the raised voices that had been uttered behind the Prophet's closed door, but she knew he would share when he was able. Right then, she had her own issues to be concerned with as she exited the building and headed for the nursery. Without fail, those assigned to keep an eye on her followed. No one tried to hide that she was being watched, everyone reporting her movements to the Prophet. She only hoped that whatever she'd done thus far didn't blow back on Marcel and add to their problems.

Inside the nursery, she paused to coo at each infant, proffering up tummy rubs and picking up pacifiers tossed aside. She acknowledged each and every child in the two rooms. It was only after feeling the adults relax, resuming their daily affairs without being concerned about her, did she venture to Sabine's crib. The baby lay on her back, staring up at a mobile constructed of wooden crosses painted in vibrant shades of the rainbow. The little girl's eyes were wide and bright, and she began to kick her chubby legs excitedly. Alexis could feel her own smile spread canyon-wide across her face.

"Hello, *cher*!" Alexis said softly as she reached to lift the child into her arms. She pulled the baby against her chest and held her tightly. "You must be lonely lying here with no one to play with you." Alexis nuzzled her face against Sabine's buttery skin and the little girl squealed with glee as she grabbed a fistful of Alexis's hair and pulled.

"Ouch!" Alexis laughed as she reached to disentangle her curly strands from the baby's small hand. "That's not fair, little girl! Be nice now." She kissed the baby's cheek.

"She will learn soon enough that life is rarely fair or nice."

Alexis turned slowly to find the woman named Felicia staring at her intently. Her arms were folded tightly across her chest and her eyes were cold. She looked from Alexis to the baby and back again.

"She has her father's eyes," Felicia said.

Alexis smiled. "All honor to the Prophet."

"Prophet claims her, but everyone knows she's your husband's child. You know, too."

"I know that we are all the children of a powerful and generous God."

Felicia's brow arched and it looked like she wanted to say something but thought better of it. As if she suddenly realized who she was talking to.

Alexis asked, "Are you her surrogate?"

Felicia snorted. "Her mother's dead," she said nonchalantly.

Alexis gasped.

"Ask the Prophet's wife if you don't believe me," she added. "The kid's mother died in childbirth. The Moral Mother keeps copious records on everyone who passes through these doors. I bet she's already started her file on you."

Alexis held Sabine a little tighter, the baby falling asleep against her shoulder as she rubbed her back. She took a deep inhale of air, the scent of baby powder wafting around her.

"I need to get back to my duties," Alexis mumbled. She turned, gently laying Sabine back into her crib. The baby made as if to cry but stopped when Alexis gently rocked her with one hand.

"I should have been his wife," Felicia quipped. Her tone was curt and bitter, the comment meant to get her feelings off her chest.

"I know nothing of that," Alexis responded.

"He said he loved *me*. He promised *me* a future," Felicia answered; the words intended to hurt, cutting like a knife in savage hands.

Had Alexis been insecure, the comment may have bothered her, but intuition told her Felicia was lying through her teeth. Or maybe Alexis just wanted to believe Marcel would never have been so expressive about loving some other woman.

"Do you love him?" Alexis asked.

"Do you? And does it really matter?"

"Then I feel sorry for you," Alexis said. "Because it does matter." She shrugged her narrow shoulders. "Either way, he married *me. With* the Prophet's blessing." Her head was tilted ever so slightly, her eyes narrowed into thin slits. "In fact, perhaps you should take the matter up with the Prophet. I've no doubt that he will have much to say about your discontent."

Felicia smirked. "Don't think I don't know what you're up to," she said.

Alexis smiled. *Don't think I don't see your games, too*, she thought to herself. Aloud, she said, "I have a meeting with the Prophet in a few minutes. I'll make sure to address your concerns." As she stepped past Felicia, she paused, directing one last comment in the other woman's direction. "Be angry, if you want," she whispered. "No one gives a damn, so you can stay angry for all I care. But Elder Marcel is *my* husband. Now stay the hell out of my way, or I will make sure you regret it."

And with one last glance toward Sabine, who was slumbering peacefully, Alexis turned and headed for the door.

When Alexis and Marcel next saw Felicia, the two were standing in conversation with the Prophet. When she entered the room, her face fell, her smug smile gone like the flame of a candle extinguished. Something like fear flickered in her dark eyes.

Alexis stared in her direction. She gave the woman the bare minimum of a smile. Marcel leaned toward the Prophet to whisper something in his ear. The Prophet tossed Felicia a quick look, his timing close to perfect. Alexis lowered her eyes when the Prophet suddenly spoke, asking her a question that had absolutely nothing to do with anything. The thirty-second exchange was enough to have Felicia shaking with fright. Alexis could see it all over her face. The conversation was nothing that Felicia imagined, but letting her believe the worst would buy them time and keep her out of their way.

Belinda gestured for Felicia's attention and the girl hurried to her side. The First Wife tossed the trio a quick glance and then both women disappeared into the kitchen. Alexis turned her attention back to the two men.

"All of our problems will soon be miles from us," Prophet Amos was saying to Marcel. "Weeding out the bad seeds will allow us to prosper in a way that befits our calling and will honor the Holy Father. I trust that I have your full support in helping to facilitate that?"

Marcel nodded. "Most certainly, Prophet."

Prophet Amos bent forward to press a damp kiss against Alexis's cheek. She froze, hoping the disgust she felt didn't show on her face or in her body language.

"All honor to you, Prophet," she said softly.

"Blessings to you both," the man answered and then, with the blink of an eye, he disappeared from the room. Harris, who'd been standing off to the side, watching everyone too closely, hurriedly followed after him.

"Sorry about that," Marcel muttered, his voice a loud whisper. "I heard you had a rough day, too."

Alexis shrugged her narrow shoulders. Much like she had already heard about his day, she knew Marcel had heard every detail of hers. The community was small and rumors were rampant. Whispering tales, true or not, was pretty much an Olympic sport among the members.

Alexis nodded her head. "I heard your day wasn't easy either. But I did have one bright spot." She smiled and Marcel's eyes widened.

"Sabine is a beautiful baby, Marcel. She looks just like you."

"You saw her? She's there?"

Alexis's smile widened. "I held her. And I'll go back for her last bottle to help put her down for the night."

"And she's good? There's nothing wrong with her?"

"She's healthy, and the sooner we can get out of here, the happier we'll all be."

"If I could grab and kiss you right now, I would," he said, smiling with his eyes. They shimmered, flecks of gold seeming as if they'd come alive. His energy felt different, bringing back memories of the old Marcel. Of the Marcel she had loved like air and water.

Alexis chuckled. "You and I both know better than that. Public displays of affection are a definite no-no. You're trying to get us both flogged."

"Not in this lifetime, or any other," Marcel responded. "Why don't we sit down and eat together before you head back to the nursery?"

She shook her head. "I'm done for the day. I need a break from all this. Once Sabine is asleep, I plan to get a hot shower and go to bed."

"I understand. I can have them prepare something for you to eat and bring it to you."

"No. I'm not hungry. I just need a shower and bed."

"I'll give you some alone time then," Marcel said. "I still have some work to do for the Prophet. I'll join you later."

Alexis hesitated, a million thoughts running through

her head. She couldn't help but wonder what work for the Prophet entailed. She would ask later, she thought. "Please, be safe," she said softly.

"I will," Marcel answered. As she turned, he called her name.

"Yes?" Alexis said, pivoting to face him.

Marcel took a step toward her, tossing a look over his shoulder to make sure no one was paying them any attention. "Please give my daughter a hug and kiss from me," he whispered.

She smiled. "I'll give her two."

Alexis could feel him staring after her as she walked away. It was the only thing that kept her from breaking into a full sprint as she made her way out of the room.

Chapter 11

Marcel sauntered through the marshes with a sense of urgency, following the length of bridges and platforms that led him deep into the swamps that surrounded the area. He thought back to his first visit. It had been unsettling, the area feeling too primitive for comfort. Now, he found solace in the natural order of the wildlife. Walking this trail, in particular, gave him time to think, to reflect on everything that had gone wrong in his life and with the Order.

Since returning, he'd invested time and energy in building what he had hoped could be a sanctuary of sorts for those converts who only wanted to live a simple life and feel like they were growing closer to God. Despite everything that had happened with his parents and his sister, there was a part of him that still believed in the good of the Moral Order. There had been a synergy between man and nature that had felt fulfilling in ways he couldn't begin to explain. Its perversion by godless people often felt like a personal failing despite his not being a part of what it had devolved into. He sometimes questioned what it could have been had he stayed to fight for all that had been good and right about the community.

Thick, low-lying fog had begun to cover the landscape,

dropping down onto the surface of the swamp's waterways. Something splashed into the water beside him and, out of the corner of his eye, he spied a gator slipping beneath the murky surface. Everything was beginning to settle down for the night and he, too, was ready to be finished and back with Alexis.

How he loved her, he thought. Just the idea of sharing air in the same room with her made his heart sing. He realized that disappearing the way he had, had been a grand mistake. Coming back from that would never look like it had before. Her willingness to help him was just who Alexis was and had nothing at all to do with him or her feelings. Now, he wasn't even certain that everything he had sacrificed their love for had been worth it. Sabine was all the family he had left, and she didn't know him. The Moral Order was no longer moral, and he couldn't find the words to pray the confusion and hopelessness away. He didn't deserve forgiveness and, being unable to give it to himself, he didn't expect that Alexis could forgive him. Suddenly, Marcel was feeling both alone and lonely.

Ahead of him, he heard a soft thud. There were hints of light flashing through the trees and familiar voices echoing in the air. He'd arrived at his destination and his timing couldn't have been more perfect. Harris stood waiting, he and another man loading a box of incoming cargo onto a flat-bottomed skiff.

The other man snapped, "Took you long enough. I was beginning to think you weren't coming."

"You knew I'd be here," Marcel said calmly. "When have I ever failed the Prophet?"

He and the man standing beside Harris exchanged a

look. Marcel gave him a nod. "Good to see you again, Brother."

"It's good to see you, too, Elder Marcel," Matthew Waters answered as if they were only casual acquaintances.

"I see you've come bearing gifts," Marcel said.

Harris grinned. "Gifts that will bring us a pretty penny on the black market." He opened the top of one of the cardboard containers and pulled out an AK-47. The select-fire, air-cooled, magazine-fed rifle with a rotating bolt was designed to be a simple, reliable automatic firearm that could be manufactured quickly and cheaply. It was now another weapon of mass destruction in the hands of the wrong parties. On the black market, it was gold.

Trafficking guns and bodies was the cornerstone of the Prophet's illicit business operations. He'd begun his career of crime trading contraband that included small arms, explosives and ammunition. With each successful deal, he had upped the ante, believing himself untouchable by the possible repercussions of getting caught. In his mind, those who served him would take the fall if things went left. As far as the Prophet was concerned, Marcel and Harris were loyal, and also expendable. *If only he knew the truth*, Marcel thought.

"I'll get these back," Harris said as he grabbed an oar to propel the skiff through the waterway. "You load the rest of those boxes onto the dingy and follow." He turned to speak to Waters. "We have cargo going out next week. Nineteen females and just as many infants headed to our friends across the border. Can you handle the shipment?"

Waters paused as if he needed to give the request consideration. "You'll need to meet me," Waters said. "I'll need a bigger boat and it won't get through that narrow passage down the way."

"Not a problem. You just be there to accept delivery."

"As long as you have my money," Waters answered.

Marcel reached into the pocket of his robe and pulled out a white envelope stuffed with cash. "When have we not had your money, Brother?"

Waters grinned. "It's always a pleasure doing business with you lot."

Harris laughed. He had already stepped onto the skiff and had pushed himself from the dock. Dropping the oar to his feet, he started the engine and chugged out into the darkness. The other two men stood silently until the sound of that engine faded off into the distance.

"I've got to get back to Alexis," Marcel said as he reached for the last few boxes and began to load them into the dingy.

"Looks like you'll be rowing back," Waters said with a slight chuckle.

"What else is new!" Marcel laughed with him.

"How's Alexis?"

"She's good. Probably better than I am actually."

"That family of hers is beastly. If they don't hear from her soon, they might blow this whole operation to come look for her."

"She found my daughter. We're ready to get out."

"That's great! Everything's set and we're ready to raid this place. Once we stop that shipment next week, the team will be here with both barrels blazing. You know what you'll need to do when that happens."

Marcel nodded.

"Meanwhile," Waters reached into the breast pocket of his jacket. He pulled out an envelope. "You need to give this to Alexis. It's from her mother."

"What is it?"

"A letter I didn't dare read and a burner phone. Make sure she doesn't get caught with either, please."

Marcel tucked both securely into the pocket of his robe.

"You know how to reach me if anything changes," Waters said.

Marcel shook the other agent's hand. "Let's pray nothing changes."

The barest hint of moonlight shimmered through the umbrella of tall trees. The landscape was pitch-black and the air around Alexis felt even darker. She didn't have a flashlight and she had missed last prayer before all the lights had been turned off. She had stayed in the nursery longer than planned, discovering that leaving Sabine behind was harder than she could have ever imagined.

The baby had been the bright spot in her day and Alexis hated that all the children were frequently left alone with no external stimuli. They cried often, or not at all, accepting whatever fate had been dealt to them. They didn't know any better, and the women who seemed to care most were too often pulled away to serve other duties. Alexis would never have believed operating a baby mill could be possible, but the Prophet had successfully done just that. For all he cared, they could have been puppies bred for profit, or feeder crickets like the ones bred to feed reptiles.

After pausing to allow her eyes to adjust to the darkness, she slowly inched her way along the short pathway to the main house. Once she reached the porch, she hurried through the entrance. Inside, it was quiet, no one willing to risk reprimand for not following the rules. She flinched when the door creaked as she closed it. She paused again and took a deep breath.

Finding her way to Marcel's quarters would be so much easier if she had light, Alexis thought. As she slowly maneuvered her way down the length of the hallway, she wished a prayer that she didn't open the wrong room door. She imagined the screaming that might ensue, someone frightened by the intrusion. That would surely earn her a flogging, or even worse. She still had no certainty that Marcel could protect her, despite his assurances that he would keep her safe from harm. Everyone knew if the Prophet ordered her to be punished, then he would get his reckoning. Just like they all knew that whoever was ordered to administer that punishment would do so at his own discretion. And some men were more brutal than others.

The light that suddenly shone in her eyes was blinding. Alexis didn't see who was holding the flashlight and she was slow to react when he suddenly grabbed her by the throat and slammed her head into the wall. The slam was followed by a fist connecting to her face. Pain shot through her skull and for the briefest moment everything began to swim in a tight circle. She gasped for air as she hit the wall a second time, large hands cutting off her oxygen. She couldn't scream, or rage, and no tears dared to fall. She was desperate to focus, to figure out who and what she was up against. Then she heard footsteps headed toward them. The man who was strangling her suddenly relaxed his grip, taking a step from her. With everything in her,

Alexis drove her knee into his groin, nailing him with the force of a Mack truck hitting a brick wall. His body folded in two as she landed a second blow to his chin. He hit the floor with a loud thump. One last strike hit near his kneecap. Bone snapped and her assailant screamed out in pain.

Moving swiftly, Alexis grabbed the flashlight that had landed on the floor and ran, not stopping until she was standing in Marcel's room, the door closed behind her. She pressed her ear against the entrance and listened, her heart pounding. The commotion at the end of the hallway never made it to where she was and it was only when things went quiet again that Alexis release the gasp she'd been holding. Then she dropped to the floor and sobbed.

An hour later, that hot shower Alexis had hoped for was everything but hot. Despite the plush towel wrapped around her, she was still shivering. She wanted to blame the chilly spray of water that had rained down over her hair and body. But being attacked probably had more to do with it than not, she thought.

After dressing in her nightclothes, she made her way from the bathroom to the bedroom. Tall pillar candles lit up the room, casting a warm glow and throwing shadows against the walls. She found Marcel sitting on the floor at the foot of the bed. His knees were pulled up to his chest, his arms draped over them. He looked dejected. His expression was crestfallen. She thought he might have even shed a tear or two, but she was mindful not to let him see that she had noticed.

He gave her a nod, his full lips pulling into the slightest smile. "Are you okay?" he questioned.

"I've been better," she said.

His eyes narrowed and he shifted his body forward as he stared at her. "What happened to your face? And your neck is bruised!"

"Someone attacked me," she answered. She walked to the bed and sat down. She spent the next few minutes explaining what had happened since they'd last seen each other.

Marcel's expression shifted from dejected to irate in the bat of an eye. He shook his head from side to side. He moved to get up, heading for the door.

"Stop," Alexis said. "Let it go."

"I need to know who did this to you."

"We need to remember what we're here to do. I'm fine and I'll be okay. I think one of the men here wanted to send us a message. But I assure you, he got exactly what he deserved."

"We need to get you out of here."

"We all need to get out of here," she responded. "Worrying about Sabine is going to drive me crazy."

"Welcome to my world," Marcel muttered.

She shot him a look. "Did you know her mother had died in childbirth?"

He shook his head again. "I honestly know nothing about her mother."

"From what I've learned, Belinda has kept meticulous records on all the women and children. We'll need to secure those records as evidence. It might make it easier to track them all down and reunite the kids with their biological mothers."

"That might not be easy to do," Marcel said. "Prophet has given strict orders for all documentation to be destroyed if we're ever raided. The First Wife might make those papers disappear."

"Then I need to find them before they come in like the cavalry."

"No," Marcel said, his head shaking from side to side. "That's way too risky."

Alexis didn't bother to respond.

Marcel cut his eye in her direction. He knew from the look on her face that Alexis was determined to do what she wanted no matter what he said. He didn't have the energy to argue, so he changed the subject.

"I saw Agent Waters tonight. He asked about you."

"How did you manage that?" Alexis asked.

Marcel gave her a quick update, detailing his own after-dark activities.

She shook her head. "Is there any chance they will sell those guns before the raid?"

Marcel answered. "Highly unlikely, but if that even looks like it might happen, I'll make sure the FBI intercepts them."

"Do you think the Prophet keeps records like Belinda?"

"Nothing would surprise me with him," Marcel answered.

"Well, we need to find them if he does," Alexis said.

"I really need you to focus on Sabine," Marcel said, his determined tone clearly giving Alexis pause. "She's got to be your priority."

He released a constrained breath and continued. "If anything happens to me, Alexis, I need you to promise that you'll raise Sabine for me."

Her eyes widened, looking like two China saucers.

"Why would you even think such a thing, Marcel? Nothing is going to happen to you!"

"You don't know that. And I need to make sure my daughter will be okay if something does happen."

Alexis rolled her eyes skyward. Admittedly, she was drawn to the little girl. It had been love at first sight. She had gone into mama bear mode, completely protective of her young charge. Going forward, Marcel would have a hard time keeping her from the child, but she had never considered *him* not being there to raise his baby girl. The very idea that such a thing could happen suddenly moved her to tears. She swiped at her eyes with the back of her hand.

"Don't cry," Marcel intoned, realizing what he had done. "Please, Alexis, don't cry."

"This is not how our lives should be, Marcel! We shouldn't be worried about things happening to us. What happened to our joy? We were so happy once!"

Marcel hung his head. There was no reason to point out the obvious. He had blown up their lives and he couldn't fix it. Alexis hadn't deserved the harm he'd caused, and she didn't deserve to be in the position he had now put her in.

"I've made a lot of mistakes, Alexis. And I'm sorry for that. We had often talked about having children together and, in all honesty, I couldn't imagine myself ever having a child with anyone else. But it happened, and now I still can't imagine you not raising any child of mine. But once again, I'm making assumptions instead of including you in the decision-making."

He hesitated, searching for his words before continuing. "Yes, I want you and your family to raise Sabine if anything ever happens to me. But I also want you to be *willing* to do that because you *want* to. For no other reason than you love her as much as I do. You don't owe me anything. You have no obligations to either one of us and I don't want you to feel like I'm putting you in another uncomfortable situation. If you say no, I'll understand completely."

The room was suddenly quiet. Marcel and Alexis both fell into thought. Time seemed to stand still. Marcel tilted his head and leaned it against Alexis's leg. When she didn't jump or pull away, he allowed himself to lean into her side a little harder. She drew her fingers through the length of his hair and then settled her palm against his shoulder. Her hand was calming, and he had missed the gentleness of her touch. They sat together in silence for the next hour. When sleep finally came, Marcel had retreated to the sofa in the other room. Alexis had slid beneath the bedcovers atop the mattress. Marcel had his answer and Alexis knew beyond any doubt what she needed to do.

Chapter 12

When morning came, Marcel and Alexis were headed in opposite directions. They missed having breakfast together. Everyone was whispering about a man named Roberts who'd been attacked in the middle of the night. His nose and leg had been broken and there was concern he might never father children after the damage done to his male member.

All the Elders had been summoned before the Prophet; Harris himself carrying out the request. Everyone else was walking on eggshells, fearful of what might come.

"He deserved it," Christiana muttered. "The man's a pig! I hope he rots in hell!"

Belinda shushed her daughter. "Someone might hear you."

Alexis shot the young woman a look, stalling the comment perched on the tip of her tongue. Christiana was still angry with the world, and with her mother, and that was going to take longer than twenty-four hours for her to get over.

"Well, I heard they castrated him," Felicia interjected.

Christiana moved to the other woman's side, clutching

her arm. She was holding on dearly for information. "The intruder?"

Felicia shook her head. "No, Roberts! And they say the Prophet did it himself. There have been too many complaints against him, so the Prophet personally took care of the problem."

Belinda gasped loudly. "Shut your mouth! The Prophet would never do any such thing."

Felicia snarled. "Do you really think an intruder cut off his testicles?"

Belinda snapped back. "I think we're done with this conversation. And you need to watch your mouth before I have you brought before the Elders."

Alexis had been sitting in one of the rocking chairs, baby Sabine cradled on her lap. She'd been feeding the infant a bottle and the little girl had drifted off to sleep. The trio turned to look at her when she commented, "I don't think Felicia meant anything by it. Did you, Felicia? I think we're all just curious to know what's going on."

Felicia gave her a look and nodded. "Yes, I was just being curious. And repeating what others told me. I apologize. I know we're not supposed to gossip."

Belinda glared at the woman before turning her attention back toward Alexis and changing the subject. "What happened to you?" she asked, pointing at the bruises on Alexis's face.

Alexis paused. She and Marcel had already prepared themselves for the questions they expected might come about her appearance. Most especially after one of the men had been, quote unquote, *attacked.* Both knew there would be no mention of *his* actions. More importantly, no one could know that she had been involved. Her expression was blank as she shook her head and rose from her seat. She carried Sabine over to her crib and laid the sleeping baby down. The little boy in the crib beside Sabine's was whining for his own bottle of breakfast. Alexis lifted him from the crib and cuddled him against her chest. She sat back down and cradled him gently. The trio of women were still eyeing her curiously.

"The Elder and I had a difference of opinion," she said.

Belinda's gaze narrowed ever so slightly.

"See," Christiana said. "Like I've said before, they're all alike. If Elder Marcel would hit you, then the rest of us don't stand a chance."

"Obedience to the Holy Father, and to the Prophet, is the cornerstone of matrimony," Alexis said. "To dishonor one's husband is to dishonor the Prophet. My punishment was deserving."

Alexis hated how that sounded; her words like an advertisement from the men's how-to handbook of male domination. Marcel had insisted it was their only option. Even she didn't believe what she was saying and from how the other women were looking at her, they clearly didn't believe her either.

"That's a load of horseshit," Felicia uttered harshly, "and you know it!"

Belinda was still staring at her, something like disbelief furrowing her brow. She didn't respond at all.

Silence did a two-step through the room. The tension was thick and stagnant. Even the babies could feel it, a chorus of wails starting at one end and rifting to the other.

Belinda finally spoke. "Settle the children down," she said. "We still have responsibilities."

When Alexis looked up, she met the woman's gaze, Belinda still studying her intently. The woman's eyes were narrowed and there was something off-putting about her expression. She was tightly wound and what looked like anger and rage rippled in her eyes.

Standing behind Belinda, Felicia stood staring in her direction as well. She stole a quick glance at the others before looking back at Alexis, and then she mouthed, *Thank you.*

There was a quick pause and, with a nod of her head, Alexis returned one baby to its bed then picked up and cradled another.

Hours later, Alexis headed back to Marcel's room. She was surprised to find him inside when she entered. He was throwing clothes into a duffel bag.

"Good timing," he said. "I was just about to go look for you."

"I was in the nursery. Sabine sent you a good-morning hug."

Marcel paused, a slow smile pulling across his face. "I can't wait to hold her," he said softly.

She smiled. "Until then, I promise to hug her for you every chance I can."

Marcel nodded then went back to his packing.

"What's going on?"

"I'm going to be gone for a day or two. The Prophet wants to take a trip to the other community. He wants to move up the transfer, so we're headed there to get things ready."

"Should I be worried?"

He shook his head. "No. Not at all. Just try not to assault anyone else," he said.

She smiled.

"By the way, look under your pillow. There's a note from your mother and a burner phone to call home. Waters brought them when he came. I should have given them to you last night, but with everything that happened, it slipped my mind. We need to move it, too. People are nosey around here."

Alexis hurried to the bedside, slipping her hand beneath the pillow. Her excitement was palpable, joy shimmering across her face.

"Be careful," Marcel warned. "You never know who might be lurking outside the door. Only use it at night after lights-out. And when you use the phone, turn on the shower and lock yourself in the bathroom. The shower will muffle any sound from your conversation."

"Where's the best place to hide it?" she asked.

Marcel gestured with his index finger for her to follow him. He led the way into the bathroom. On the wall beside the commode, he pulled at one of the wood panels. When it opened, he removed a metal box from the interior. Inside, there was cash, papers and a small handgun with an extra clip.

Marcel counted off three one-hundred-dollar bills from the roll of cash and stuck them deep into the pockets of the denim jeans he'd changed into. He held out his hand for the phone and when Alexis placed it against his palm, he dropped it into the container. He closed the lid on the box, tucked it back into the wall and secured the panel. Alexis followed him out to the bedroom.

"Thank you!" she whispered, her excitement like a beam of light.

He nodded. "I've got to go," he said, tossing the duffel bag over his shoulder. "If you need anything, use that phone. I programmed Agent Waters's cell number into the call list. He'll be able to get to you faster than I can."

"Sabine and I will be fine," Alexis said, although her tone wasn't overly confident. She opted not to share the details of her morning least he be worried about them more.

"Just keep your head down, please." He took a step toward her, closing the gap between them until they were standing toe to toe.

The two stood eyeing each other intently. Alexis smiled. "You be careful, please," she said, her voice a low whisper.

Marcel took a deep breath and held it. He stared, his eyes skating back and forth across her face. He looked deep into her eyes and held the gaze, wishing things were different for them. He slowly eased an arm around her waist, inching himself closer to her. When she didn't resist, he drew her to him, feeling her body settle warmly against his own. His eyes danced along the line of her profile and then he felt his heart sync with hers. It skipped one beat and then a second, and then every muscle in his body tightened as he captured her lips beneath his own.

Lost in the memory, Alexis pressed her fingers to her lips. They still burned hot from Marcel's touch and the sensation was distracting. She had wanted him to kiss her as much as he had and when he'd initiated the touch, there was little thought to stopping him. As his tongue entwined with hers, his arms holding her tightly, every fiber in her body acknowledged not only how much she had missed him, but also how much she wanted him.

The intensity of that kiss had left them both panting for air and wanting more of each other. The desire they shared was undeniable. It was a deep craving, decadent and sweet. Allowing it to happen felt as natural to Alexis as breathing and now that he was gone, she found herself missing him. But she had missed Marcel before, and remembering where that had gotten her left her conflicted.

Energy throughout the community altered the moment the Prophet and the Elders passed through the gates and disappeared past the heavy growth of foliage. The congregation was able to relax and hints of laughter bubbled through the air.

Alexis was anxious to get back to that phone to call home but knew she couldn't risk being caught. She needed to be patient and biding her time would be well worth the annoyance. She looked out the nursery window. Sabine was in her arms, eagerly scanning the outside with complete wonder. Her wide eyes darted back and forth and her innocent exuberance felt like Christmas morning with a personal visit from Santa Claus.

She kissed the little girl's cheek and she giggled. Alexis had tried to imagine what the child's mother had looked like. But Marcel's gene pool ran deep. Every one of her features was as if she'd been cloned from his DNA. He couldn't have denied her if he had wanted to because she looked like he had spit her out by himself. Alexis couldn't stop herself from wondering if a child of theirs would be more him than her. Then she wondered if there would come a time when they might find out. She hugged Sabine a little closer and the baby drooled and giggled around the small fist she'd pulled into her mouth.

"You shouldn't let yourself get attached," a voice said from the other side of the room.

Alexis turned to find Felicia coming up behind her. Her arms were crossed over her chest, as if she were ready to pick a fight.

Felicia continued. "They don't want us to get attached to them. They don't stay long enough to make any kind of connection that they'll remember. This lot is all scheduled to leave next week. The Prophet says we're not going to keep any more babies or children here."

Alexis shook her head from side to side. "Doesn't that bother you?"

Felicia shrugged. "I grew up in the state's foster care system. By the time I was seven, I'd already learned that life is about survival. Especially for females. Ours is a life-and-death situation from one day to the next. Connecting with other people will either get your feelings hurt or get you killed. I've never found them to be worth the risk."

"You were willing to risk it for Elder Marcel," Alexis said, her brow raised.

"You really are naïve! I only wanted the power that comes with being an Elder's wife. Especially if that Elder is on the path to being Prophet. You don't even realize what you could do around here if you wanted."

Alexis sighed. "I probably don't."

"Well, I wouldn't waste my time around here rocking these kids if I were you. You still have a lot to learn."

"Would you be willing to help me?" Alexis asked.

Felicia laughed. "You really are too smart to be that stupid. Hell no, I won't help you! I'm busy trying to figure out how to take your man, short of killing you and feeding you to the gators out there." She turned, heading for the door.

Alexis laughed with her. "Good luck with that."

Felicia paused, swiveling back to meet the look Alexis was giving her. "Watch your back. No one's safe around here. You wives can be dangerous."

"Any wife in particular?"

Felicia smiled, saying nothing else. With the slightest skip, she made her exit, still laughing as she closed the door behind her.

Alone again, Alexis hugged Sabine until the little girl dozed off to sleep. She held her close, counting her fingers and toes and noting the hint of dimple in her cheeks. She suckled her tongue and wound Alexis's hair around her little fingers. She had the sweetest smile and a laugh that could melt ice. Alexis knew there was so much she and Marcel needed to work through, but what was certain was that she was firmly bonded to Sabine, and nothing was going to keep her from protecting Marcel's precious baby girl.

When the day ended and Alexis finally found her way back to the room, she was surprised to find Belinda inside. The bed had been stripped and the woman stood with a pillow and case in her hand.

Alexis took a breath, assessing the situation before she reacted and snapped. "This is a surprise," she said.

Belinda shrugged. "I thought I'd be done by now. I was changing the bed," she said. She gestured toward the pile of bedclothes on the floor.

"I could have done that."

Belinda smiled. "I know. But I try to help with all of the chores. It lets me know where we may need to put additional hands. The young woman who was responsible for all the Elders' rooms will be leaving us soon and we will all need to pitch in until I replace her."

Alexis nodded slowly. "Since most of the Elders are married, put the responsibility on their wives. I don't think we'll disappoint you."

"I'm sure you won't, but there are a few younger women who are spoiled and selfish and wouldn't know a top sheet from the bottom if both were labeled."

Alexis laughed. "I'll try not to disappoint you."

"Prophet inspects rooms for contraband every few weeks. Elder Marcel has never been a problem. I hope that continues."

"I understand you might be concerned. But I assure you, there will be no problems."

Belinda grunted. The sound was harsh and not meant to inspire confidence.

"I know you have doubts, but I will be a good wife to Elder Marcel. I understand everything that is required of me."

"Is that why you two are not sharing your bed?"

It was not the question Alexis had been expecting. She was certain her cheeks were a brilliant shade of embarrassed red. She faltered, her eyes shifting back and forth as she searched for an appropriate answer.

"It's not what you think…" Alexis stammered. "We… I…the Elder…"

Belinda waved a dismissive hand. "I understand," she

said. "But you need to remember that the Prophet teaches procreation is necessary to honor the Holy Father. There can be no babies if you deny your husband." She bent to gather the dirty linens. When she stood back up, her expression was smug. "I'll let you finish the bed."

"Thank you," Alexis said, the words uttered softly.

When Belinda was gone, the door closed after her, Alexis hurried to inspect the bathroom. The panel was still in place and nothing looked as if it had been disturbed. She heaved a deep sigh. She would have been devastated if Belinda had found the box hidden in the wall. She would have to wait until lights-out before she could call, she realized, but she was grateful for the note tucked deep into the cotton bra she wore. Her mother had only written three words. Reminding Alexis that she was loved.

Returning to the outer room, Alexis dropped down onto the bed, throwing herself backward against the mattress. She replayed the conversation over and over again in her head. She wondered what had precipitated Belinda's comments and just how much snooping the woman had done before Alexis had entered the room. Thinking it through, Alexis was certain of one thing. They were quickly running out of time and she desperately wished Marcel was there so they could take Sabine and head back home.

Boarding the private Cessna Citation CJ4 had Marcel feeling out of sorts. The Prophet had still been berating them all when they'd arrived at the New Orleans Lakefront Airport. The private airstrip was just under two hours from the compound's front door and the van ride had been one rant after another. Elder Harris was their pilot and, despite his enthusiasm, the Prophet hadn't shown an ounce of emotion. One didn't need to look hard to know that his mind was racing and that none of his thoughts were good. He had finally contained his anger and now the religious leader was plotting. Plotting what was the question Marcel had no answer for.

Marcel had no level of comfort about this trip. He worried for Sabine and for Alexis. Neither was truly safe until they were far from the Order and back among family and friends.

Her encounter with Brother Roberts however had served to remind him what she was capable of doing if pushed. He had no concerns about Alexis holding her own in hand-to-hand combat. Her parents had made certain she'd had more than enough physical training to take on any opponent. Years of karate, jujitsu and weapons training had proven to be an asset more times than not. She had multiple black belts and was ranked a top sharpshooter. Her even temperament ensured that, in a trying situation, she responded versus reacted. It often gave her an edge over an opponent. Alexis was tough as nails and Marcel loved that she didn't waste time depending on someone else to rescue her. Alexis could easily save him, Sabine and herself without breaking a nail if need be.

Yet he still worried. No one could be trusted, and Alexis eagerly sought out the good in people, whether any existed or not. She had the biggest heart and the most giving spirit, and he worried that she'd be taken advantage of when she least expected it. But who was he to talk about someone taking advantage of Alexis, most especially after everything he'd done to crash and burn their relationship.

Nonetheless, he had kissed her. He felt the slightest smile pull across his face. Thinking about how his lips had danced so easily against hers left him giddy. The nearness of her had always been everything to him. Their physical connection had been intoxicating and he'd missed her sweet caresses. Missed how she'd quiver if he touched that spot behind her knees or ran his tongue against her inner thigh. Each time he had ever kissed her had always felt like the very first time. It was magical and it took his breath away. Kissing Alexis was buttercream icing on some very sweet cake and he looked forward to an opportunity to do it again. He worried that might not happen if anything at all went wrong, and he couldn't stop himself from imagining everything that could go wrong.

"We need to shut down our N'Orleans location," Prophet Amos said suddenly. He sat in the window seat beside Marcel.

Marcel turned to look at the man. He sat staring out over the bright blue sky. Outside the window, it was as if they were gliding through the late morning air.

"What concerns you?" Marcel questioned.

The Prophet shook his head. "God spoke to me and he said the time is now."

Marcel nodded. "We've accomplished so much here. It's central to our distribution network and key to the entire operation. It would be a shame to lose that."

"I agree, but I believe we've been exposed here in New Orleans. To save the Order, I feel it's time for us to get everyone moved and settled in the Midwest. Fewer eyes checking for us and all we do."

"Something I need to know?" Marcel asked.

"Too much is happening. The devil is always busy, and we need to stay two steps ahead of him. I worry for our people. We can better keep them safe if we can see what is coming for us."

Marcel took a deep breath before responding. "Do you know who might have told the Feds about our shipment?" His face was expressionless.

"I have some ideas, and I'll handle it."

"Is there anything I can do to help you, Prophet?"

"Just keep handling business the way you have. I need someone looking out for our interests. You've proven yourself multiple times and I am very happy with your dedication to the church and to our congregants."

"Thank you, sir!"

Leaning back in his seat, Marcel gave the slightest sigh, allowing his body to relax for the first time since boarding. Thinking back over the conversation and over everything that had happened, he was certain of only one thing. They had officially run out of time.

Chapter 13

The lights had gone out and everyone had begun to settle down for the night. Somewhere, someone was laughing and giggling, and Belinda had scurried off to put it an end to it. Alexis was grateful for the diversion, something else to keep the woman occupied.

Alexis had put Sabine and the other babies to sleep and was headed back to her room. No one accosted her this time and she used the flashlight that she'd taken from Brother Roberts to maneuver her way. She had just passed the Prophet's quarters when the door suddenly swung open and Christiana peeked her head out. She looked left and then right. Surprise crossed her face when she noticed Alexis standing in the hallway.

She gestured for Alexis to enter the room, peering back out the door one more time before closing it behind them.

"What are you doing?" Alexis asked, whispering loudly.

"I'm leaving," the girl answered. "With the Prophet and the Elders gone, this is my chance. If I go now, I can get a head start before my mother figures out I've left."

Alexis shook her head. "And then what? You get lost out there in the dark? You fall into the swamp and something eats you? This is not a good idea, Christiana."

"I hate it here. I can't stand one more minute. If I have to grovel to one more man, I will cut my own throat."

"I told you. Don't grovel. It's a game and you have to play it better than they do."

"By being a doormat for them to keep stepping on? No thanks."

"Why now?" Alexis questioned. "What's happened? Just yesterday you were willing to trust me and play along."

"Yesterday I didn't know the Prophet is planning to move us all to the other community. I'll never get away if we're transferred there. And neither will you."

"Who said I was planning to get away?"

Christiana shrugged her narrow shoulders. "They don't trust you. In fact, my mother believes you brought all these new problems to their doorstep. And she doesn't believe you want to be a true wife to Elder Marcel. She doesn't like you and I don't know why."

"Thanks for the heads-up," Alexis muttered.

"You really need to go now. The Moral Mother will be back soon."

"Answer a question for me. Do you know where your mother and the Prophet keep their files?"

Christiana pondered the question for a split second. "There's a secret room attached to the Prophet's office. Access to it is beside the bookcase. You'll need the code for it and a key for the file cabinet inside. He keeps both taped under the drawer in his nightstand. If he has files, I imagine they'd be there."

"Thank you." Alexis nodded her head. "Please, don't run, Christiana. Not yet. It's not safe."

"I can't make you any promises." Teenage indignation

was wrapped around the girl's shoulders like a wool blanket. Her expression said she'd already made her decision and nothing anyone else said was going to change her mind.

Christiana suddenly threw herself toward Alexis, flinging her arms tightly around the woman. "Thank you," she said. "You're the only one who has ever really cared."

Alexis held her back, squeezing her tightly. When she let go, tears pressed hot against her lashes. "Your mom does care," she said softly. "She cares more than you give her credit for. She loves you."

The young woman rolled her eyes skyward. "My mom tolerates me. My brother was her favorite. I was the 'change of life baby' she wished she'd never had."

Surprise wafted over Alexis's face. "You have a brother? Did he leave the church?"

"He's still a disciple. He's the other reason my mother won't leave. She's waiting for him to come back."

"Where is he?"

Christiana shrugged. "Dead, for all we know. Prophet won't say, but I think it's because he doesn't know either. He says my brother is out sowing the word of the Moral Order and claiming souls for the ministry. The last time the Prophet supposedly heard from him, he was somewhere in South America."

The young woman moved to the door, pulling it open ever so slightly. She peered out a second time. "Goodbye, Sister," she said as she gestured for Alexis to exit.

Alexis pleaded one last time. "I really need you to trust me," she said. "I understand your frustration, but you can't put yourself in harm's way without a plan. How are you even planning to travel? You don't have a car. And you can only walk so far. You don't have a clue what you're up against!"

Christiana shrugged. "Neither do you," she said snidely. "And if you did, you should have gone through with it yesterday because something's coming and it's not going to be good. I'm not waiting around for things to blow up or for them to start passing out the Kool-Aid. I'll take my chances."

Alexis paused, reflecting on the comment. Years earlier, she had been Christiana, desperate to get away from the torment that had become her daily existence. Petrified of what one man could entice the entire group to do. She understood, knowing that she would not have listened to anyone who might have tried to convince her not to run either. Running was all the hope she'd had. Christiana was clinging to the last bit of hope she believed could save her.

With a nod of her head, she leaned to give Christiana one last hug. "Be safe," she said. "Follow the tire tracks and stay on the main roadway. Do not wander off-road. If you do, you risk getting turned around in these swamps and, if that happens, you won't make it out of here alive. And wait until dawn. You'll need as much light as you can get. I'll have someone waiting for you when you get there. Do you understand me?"

Christiana nodded. Then Alexis eased out the door and down the hall to her room.

There had been a meeting of all the Elders. The Prophet had prayed over them and then he'd detailed the plans that were to take effect immediately. The acolytes from New Orleans would arrive within the week and space needed to be made for those who were staying. Many of the women were being sent elsewhere, but at no time did he note where "elsewhere" actually was. With the arrangements made, he demanded to see those persons who'd been labeled "problematic" within the community. Problems would be eliminated immediately, he'd professed.

Marcel stood by the Prophet's side, listening to complaints of abuse and harassment. Victims pointed out abusers, and abusers denied the allegations. It was a vicious cycle, feeling like they were all riding a roller coaster of highs and lows, with no one wanting to get off. When all was said and done, the *problems* were scheduled to be transferred out, their services to the Order needed elsewhere.

Along with Marcel and Harris, there were three other Elders from the Midwest community standing with the Prophet: Elder Jenkins, Elder Franklin and Elder Charles. All were waiting to be excused before the lights went out. Prophet suddenly turned his attention to Elder Harris.

The Prophet stared at his friend, but his comment was for Marcel. "We have found a snake in our midst," he said, his tone casual.

Marcel's brow creased. "Excuse me?"

"A snake. One who has betrayed us."

"I don't understand," Marcel said.

"It has come to my attention that Elder Harris has not been a faithful follower."

Harris laughed; a nervous titter that echoed through the late-night air. He laughed, but he didn't utter a word in his defense.

"What are his crimes?" Elder Franklin asked. He was a tall, thin man who reminded Marcel of that actor Tom Hanks.

The Prophet spent the next few minutes detailing a lengthy laundry list of allegations against Harris. At the top of that list was embezzlement of funds from the church. At the bottom was an inappropriate relationship with one of the young men who'd been exiled from the community.

Harris stood defiant. He lifted his chin ever so slightly as he responded, staring the Prophet in his eyes. "I did nothing that you didn't approve or have knowledge of," he snapped.

The Prophet snapped back. "Did I know about you talking to the FBI?"

Harris's eyes widened and he stammered. "I…didn't… I…" he started.

Marcel's gaze shifted from one man to the other. The tension in the room had risen substantially, an electrical current that felt dangerous at best. "What about the FBI?" he questioned.

The Prophet shot him a quick look. "Elder Harris met with a federal agent recently. Shortly before our last shipment was intercepted."

"I had nothing to do with that," Harris said, his expression suddenly nervous. "I told you, he's an old friend. I was hoping to turn him. If he joins the ministry and is willing to work for us, we'd have an upper hand against law enforcement. He could be our eyes and ears."

"And you needed to spend the night in his hotel room to make that happen?"

Marcel didn't miss the resentment in Prophet Amos's tone. It reeked of bitterness and rage. Jealousy was playing out like a movie on a big screen. Marcel was starting to feel anxious, the situation unsettling. Whatever was happening had nothing at all to do with the Saints of the Moral Order and even less to do with the church's congregation. "We should probably table this discussion until morning," Marcel said, hoping to diffuse the rising tension in the room.

"I have nothing to say," Harris said. "I did nothing wrong."

"You betrayed me!" Prophet Amos suddenly shouted.

Marcel was not prepared for the rage that seemed to swallow them all whole. It flooded the room like a tornado gone awry. Nor was he ready when the Prophet suddenly drew a .38 revolver from his pocket and pulled the trigger, sending five rounds into Elder Harris's chest.

Alexis had propped a chair against the room door and secured the lock on the bathroom. The shower had only been running for a few minutes when she dared to pull the burner phone from its hiding spot. Everything was as Marcel had left it; nothing looking like Belinda might have discovered it while she'd been snooping.

She was anxious as she pushed the speed dial button for her mother. Her hand was shaking as she pulled the device to her ear and waited as it rang once and then a second time.

Claudia answered on the third ring.

"Tell me you're safe," her mother said, not bothering to greet her with a hello.

Alexis laughed. "I'm fine," she whispered loudly.

"Thank goodness!" Claudia said, slightly breathless. "I've been worried sick."

"I'm good. But I'm ready to come home."

"Did you find the baby?"

"She's beautiful, Mom." Alexis gushed. "Marcel was right. She's definitely his and we have to get her out of here.

The children don't stand a chance under the current Prophet. He's killing them all slowly. I've never seen anything like this. It's a baby mill. He's breeding them for profit."

"I haven't liked anything I've read about him. How can we help?"

"Some of these babies are going to need homes. I don't know if we're going to be able to find their mothers, but if we can, they need to be reunited."

"Even Sabine?"

"They say her mother died in childbirth. But if she didn't and she's alive, she deserves to know her daughter."

There was a moment of pause before Claudia responded. "How are things with you and Marcel?"

"I don't know. But we're making it work."

"He loves you."

Alexis paused. "I still love him, too, but I don't know if I can get past the fact that he left me."

"He would have come back sooner, I think, but..." Claudia hesitated.

Something in her mother's voice gave Alexis pause. "But what?"

Claudia heaved a deep sigh. "Your father found Marcel shortly after he disappeared. He threatened to kill him if he returned. He was afraid that Marcel might hurt you again."

"And he didn't tell me?" Her voice rose an octave, anger intensifying her tone. She bit back the anger that threatened to spew out of her mouth.

"You know how your father is, Alexis."

"Did you know?" Alexis asked.

"Your father told me after you left with Marcel. I had a

few choice words for him, and we haven't spoken since. I thought you should know."

"What is it with these men?" Alexis snapped. "Do they ever think about how their decisions impact us?"

"They don't think," her mother answered. "At least not with the head that matters," she added, chuckling softly. "Thankfully, though, what they do is usually done in love, even when they're being selfish."

Silence shifted between them, Alexis and her mother dropping into self-reflection. Claudia broke through the quiet.

"Cash is standing here at my elbow. She says there's something she needs to tell you. Something urgent."

"Put her on," Alexis replied.

She listened as her mother passed her own phone to their friend.

"You good?" Cash asked.

"Hanging in here. What's up?"

"I hacked into the FBI's database like you asked."

Alexis could hear her mother swearing in the background, cursing her and Cash. "Are you two trying to go to jail?" Claudia snapped.

Cash continued, both women ignoring the outburst. A convicted computer hacker turned professional technical guru to legitimize her sometimes-illegal operations, finding hidden data was what Cash did best. There wasn't a private operation, or a government agency, that Cash couldn't find a backdoor entry into. She'd only gotten caught one time and only because a former lover had snitched on her.

"The case against Amos Lee is solid. Marcel has done a great job providing them with intel."

"Anything on the Prophet's inner circle I need to be aware of?"

"Yeah, the prophet's wife, Belinda Bradley Lee, is wanted for questioning in the murder of a woman in California. She's a person of interest. The case went cold when she disappeared."

"Murder?"

"It gets better. Allegedly, the woman murdered was involved with her adult son."

"How long ago was this?"

"It's been a few years. But that's not what you need to know," Cash said.

"What am I missing?"

Cash said. "Her son is Stefan Guidry, the renowned prophet of the Moral Order. She is Prophet Symmetry's biological mother."

Alexis felt her face begin to heat, her cheeks reddening as if on fire. "Are you sure about that?" she queried.

"She was a teenage mother who lost custody of her son to his father, Paul Guidry. Paul was a religious zealot who homeschooled the kid to prepare him for doomsday. The child protective services report about him abusing the boy is inches thick. The parents never reconciled. She married Amos shortly after they began investigating her for multiple murders. Then she disappeared."

"And her daughter?"

"Daughter?" Cash suddenly sounded confused. "What daughter? I didn't find anything about a daughter. Everything I reviewed says she only had one child."

The confusion carried over the phone line, thoughts racing through Alexis's head. "Is it possible she had the baby here or at the other community and there's just no record of the child's birth?"

"Anything's possible," Cash replied, "but her medical records said she had a hysterectomy after the birth of her son due to postpartum hemorrhaging. How old is this daughter?"

"Christiana is sixteen."

Alexis sensed Cash shaking her head. "It's possible she stole someone's kid," the other woman said. "I'll dig a little deeper to see if I can find anything."

What it could all mean was suddenly spinning in Alexis's head. "Thanks, Cash. Can you put Mom back on please?"

"You be safe," Cash said before she passed the phone back. "And remember, she may very well know exactly who you are and your connection to her kid."

Cash saying what Alexis had already been thinking only served to raise her anxiety level another notch.

"What's next?" Claudia asked, returning to the call.

"Daddy put a tracker on Marcel's van. The van's not here now, but he should have a lock on its previous location. We're not too far from Lafayette, I think. Can you please put someone out on Interstate 10 near here? Have them looking out for a teen named Christiana. She has waist-length, red hair that she keeps pulled back in a ponytail. She should show up sometime in the morning if she makes it and she'll probably be hitchhiking. Tell her, please, that I sent them to help her."

"We'll make sure she's safe," her mother answered.

"Thank you."

"When are you coming home, Alexis?"

There was a moment of hesitation as Alexis considered the question. She didn't bother to answer. "I've got to go, Mommy. I love you," she said. And then she disconnected the call.

Chapter 14

"We need to move quickly," Prophet Amos was saying. He'd been ranting while Elder Harris's dead body lay on the floor at his feet.

Marcel was still reeling, not having anticipated the religious leader would execute the one person he had seemed closest to. Standing by the Prophet's side as others made that body disappear, he watched as Elder Harris's legacy perished in the large hog enclosure. The massive animals made a quick meal of the body, not a single bone left when Marcel finally found his way to bed.

Needless to say, there had been no sleep. For all he knew, he might have been next, so closing his eyes was the last thing he was thinking of. That following morning, Marcel had a dozen questions and no answers. Waters had said nothing of Harris talking to the Bureau, which potentially put him, and Alexis, at risk. What had Harris said to this "agent" friend? What had the friend told him? Had pillow talk been just that? Talk and nothing more. Or had the Prophet gotten it wrong? Did he lay blame on Harris for something Marcel had done? It wasn't a risk he was willing to take with Alexis and his daughter. All he wanted was to get back to Louisiana and get them both the hell out of there. He heaved a deep sigh, suddenly feeling the Prophet's gaze laser-focused on him.

"What are you thinking, sir?" Marcel asked, refocusing his attention.

"I'll be staying here. You'll need to make travel arrangements for our congregants the minute you get back. Those heading here to the commune will travel by bus. Those designated to be taken in by our Mexican associates will travel to the Gulf and be met there. Once everyone is gone, burn it to the ground. I don't want anything left that might incriminate me. The Moral Mother will be able to tell you who is going where."

"We also have cargo…" Marcel started, thinking about the guns hidden beneath the floorboards of the prayer room.

"Burn it all," the Prophet snapped. "For all we know, the Feds are already headed there to take us down. I can't believe he would do this to me. After everything I risked…" His words caught in his throat and he looked like he was about to vomit. He stood staring off into the distance, shaking his head vehemently as he reflected on the betrayal that undoubtedly felt very personal.

"Consider it done," Marcel said.

"I am trusting you to get this right," the Prophet concluded.

"All honor to you, Prophet!"

Alexis bypassed breakfast and headed straight to the nursery. She could feel that something was amiss and, despite her concerns that Christiana had indeed run, she knew that whatever was going on was even bigger than that.

Felicia had beat her to the room, holding the baby boy

they'd named Marcus in her lap. He suckled a bottle, his little hand resting atop hers.

"Good morning!" Alexis said as casually as she could muster.

Felicia simply nodded, saying nothing in reply. She nuzzled the baby closer to her heart and pressed a damp kiss to his forehead. The gesture made Alexis smile as she watched. Not bothering to hide her intentions, Alexis went straight to Sabine's crib, greeting the infant with a bright smile and a snuggle.

"Good morning, *cher*! I missed you so much!"

Sabine cooed, clutching the front of Alexis's dress between her chubby fingers.

"I think someone needs a fresh diaper," Alexis said, wiggling her nose.

Sabine laughed and the sweet treble in her voice moved Alexis to laugh with her.

Minutes later, the two were snuggled together in one of the wooden rocking chairs, Sabine clutching a bottle of fresh milk between her small hands. Alexis marveled at how tiny, and how strong she was, the glass container clutched tightly within her fingers. She was a good baby, with a sweet disposition, and this was not where she needed to be raised. The powers in charge had sapped the joy out of the ministry, and most of the congregation was barely able to endure the hardships the Prophet had placed on them. His tight ship had slowly begun to sink, many members ready to run if the opportunity presented itself. That they were scared to stay, and even more petrified to leave, should have been a warning for the leadership. But no one was paying attention, and few seemed to genuinely care. Alexis found herself wondering where it had all gone wrong.

She whispered into the baby's ear, casting a quick glance toward the other women in the room. "I sure hope your daddy gets back here soon, *cher*. If he doesn't, I may have to take matters into my own hands and you and I are getting the hell out of here."

The quiet moment of reverie was broken when Belinda suddenly barged into the room. She glanced at each of the women and their charges before settling her eyes on Alexis.

"Have you seen Christiana this morning?" she questioned. There was an air of anger and hostility in her tone.

Alexis shook her head. "No, I haven't seen her. Not since yesterday afternoon."

Felicia suddenly spoke. "She was here earlier. Then she said she was going to the kitchen to help prepare breakfast."

Belinda frowned. "The kitchen?"

Felicia shrugged. "That's what I thought. But Sister Alexis has been preaching to all of us that we need to widen our horizons. Find ways to help carry more of the workload. That we need to volunteer in other areas. I plan to go help in the greenhouse after all the babies are fed. I figured Christiana was going to try her hand at cooking."

Belinda shot Alexis another look. Her eyes dropped to Sabine, who was playing in her lap. Alexis straightened her shoulders and stood up. She carried Sabine back to her crib, tucked a pacifier between her lips and then lifted another infant to feed. Without another word, Belinda hurried to the door and stormed out.

Alexis turned to Felicia. "Did you really see her in here?"

Felicia smiled. "Was yesterday afternoon really the last time you saw her?"

The two women exchanged a look. With nothing else to say, both went back to doing what had to be done, losing themselves in their own thoughts.

Marcel was already feeling out of sorts when he arrived back at the New Orleans compound. He and the select Elders who had also returned were already preparing for the work that needed to be done. When they'd left the Midwest facility, Prophet had been eating strawberries and Greek yogurt and laughing with one of the new congregants. That he had murdered a man in cold blood just hours earlier seemed lost on him and all the others who had been witnesses.

Belinda was standing at the front entrance, waiting to deliver the bad news that three of their teens had run off. Belinda was fuming that the Prophet hadn't returned and that suddenly their plans had been disrupted.

"I don't understand," she said. "Why is he rushing?"

"It was not my place to ask," Marcel answered.

"Well, what of Elder Harris? Why didn't he come back to help?"

Marcel gave her a look. "Elder Harris is no longer with the Moral Order. He has ascended to the Kingdom of God."

Belinda's eyes widened. "I don't understand…" she repeated.

Taking a deep breath, Marcel's tone changed. "It is not for you to understand," he snapped harshly. "Neither you, nor any other woman, will question the Prophet's commands. I think you forget your place!"

Belinda bristled. She visibly bit back the thought that

was perched on the tip of her tongue. She dropped her eyes to the floor and took a step back. "My apology, Elder," she muttered.

Marcel continued. "The Prophet says you have the list of congregants and where he wants them sent?"

Belinda nodded. "Yes."

"Bring it to me. I'll be in my quarters. And contact the travel agent. He'll be expecting your call to arrange for transportation."

"Yes, sir, Elder."

Backing away, Belinda turned and disappeared from the room. Taking another deep breath, Marcel headed in the opposite direction, ordering one of the other women to find Alexis and send her to him.

Marcel had returned and Alexis could barely contain her excitement. After one last check on Sabine, who had dozed off into a peaceful sleep, she practically ran back to the main house to find him.

When she entered their room, he was standing in conversation with Belinda. She wasn't happy and, clearly, from the expression on his face, he didn't much care. She held a manila folder in her hands, explaining what he would find inside. Marcel nodded then gestured with his hand to dismiss her. His gaze was focused on Alexis's face, his eyes smiling brightly at the sight of her.

"What about Christiana and the other two children?" Belinda asked. She stood her ground, not yet ready to be moved.

"What about them? This isn't a prison, Mother Belinda. They are free to leave if that's what they desire."

"Christiana is only sixteen!"

"And the other two with her are both eighteen. Legally, there's nothing much we can do. Prophet is not going to allow the police to become involved and you know that."

"We can send out a search party!"

"It's my understanding that you already did that, and they didn't find anything. Am I correct?"

"I just requested help in case they became lost in these swamps."

"And did anything come of it?"

"No," Belinda quipped. "But that doesn't mean—"

Marcel cut off her statement. "It means we're going to focus on what we need to do here."

"What if she comes back and we're gone? What then?"

Marcel sighed. "Do you want to stay here alone and wait? Or are you going to stand by your husband's side as he begins to build up the Order in the Midwest? I don't doubt you know what the Prophet has planned for this place, so you need to decide."

"I just need to know that my daughter is safe!" she railed.

Marcel stared at her intently. "You have no daughter," he barked harshly. "All the children are the offspring of the Prophet. Isn't that what you told me?"

Belinda bit down against her bottom lip. Alexis could see the argument building on her face. She wasn't ready to back down and Marcel wasn't going to give her an upper hand.

"I think you need to remember who you're talking to," Belinda snapped.

Marcel snapped back. "You have no authority here and you have no authority over any Elder in this place."

"The Prophet—"

Marcel cut off her comment. "The Prophet isn't here. And you know better than anyone else that his leadership within the Moral Order is standing on very thin ice. I would tread very cautiously if I were you."

Belinda threw her gaze back to Marcel. Ire washed over her expression, and she was visibly shaking with rage.

"Leave us," Marcel finally said, his voice loud as he punctuated each word. "I will call you if I need you."

"Yes, *Elder* Marcel," Belinda said, her snide tone ringing with hostility as if she needed to remind him of his lane. Making it clear that he might have been in charge, but he was not the Prophet. Not yet.

Alexis's eyes narrowed, the woman's attitude striking a nerve. In the short time she'd known the First Wife, Belinda had never been mean or nasty. She could be abrupt, sometimes brash, but this side of her was new. What bothered Alexis most was that it felt natural, like she was seeing Belinda's true self for the first time.

Marcel followed the woman to the door. He stood in the entrance peering out, watching until Belinda turned the corner at the end of the hallway. When she was well out of his sight, he closed and secured the door. Turning, he moved swiftly to Alexis's side and pulled her into his arms.

He pressed his forehead against hers, his face brushing lightly against her skin. His mouth was a sliver away from hers and his breath was warm and minty. "I really want to kiss you," he whispered, the comment said to seek her permission.

Alexis smiled as she lifted her face forward and pressed her mouth to his lips. She answered him with her tongue.

When Marcel set his lips to hers, every ounce of anxiety

he had been feeling billowed away. Both were reminded of everything that had been good about them together. It awakened feelings that they had thought gone forever. It was cotton candy and waterfalls and sunshine on a spring day. It was safe and easy and comfortable, like a plush blanket on a chilly morning. It was midnight runs for strawberry-glazed donuts, and sugared beignets in bed on a Saturday morning. It was all those things that had ever brought them joy. Marcel was home and Alexis welcomed him in without a moment of hesitation.

They were both breathless when Marcel finally pulled himself from her, taking two steps back to put some space between them. Alexis inhaled swiftly, drawing air deep into her lungs. She would have given anything to magically be back in her home, with Marcel and Sabine, the last few days and what they would soon face nothing but a bad memory. But losing herself in Marcel's embrace wasn't possible, or smart, for either of them with everything going on.

Outside the room door, the noise level had risen substantially. People were rushing to pack. Many would be leaving on a bus first thing in the morning. The others would be traveling by boat. If Marcel kept the Prophet's commandments, the entire facility would be in flames just hours after their departure. It was just crazy enough to be unfathomable.

"He expects you to single-handedly burn the entire place down?" Alexis's incredulous expression made Marcel smile as he nodded his head.

"Those are my orders," he replied.

She shook her head. "So, what are you going to do?"

"I need to get a message to Waters. He will have to intercept that boat and raid the Midwest property. Hopefully, before the bus gets there.

"And the Prophet just plans to hide out there?"

"He thinks we're about to be raided here. I don't think he's even considered that the other communities might be on the FBI's radar, too. That, and he murdered Harris. I don't think he's counting on getting caught for that crime."

Alexis's eyes widened. Her jaw dropped as her mouth fell open in shock. "He killed Harris?"

Marcel nodded. "He shot him *dead*. Emptied an entire clip into the man's chest. He claimed Harris was working with the Feds, as well as having a relationship with one of the agents. He was angrier about that than he was about Harris possibly giving away our secrets."

"Was Harris working with the FBI, too?"

"I honestly have no idea. But if he was, I'm worried about what that agent he was sleeping with might have told him about us."

Alexis rolled her eyes skyward. She took another breath and blew it out with a loud exhale.

"What's the deal with Belinda's daughter? I thought you were planning to mentor her?" Marcel took a seat against the side of the bed. His hands were folded together in his lap.

"Teenage angst! She's sixteen and pissed off at the world. She wanted out and there was nothing I could say to change her mind. She was planning to walk out of here earlier this morning. She promised to follow the tire tracks and stay on the road, and I did ask my mother to have someone on the lookout for her when she reached the interstate. Hopefully, they'll convince her to let them help."

"The First Wife isn't going to leave easily if she doesn't know what has happened to her daughter."

Alexis thought about the woman and how she'd left them. Rage would be a kind descriptor, but she had been anything but kind. Belinda had been irate. Alexis sensed that she could be vindictive, and that scared her.

"Belinda may be an even bigger problem," she said, relaying the information Cash had shared about Belinda's maternal connection to the former prophet and there being no record of Christiana being her biological child. "There's also a warrant out for her arrest. Apparently, she's a person of interest in a murder investigation," Alexis concluded.

Marcel cursed, frustration worrying his brow. He shook his head. "Let's just focus on getting out of here right now. We can worry about the rest of it later. There's going to be a lot of activity around here tomorrow. You and Sabine need to get lost in that shuffle and slip away unnoticed. I'll arrange for someone to meet the two of you."

"What about you?" Alexis asked, concern in her voice.

"I need to hang back until everyone's out of danger and Waters and his team are in place. I'll meet you both after."

"You're not seriously going to pyro this place, are you?"

"I don't plan on it, but I'll need to make it look real for anyone reporting back to the Prophet. We can't risk anyone warning him about what's happening here or what's coming his way. And we need all the evidence here that the Feds can find. If he has records of anything, I need to make sure nothing happens to them."

"How can I help?" Alexis asked.

"I just need you to watch over Sabine, please. And try to keep yourself out of trouble. I'll be worried enough about the both of you."

Alexis smiled.

Chapter 15

Alexis didn't see Marcel for the rest of the afternoon. The energy throughout the buildings was frantic; people confused, and frightened, and uncertain about their future and where they might land when things finally settled down. Outside, the weather seemed to be reading the mood. The winds had begun to kick up and not a sliver of sunshine was breaking through the tree cover. The humidity had risen and the evening air felt damp and sticky.

Alexis was also unsettled despite knowing more about what was happening than the others. Though she and Marcel had a plan, she couldn't stop herself from imagining the worst. After checking in on Sabine, she hadn't been able to spend the afternoon in the nursery. Belinda had commanded her assistance with packing up supplies. The older woman had pointed her to the oversized pantry and had handed her a corrugated box.

With a bright smile and a nod, Alexis had packed boxed goods and canned foods for over an hour. She hadn't complained or given anyone a hard time. When she was done, she'd followed everyone to the community room for evening prayer and an update on what would happen the following day. A surge of energy permeated the air as Marcel relayed a message from the Prophet and assured them all that everything going forward came with the Holy Father's blessings and would better serve them in the future. For just a brief moment, Alexis thought he sounded like a snake-oil salesman hawking his wares. And then, just like that, there was an air of honesty and determination that swept over him. Marcel genuinely wanted things to be well for them and you could hear it in his words. His sincerity was palpable and seemed to ease everyone's concerns. Even Alexis felt less anxious as she listened to the soothing timbre of his voice as he led the congregation in prayer then wished them all well on the next phase of their journey.

Sneaking around in full view of everyone wasn't something her training had prepared her for. Alexis carried a laundry basket filled with clean towels. It wasn't the best cover, but it would serve its purpose if she were caught, she'd thought. As Alexis headed toward the Prophet's quarters, she hadn't anticipated running into as many people as she had. There was a burst of activity still going on, the congregation readying themselves as they gathered up the last of their personal belongings. Evening prayer and Marcel's enthusiasm seemed to have boosted everyone's morale.

She stopped once to help an elderly woman who was panicking that she might be left behind. Guiding her to her bed and assuring her that she would personally check on her in the morning had eased the woman's anxiety and added one more item to her list of things to do. Then there was the couple blocking the hallway as they bickered about absolutely nothing. She lowered her gaze as she passed by the man but tossed the woman a supportive glance. By the time she arrived at the Prophet's door, she reasoned that at least a dozen people had seen her, most pausing to speak and acknowledge her as she sauntered by.

She tossed a look over her shoulder before reaching for the doorknob and pushing the door open. She knew that Belinda was still in the community room with Marcel and the Elders, finalizing the details of the move. She reasoned she had at least twenty minutes before she would have to worry about being caught. Marcel would have a fit if he knew what she was up to, which was why Alexis hadn't bothered to tell him. But she had made finding those files a personal mission and she was determined to complete that task.

Inside, the room was as nondescript as all the others. There was a queen bed, one nightstand and a desk. The décor was bland, looking like white toast with peanut butter. A hairbrush rested atop the desk, sitting beside a notepad and a number two pencil. There was also a pack of chewing gum and an unopened bag of sunflower seeds.

Resting the laundry basket atop the bed, Alexis went swiftly to the nightstand and pulled open the drawer. There was a collection of medicine bottles and pamphlets inside. She took one into her hand and read the label. Then she looked at a second. Both were used for the treatment of prostate cancer. Processing what she knew about the medications, she reasoned that the Prophet was sick and trying to keep it a secret. That information and the questions about his sexuality were more than enough to unseat him from his position if it were ever to go to a vote.

Reaching beneath the drawer, she felt for the key and discovered an envelope taped to the bottom. Taking it from its hiding spot, she found what she'd been looking for inside. Easing over to the bookcase, she located the door hidden behind a heavy velvet curtain. She punched in the code, and it opened easily. Stepping inside, she came to an abrupt halt.

The adjoining room was a lavish extravaganza of expensive fabrics and vintage furniture. It was a collaboration of all things gaudy and over-the-top, starting with the oversized portrait of Amos Lee in all his naked glory and ending with the life-sized, anatomically correct, silicone male doll posed on a velvet settee. The addition of Persian rugs and the excessive gold adornments was more than Alexis could have ever imagined. Unexpected, it was a lot to take in when she considered the limited time she had to search.

She shook her head, focusing her attention on what she was there for. She moved to the file cabinet and used the key. Everything she'd hoped to find, and more, was inside. The Prophet, or Belinda, had kept detailed records on all their operations. There were names and dates and pages detailing every dirty secret the duo had. It was a gold mine of information and although she couldn't take it all, she was determined to take as much as she could.

Alexis grabbed the most recent notebooks and the file of birth records. She snatched manila folders and bank registers. Closing the file cabinet, she exited the room and tucked everything between the bottom layer of towels in the laundry basket. She had barely replaced the envelope and closed the nightstand drawer when Belinda pushed open the door and stepped inside.

"What are you doing in here?" Belinda questioned, her eyes wide. Her voice had risen, annoyance exploding over every word.

Alexis met her query with a bright smile. "They were short-handed in laundry and asked me to deliver towels. I was just leaving them on your bed for you."

Belinda looked at Alexis and then at the cotton towel she had gestured with. Her gaze rested on the plastic basket. "Why are we short in laundry?" Belinda prodded. "We should have had enough coverage."

Alexis took a deep breath. "From what I was told, someone was sick and wasn't able to work. With everything going on, I was just trying to help out where I could. You've had so much on your plate, I was hoping to lighten your load a little, Moral Mother."

Belinda's gaze narrowed slightly. She stared, pondering Alexis's comment. "My load…?"

Alexis smiled again, the bend to her lips widening. "As our Moral Mother, your duties are never-ending. Watching how you handle yourself with such grace is commendable. I hope to be as inspiring to the young women who will come after me. So, how can I not help lessen your burdens when I can?"

Belinda was still eyeing her suspiciously. After a moment, she nodded. "Just leave the towels and finish your chores. We all need to rest well tonight."

Alexis removed two towels from the top of the basket and rested them against the bedcovers. She lifted the basket and headed for the door. "I've only a few more deliveries," she said. "It shouldn't take me too much longer."

Belinda continued to glare in her direction.

Alexis gave her one last smile. "All honor to the Prophet," Alexis said as she made her exit, hurrying quickly back down the hallway.

* * *

Before the lights went out, Alexis headed to the nursery to put Sabine down for the night. Even she seemed to sense that things were different, the little girl fretful. She whined and cried and clung to Alexis, her tiny body shaking with distress. It took everything Alexis had not to cry herself as she did everything, she could to soothe the baby.

"I think you're teething," Alexis asked. She ran her index finger against Sabine's gums. The baby began to gnaw on her finger, drool flowing past the corners of her small mouth.

Felicia was there with baby Marcus and pointed her toward the supply cabinet. "There's teething oil on the top shelf. Rub some on her gums. That should calm her right down."

"Teething oil?"

"It's coconut oil mixed with chamomile, clove and peppermint. It'll soothe the pain and give her some relief. There are also frozen chew toys in the small freezer. Those are popular around here."

Alexis smiled. "Thank you," she said, rising from her seat and heading to the pantry. She shifted the baby in her arms, caressing the child's back with her palm. Sabine was fussy and irritable and clearly not happy with her situation. She dropped her head against Alexis's shoulder, pulling her thumb into her mouth.

Minutes later, she was giggling like nothing at all had pained her. Her bright smile moved Alexis and Felicia both to laugh.

"Don't get too excited," Felicia said. She shifted Marcus against her shoulder and patted his back. "It's only a temporary relief. If you're lucky, it will last long enough for her to fall asleep and rest for an hour or so before she wakes up crying again."

Alexis nodded, still cradling the baby girl in her arms. "How are you feeling about the move?" she asked, turning toward Felicia.

"I view it as an opportunity to upgrade my status."

"Still looking to marry an Elder, I see."

"I hear there will be a few more to choose from. I have high hopes."

Alexis chuckled softly. "Seriously, though. Are you concerned at all?"

"I'm more worried about having nowhere to go. It's hard out there on the streets. The Moral Order isn't perfect, but it's better than nothing at all."

"What brought you here? How did you join the Order?"

Felicia shrugged. "I followed a man. It didn't work out."

"It rarely does," Alexis muttered, an air of empathy in her tone.

"Looks like you made out all right," Felicia said. She smiled.

Alexis let the moment sweeping between them settle. Outside, the wind had picked up and trees were blowing harshly. The tin roof on the building rattled loudly. "Feels like we might get some rain," Alexis said, her head tilted as if it might help her hear better.

"Most of the babies are settled for the night. You can probably lay her down now without any problems." Felicia gestured toward Sabine with her head.

The little girl was snoring softly against her shoulder. Alexis smiled again. Sabine had that in common with her father, too.

* * *

When Alexis made it back to the room, the lights had already been shut down for the night. Inside their private space, Marcel had lit the candles, the glow around the room feeling slightly eerie. He was talking on a cell phone she didn't recognize, and Belinda was standing at his elbow. The other woman didn't bother to acknowledge her, barely looking in her direction. She was focused on Marcel and the conversation he was having. Pausing, Alexis realized the Prophet was on the other end and Marcel was not happy about the conversation.

"We are responsible for their safety," Marcel said, his voice raised. "Why would we..."

The Prophet was shouting into the other end. His words were mumbled, but the rage in his tone was clearly evident. Marcel listened until he heard an opportunity to interject a comment.

"I will make sure things go smoothly as planned, Prophet. You can trust me. This storm has just put a small roadblock in our way. We need to make some slight adjustments. What we don't want to do is put our congregation in harm's way. Heaven forbid if something happens to them. The police will be all over us and we can't have that happen."

The Prophet's murmured voice sounded over the line, but his rage had been replaced with an air of calm. Marcel nodded into the receiver. "All honor to you, Prophet," he said and then he disconnected the call.

Marcel looked like he had just waged war with Satan himself. Alexis sensed he was ready to explode but he maintained his cool. He handed the cell phone back to Belinda.

"What are we doing?" Belinda questioned. "Will we stay?"

"No," Marcel answered. "That's not an option. We aren't safe. Buses will be here in the morning for everyone. We're vacating the premises."

"What about the boats?"

"Everyone will be on the bus."

"The Prophet will not be happy," she said.

Marcel paused. Then he looked her in her eye. "I really don't give a damn," he said, a brow raised as he stared at her. "Now get everyone ready. We need to get moving at first light."

"What's happened?" Alexis asked.

Belinda shot her a look but said nothing. Instead, she gave Marcel the slightest bow then turned and exited the room.

"Are you okay?" Alexis queried. She took a step toward him, pressing her palm to his chest. "What's going on?"

"There's a hurricane headed right for us. Amos thinks I'm going to put half the women and all the children on a boat to Mexico but with the winds, rain and floodwaters rushing through the channels inland, that's a formula for disaster. It won't happen on my watch. That's not a risk I'm willing to take.

"When is the storm supposed to hit?"

"Tomorrow afternoon." His voice dropped two octaves to a low whisper. "I've already been in touch with Waters. We're still on schedule."

"How'd you hear about the storm?" Not having access to television or radio, Alexis could only imagine what might have happened if they hadn't had a heads-up. Her curiosity burned feverishly.

"Agent Waters. Belinda knows him as Harris's contact for transportation. She called him about the boats and he let her know it might be a problem."

"So, just how much does she know about the Prophet's operation?"

"I assume most of it. Prophet has put her in charge of everything he has no interest in dealing with. She's the point of contact for anything dealing with the outside world. She has a great amount of power and she's not ready to give that up. It's why she's been challenging everything I say."

"Has she mentioned Christiana again?"

Marcel shook his head. "Not one word."

That wasn't the response Alexis had expected. She'd imagined Belinda would still be hounding him to track the young girl down. Alexis would have expected that news of the storm would have made her even more anxious. She knew if she were in the woman's shoes and it was Sabine, nothing and no one would keep her from searching the child out. She suddenly wanted to head back to the nursery but knew that would only draw unwanted attention to them both.

"I should call my mother," Alexis said, whispering with him.

Marcel nodded. "I'll be right here. Just lock the bathroom door. If Belinda comes back, I'll knock twice."

Minutes later Alexis called Marcel's name. There was a hint of panic in her voice, the tone disquieting.

"What's wrong?" he asked, moving quickly into the space.

Alexis stood with the metal box in her hands. The lid

was open and she held it out for him to see. Peering inside, Marcel's eyes widened, rising anxiety washing over his expression. The money, cell phone and pistol that had been hidden inside, were gone.

Sleep didn't stand a chance. There was no counting sheep or warm milk, or any of those things that would give them a good night's rest. Marcel had paced the floor from one side of the room to the other, he and Alexis trying to figure out who had been in their room, going through their things. Who knew what they'd kept hidden, and where? And where was that damn gun?

Belinda was at the top of their suspect list, but if they were honest, it could have been anyone. But more important than not knowing who, was not knowing what the intruder's intentions were.

"For all we know, it could have been one of the women on the housekeeping staff," Marcel was saying.

Alexis shook her head. "Or one of the men in maintenance."

"Well, whoever it was doesn't want us to know they have it. Or they would have outed us by now."

"What are we going to do?" Alexis asked.

"Stay steady the course. "I'll worry about it once I know you and Sabine are safe."

"We still need to get those files."

"We can't risk it. Let's hope Waters's team finds everything once we've cleared out."

"If there's anything left to find," Alexis muttered.

"I'll make sure Belinda is one of the first on the bus.

Once she's out of the way, I'll better be able to see what I can find."

"I want to help, Marcel."

"Keep Sabine safe. That's the help I need from you.

Alexis rolled her eyes. She said, "The Prophet has a secret room connected to his private office. Inside, there's a locked file cabinet and a safe. He keeps the key to the cabinet and the code to the door taped to the underside of the top drawer in his bedside nightstand. And don't let his blow-up dolly thing throw you. I'm sure it's harmless!"

Marcel's expression was judicious mixed with skepticism. He tried to keep the surprise out of his voice. "How do you know that?" he questioned.

"I have my sources," Alexis answered. Her smug expression moved him to laugh despite the seriousness of their situation.

"If you did what I think you did…"

"I did what was necessary," she said with a shake of her head.

Marcel gestured toward the bed. "Do you mind if I sit and put my feet up?" he asked.

She shrugged. "As long as you keep your hands to yourself, we're good," she said.

Marcel laughed. "I won't make any promises, but I'll make every effort to do my best."

She smiled as she watched him kick off his shoes and ease his body atop the mattress. He shifted himself upright until his back rested against the headboard, his legs extended out in front of him. He folded his arms across his broad chest and tucked his hands beneath his armpits. He winked his eye at her and Alexis laughed. She rolled her eyes skyward. "You are so foolish!" she said.

"Just trying to lighten the mood. I appreciate being able to laugh with you. There isn't a lot of laughter that goes on around here."

Alexis moved to the other side of the bed and sat down. "Why is that? From everything you told me about when your family first joined, it was idyllic."

"It was idyllic in the beginning. I was about twelve years old when you could begin to feel the shift. And it only took one leader to effect those changes. Think about Charles Manson, David Koresh or Jim Jones. When you have leaders who are charismatic and highly convincing, people will listen and follow them. They build their image on lies and it all goes to hell from there. My father got us out when the ideology shifted right and no longer meshed with his values. It's gone downhill ever since."

Alexis slid her body closer to his, leaning her head against his shoulder. "It was bad when I followed Symmetry into the fold. Really bad. There was no respect for women, everyone was treated badly, and he considered himself above reproach."

"The Prophets that followed weren't much better. In fact, it seems like every last one of them was worse."

"There's no way we can raise Sabine here."

Marcel hesitated for a brief moment. "We?" he questioned, his voice barely a whisper.

"You don't think I'm going to let you raise her alone, do you? I plan to be a very active auntie."

"What if I wanted you to be a very active mommy?" Marcel questioned.

Alexis took her own sweet time to consider his query. When she finally answered, there was a joyous lilt to her tone. "I'm still very angry with you, Marcel. But I can't deny that I still love you. I love you. And I already love Sabine as if she were mine. I want the best for her and for you. But you and I have a lot to work through to figure out if you and Sabine are what's best for me."

"So, you're not going to make it easy for me?" His brows were lifted teasingly.

Alexis smiled. "Oh hell no!"

Marcel bent to kiss her forehead. "I promise that I'm willing to do whatever I need to do for you to take me back, Alexis. I will not disappoint you."

"Don't make any promises you can't keep, Marcel."

"I promise that I will regain your trust no matter how long it takes me. Because I still love you, too, Alexis. I never stopped loving you. Loving you is the only thing that kept me going." He pressed a kiss to the tip of her nose, his hand gently cupping the side of her face. His warm breath floated against her skin, teasing her lips. When he kissed them, everything else was nonexistent, nothing but the sweetness of it fueling their thoughts.

Outside, the rain was coming down harder, pelting the tin roof and sounding like a myriad of drums. Dozing here and there, the duo spent most of the night talking. There were discussions about the past and about future ambitions. They reflected on each other's hopes and dreams and readiness to risk it all for a second chance at forever. They laughed together, prayed together, debated politics and religion and found consensus on their goals for Sabine and her future. If it had been possible to make up for lost time in those few short hours, the two had come close.

"So, what now?" Alexis asked, snuggling even closer against him.

Marcel answered. "When we get back, I think we should consider couple's therapy."

"I think that's a good idea. I think it's a really good idea."

It was quiet for a moment, both falling into thought. A rumble of thunder sounded in the distance.

Alexis sat up, pressing her hand against his chest as she stared at him. "I'm scared," she said softly, the emotion seeping out of her eyes. "I'm terrified that this isn't going to go well."

"You should be scared. Don't be complacent thinking we have things under control. A dozen things could go wrong. We don't know who can be trusted and who can't. And then we have to battle this storm. Nothing about getting out of here is going to be easy," he said. "I know enough about how the Prophet thinks to know he's got someone watching and ready to take us out if he feels threatened. But you just remember, I'm not going to let anything happen to you or Sabine."

He took a breath and continued. "Make sure you're on that first bus with the other women and children. They'll be making a pit stop somewhere down the road where it's safe for everyone to stretch their legs and take a bathroom break. When you get off the bus, your father will be there to pick up you and Sabine."

"My father?" Surprise rang in her tone.

Marcel nodded. "I needed someone I could trust."

She shook her head. "Why didn't you tell me my father had found you and threatened you to stay away?"

Marcel smiled. "Because that was between me and him. He was doing what he thought he needed to do to protect both of us. Most especially you. If the situation ever arises, I will do the same for Sabine."

"You men make me sick!" she muttered under her breath.

Marcel chuckled. "We'll work on that in therapy."

Alexis nodded as she lay back against him, resting her head on his chest. Marcel wrapped his arms around her torso, hugging her tightly. Minutes later, both had dozed off to sleep, the patter of rain lulling them into slumber. Outside, Mother Nature was waging a war of her own making. It was ominous and foreboding, oblivious to their cares and concerns.

Chapter 16

Marcel rose early. Stepping onto the porch of the main building, he watched the rain that continued to beat down above them. It was clear the weather was not going to cooperate and he was prepared for something to go wrong. The cloud-filled sky was dark, little light shimmering through the awning of trees that surrounded the area.

His calls to the Prophet had gone unanswered, no one bothering to pick up the line. He found it concerning that the man who was dead set on exercising full control, even from a distance, wasn't available to give them any direction. Even Belinda had expressed concerns about not being able to reach her husband for guidance.

They had started the morning with prayer, everyone gathered together in the common room. Afterward, the women had made them all a quick breakfast of toast, fresh fruit and juice. Now, everyone was milling about inside, waiting for direction. Alexis had stayed to assist with Sister Hannah and the elderly before heading over to the nursery to help bundle up the babies and get them ready for travel. There were bottles of fresh milk and clean diapers they had to be concerned with.

In the distance, Marcel could hear the rush of water spiraling along the waterways. It was rising faster than anticipated, the threat of flooding becoming very real. He and Waters had touched base before sunrise. He'd called his friend to make sure everything was still on track. Waters had promised help would be there to get them out safely and, as the first bus rolled into view, Marcel breathed a sigh of relief.

He began shouting orders to the men standing in wait beside him. "Start loading everyone on the buses. If they can't carry it, then they'll have to leave it. We're only taking necessary supplies with us. Gather the seniors, the women and the children, and get them on first. Everyone move it!" he called out.

Sister Hannah, the elderly woman from the previous night, was thanking Alexis profusely. In the span of fifteen long minutes, Alexis had heard her entire life story, ending with how she hoped the Prophet would be there to hold her hand when she took her last breath. When the call came for them to start getting onto the first bus that had arrived, Alexis guided her to the front door and pointed her in the right direction. One of the men took the woman's hand, slipped his arm around her shoulders, and led her the rest of the way to the bus.

For the briefest moment, Alexis watched as Marcel issued commands and helped where he was needed. She watched, pride gleaming from her eyes as he led and the others followed. He had a calling in ministry, and she realized that he had yet to see what she had been seeing since the day she'd met him. For a brief second, she wished she could take a moment to touch his hand and draw from his inner strength, but she needed to get to Sabine.

Hurrying along the walkway to the nursery, she passed by the women already heading to the bus with one of their charges. The babies were bundled tightly against the weather to ward off the rain. Rushing through the door of the first room, she found all the cribs empty. As she passed through the door into the second space, it, too, had been cleared. Concern suddenly buckled like a tight fist in the pit of her stomach. She turned back, rushing after the last woman she'd passed.

"Sister Delphine!" she yelled as she grabbed the woman's arm, practically swinging her about. "Where's Sabine? Does someone have Sabine?"

The woman named Delphine shrugged her narrow shoulders. "The Moral Mother took her. She's probably on the bus already," she said, pulling the baby she was holding closer.

Alexis forced the slightest smile on her face. "Thank you," she said. "You better hurry."

Alexis ran toward the front, racing past the other women who were making their way. Her mind was a jumble of questions. Why would Belinda have taken Sabine? And *where* had she taken the child to?

As she reached the front door, the first bus was pulling away. Marcel and the men were helping to load the second bus, the last of the congregation anxious to get on board. She hurried out into the weather, barely aware that she wore nothing to protect her from the onslaught of rain.

She cried out for Marcel. "Was Belinda on that bus?" she yelled.

He shook his head. "I haven't seen her. She should still be inside. She changed her mind about getting on the first bus. Now she insists on riding in the van with me. Why? What's wrong? And why aren't you and Sabine on that damn bus?" he suddenly barked.

Alexis should her head. "Belinda took her!" she screamed before turning on her heels and heading back inside.

Alexis ran to the Prophet's living quarters. It was the first place she could think to look for Sabine and Belinda. The room was empty. The door to the Prophet's private office had been left open and there was a strong scent of gasoline that filled the air.

Alexis shouted for the two of them. "Mother Belinda! Where are you?"

When no one responded, Alexis raced back to the prayer room, poking her head into each of the rooms along the way. Everyone had cleared out like planned and the First Wife was nowhere to be seen. Guilt hit Alexis like a tidal wave. She should never have stopped to help the others without making sure she had Sabine first. She'd earnestly believed Sabine would be well until she got to her, and she'd been wrong. Their baby was gone, and she couldn't begin to know where.

Marcel suddenly flung himself into the room and rushed to her side. "Where are they?" he cried.

Alexis shook her head. "I don't know. I was headed to the nursery to see if she might have gone back there."

He was suddenly screaming in her face. His tone was accusatory and abrasive. "You had one job, Alexis! One thing to do. I can't believe you let this happen!"

Alexis bristled, her eyes widening. "Don't you dare scream at me like that," she hissed through clenched teeth. "I didn't purposely let that woman take that baby. And I'm trying to find Sabine just like you are. I'm scared, too, so don't you dare!"

Contrition painted his expression. He reached his hand out, but Alexis snatched herself away. In her eyes, he was suddenly the biggest jerk in the world.

"I'm sorry," he said. "I never meant…"

Alexis turned. "I don't care what you meant," she snapped. "But we will talk about it later. Right now, I need to go back to the nursery to check if they went there."

Marcel nodded. "There are some places I can check on the other side," he said. "Just please, meet me back here in five minutes. Things are changing fast out there."

Alexis nodded, rushing off as quickly as she could. Marcel hurried in the other direction.

Making her way to the nursery, Alexis found one of the other Elders headed out. He carried a red can filled with gasoline and was pouring the noxious fluid over the furnishings and the floor.

He stopped what he was doing to bellow at her. "What are you doing here? You shouldn't be here!"

"I'm trying to find Mother Belinda. No one knows where she is!"

"She's fine," he said with the slightest sneer. "She's taking a boat upstream and will meet us at the Midwest compound."

Alexis's eyes widened. "A boat?"

He snapped at her a second time. "Head out now. Don't make me tell you again." He resumed splashing gasoline around the space.

Ignoring him, Alexis made a beeline for the rear entrance. When he reached to grab for her, she slammed him hard in the face with the butt of her palm. Every ounce of ire and fear she was holding was unleashed in that punch, breaking his nose. Before he could recover from the blow, she disappeared through the door and out of the room.

The wind and rain had intensified and the noise outside was thundering. The structures around them creaked and groaned, paying tribute to the workmanship of their building crew. But Marcel knew that even the best work in the world might not hold in these conditions. The tin roof rippled, sounding like the low pitch of African drums.

He had not meant to shout at Alexis the way he had, but fear for Sabine had had him ready to pull his dreads out. He'd anticipated something going wrong, but Belinda absconding with his daughter had not been on his bingo card. All he wanted was to find them both and hug his child to his heart. But now, not only was Sabine gone, but because of his temper, he might have lost Alexis, too.

After searching all the rooms in that last wing of the building, he raced back to the common area. Alexis was nowhere to be found. Overhead, the tin roof had begun to screech. Loudly. Realizing time was not their friend, he ran in the direction of the nursery.

Alexis pushed her way through the torrential rain. The wooden walkways were slippery and the waters beneath them had risen to dangerous levels. Tears were streaming down her face. She had to find Sabine. She couldn't fathom going back to face Marcel, not knowing what had happened to his daughter. She couldn't blame him for being angry. She was angry. Despite her understanding of his pain and emotions, he'd still had no right to speak to her the way he had. Men like Prophets Amos and Symmetry lambasted women so callously. Not Marcel. Not the Marcel she loved. But this Marcel hadn't batted an eyelash before spewing vitriol in her direction. Getting past that was just one more thing that could potentially curtail their reconciliation even if Sabine was found and all else was well.

Alexis suddenly came to a halt, tilting her head to listen. There had been the faintest noise in the wind; a small cry that seemed out of place. She swiped her hand over her face, wiping at the water that rained over her head. The traveling clothes she'd been allowed to wear, were saturated, her dress clinging to her curves. She hadn't bothered to find a coat and the running shoes on her feet were soaked. She was cold and shivering. The water was higher, and she knew it was only a matter of time before the walkway would be completely under water. She listened again, hearing the cry one more time.

Panic suddenly washed over her. She was certain it was Sabine, the little girl crying. She couldn't begin to imagine what the First Wife had to be thinking. And then it didn't matter. Alexis pushed forward, fighting against the strong winds. Sabine needed her and neither hell nor high water was going to keep her from finding her.

Elder Paul was pulling himself up off the floor when Marcel rushed into the room. Blood was spewing out of his nostrils and rage pierced the glare he gave Marcel.

"What happened?" Marcel asked.

"Your wife. The Prophet will hear about this!" he shouted.

Marcel took a deep breath. "Where is she?"

The Elder pointed toward the door.

Confusion washed over Marcel's face. "Where was she going?" he questioned.

"How should I know?" the other man snapped.

Marcel suddenly snatched him by his collar. "Where was she going?" he repeated through clenched teeth.

"Looking for the Moral Mother! She was headed to the docks."

Marcel threw the man back to the ground. He rushed for the door and outside. He'd barely made it through the entrance when the sound of tin vibrating and wood cracking screamed for his attention. He turned to look just as the roof suddenly caved in, a massive tree crashing down against the building. He heard Elder Paul scream and then nothing but the sudden quiet of the rain falling. Turning, he ran toward the docks, shouting out Alexis's name.

A tree had fallen across the pathway. The rain had eased just enough for Alexis to clearly hear Sabine crying. "I'm coming, baby," she whispered as she navigated herself across the top of the fallen tree trunk and regained her footing. As she drew closer, she realized where the sound was coming from, and she felt her heart drop into the pit of her stomach. She wanted desperately to be wrong but as she drew closer, she knew exactly where Belinda had taken the baby.

She could see the hotbox in the distance. It hung low, the branches that held it bending with the wind. Water washed against the sides of the box. The bottom of the torture chamber kissed the rise of water. It was only a matter of time before it would be engulfed beneath the tributary.

Sabine was sitting upright inside. The little girl was crying hysterically, her face beet-red. Alexis rushed to her, only to discover the box was locked. She looked around, hoping to find Belinda and the key, but there was no sign of her.

"It's going to be okay, *cher*!" Alexis murmured. "I'm here now," she said. She pulled at the lock, her heart breaking as Sabine reached for her. She had to get the thing opened and she couldn't begin to figure out how. The child was now sitting in a good inch of water, and the rain and wind had picked up even harder.

Turning, Alexis searched for anything that she could use to pry the box open. She knew she was running out of time. So focused, she wasn't paying attention until it was too late. The blow to the back of her head was blinding. Pain shot through every nerve ending in her body and she couldn't focus her eyes. She fell forward, the cold water rushing up her nose. She forced herself to roll onto her back and realized she had landed in the water. In the distance, Sabine was crying even harder. Pushing herself upward, Alexis crawled back onto the walkway. With every ounce of energy she could muster, she headed in the direction of Sabine's screams.

"Please, dear God," she whispered. "Please help me get my baby!"

Alexis was suddenly aware of someone standing above her. She didn't know when she had fallen again, or even why she was lying on the ground. She didn't know how far she was from Sabine and that cage. The water around her was choking. She couldn't catch her breath and each inhalation felt as if she were drowning. Alexis cried out for help. She called to the baby, wanting to assure her that she was coming. That she was fighting to get to her. Her eyes flickered open then closed and then open. She saw double and then everything went black.

When Alexis opened her eyes again, Mother Belinda was standing above her. She was talking, saying something, but Alexis couldn't make out a single word. Gunshots suddenly rang through the air. One, and then a second, and maybe a third. Belinda took off running from the bullets that flew over their heads. Someone, or something, ran past Alexis, close on Belinda's heels. Alexis struggled to sit up, determined to save the baby. She reached forward, her hand grasping at air. In the distance, thunder rolled across the dark sky.

Chapter 17

Hurricane Bruno had been downgraded to a tropical storm when it actually hit the New Orleans area. The sustained wind speeds had averaged under seventy-four miles per hour. It had hit hard enough to do just enough damage but not destroy anything major, and no one's life had been lost to the storm. It had been a blessing.

As Marcel had rushed to find Alexis, panic had begun to set in. The wind and rain had made everything difficult. The rising waters had made the walkway virtually impossible to see. Blinded, he'd had to slowly feel his way along the path. When those gunshots had rung out, everything imaginable had crossed his mind. Who was shooting? Who were they shooting at? And then he'd seen the Prophet's wife running in the distance and another woman running behind her. But he had not seen Alexis. Not at first. And that had set his panic level escalating.

Sabine's screams had been gut-wrenching. He'd found the little girl submerged in water up to her waist. Beside her, Alexis had lain unconscious, her body half in the water, half atop what was left of the platform. Her arms had been outstretched, as if she were reaching for the baby. But reaching hadn't been enough.

He'd pulled the keys for the lock from his pocket. When he'd taken Sabine out of the box and into his arms, she'd been shivering with fright. She'd clung to him, and he'd wrapped himself tightly around her. Dropping to his knees, he'd checked Alexis for a pulse, grateful that he'd found no bullet wounds. She'd been very much alive but unconscious. There was a gash on the back of her head, blood beginning to coagulate along the wound. He'd known that there was no way he would risk leaving her, so with strength that surprised even him, he'd heaved her up and over his shoulder like a sack of potatoes and slowly inched his way back along the watery path. He had almost made it, carrying them both, when he'd felt his knees wanting to give out beneath him. And then, out of nowhere, like a knight in shining armor, an FBI agent had appeared to assist him. A rescue team had swept in courtesy of Agent Waters.

Now, Marcel paced the hospital floor. They were still denying him access to Alexis because he wasn't family. Unable to prove his paternity, they also refused to let him see Sabine until he could provide documents confirming that he was her father. His frustration was mounting and he hadn't been able to reach Agent Waters for help. All he could do until the pieces fell into place was pace the floor and he was becoming proficient at doing just that.

"Where's our daughter?"

Marcel turned in time to see Alexis's parents barreling in his direction. Both wore their emotions on their sleeve, concern and worry branding their expressions. He couldn't begin to articulate how happy he was to see them. They stopped at the nurses' station.

Josiah Martin's voice was booming. "I need someone to tell me what's going on with my child. Now!"

A nurse rushed forward to calm them both down. "Mr. and Mrs. Martin," she said, "you can follow me. I will take you to see her."

Turning, both started to follow the woman. Josiah paused to toss Marcel a look over his shoulder. "What are you waiting for, son?" he said.

Gratitude washed over Marcel's face as he hurried after them. Claudia grabbed his hand and squeezed it. "Are you okay?" she questioned.

"I'm much better now. Thank you for asking."

She squeezed his hand a second time as she pulled him along beside her.

Dr. Robert Jackson met them at the door to Alexis's room. He was a muscular man with a distinguished mustache and goatee. He reminded Marcel of an older version of Dwayne Wade, the professional ball player. It quickly became clear that he was a friend of the Martin family.

Dr. Jackson explained. "Alexis is going to be just fine. She suffered a serious blow to the back of her head, but I anticipate she will make a full recovery. For now, we plan to keep her here. We want to keep an eye on her. She inhaled some water into her lungs, which wasn't good, but I don't anticipate there will be any lasting concerns. She's awake and has been asking for her baby. In fact, I wasn't able to calm her down until I promised they would bring the little girl to her."

Marcel interjected. "And the baby, how is she?"

"Are you the child's father?" he asked

Marcel nodded his head. "Yes."

"The beauty of babies," Dr. Jackson responded, "is that they are very resilient. Once she was dry, fed and had herself a nap, she has been a very happy little princess. But we want to keep an eye on her also. Just in case."

"Can we see Alexis please?" Claudia asked.

"Yes, ma'am! I have to make my rounds, but if you have any questions or if you need me, just let her nurse know."

Josiah shook Dr. Jackson's hand. "Thank you."

Marcel echoed the sentiment. "Thank you so much, Dr. Jackson."

As Claudia pushed the room's door open, Marcel took a step back. "I'll give you some time with her," he said softly.

Josiah looked him up and down. "What's wrong? Did something happen we should know about?"

"No, sir," Marcel answered. "Things were tense for a while there. We had words and I admit that I didn't respond kindly. But Alexis put me in my place. I just figured you would want a moment with her alone. And she might not want to see me."

The patriarch grunted. "I swear, you young people are going to send me to an early grave!"

Claudia laughed. "You men need to be checked a time or two. Marcel will be fine. I know my daughter. She will cut you until you bleed, but if she loves you, she'll help bandage the wound."

Marcel nodded. "I just think you should go in first."

Josiah chuckled softly. "I never took you for a coward, son!"

Marcel couldn't help but laugh with him.

"Mommy! Daddy!" Alexis couldn't contain her excitement over seeing her parents. It was if she were seven years old and it was Christmas morning. She reached for both of them, settling into the warmth of their hugs and kisses.

"How are you feeling?" her father asked.

"I feel fine," Alexis answered. She turned to give her mother a look. "I asked for Dr. Jackson and dropped both your names. He's been wonderful!"

Claudia smiled as she leaned to kiss her daughter's cheek. "We saw him in the hallway," she said.

"I want to go home, but he says I need to spend at least another night here. Maybe even two."

"You had us so worried," Claudia said. "If I hadn't known that your father and Marcel were working together to keep a close eye on you, it would have driven me crazy."

"About that," Alexis said, turning toward her father. "How could you not tell me where he was? Why would you keep that a secret from me?"

Josiah heaved a deep sigh, blowing warm breath past his full lips. "I did what I thought was in your best interest. Marcel was on a mission, and you didn't need to get caught up in the middle of it."

Alexis threw up her hands. "Yet here I am," she said. "Do you have any idea how many tears you could have saved me from crying?"

"A good cry is good for the soul," her father responded.

"And now I'll have to go to counseling to get over how angry I am at the two of you."

Josiah shook his head. "Well, send me the bill. And know that as a parent you'll do whatever you think is necessary to protect your babies." He leaned over to press a kiss against the top of his daughter's head.

Alexis was so overjoyed with love to be with them again

that she couldn't even consider staying mad. "Have you seen Marcel? They haven't let me see him or Sabine and I'm worried about the two of them. Is he okay?"

Her mother fanned a hand toward the room's door. "That boy is hiding out in the hallway, afraid you won't ever talk to him again."

Her father interjected. "He said he messed up, but that you put him in his place."

Alexis shrugged. "We had a moment. He was upset about the baby being missing."

"Moments add up," her mother said.

"I was told he carried me out of that swamp over his shoulders as he held on to the baby. He should have gotten Sabine to safety first. He could have come back for me."

"He did exactly what he needed to do," her father said. "You might not have made it if he'd left you."

Her mother sat down against the bedside. "Only you know what you and Marcel need to work on in your relationship. And only you know what you're willing to accept from a man. As I've told you and your sisters many times, a man will only do what you allow him to do. My only advice is know what you'll allow and what you won't allow."

"And mine," her father added, "is that I can shoot him first and you can ask questions later."

"You are an old fool!" Claudia laughed.

"And you still love me!"

"I'll always love you, Josiah. You gave me four beautiful daughters. I'll just never marry you again."

"You keep telling yourself that lie." Josiah kissed her cheek and the two laughed heartily.

Eyes wide, Alexis gave her parents a look. "Something we need to know?" she asked.

Her mother rolled her eyes skyward. "No. Worry about your relationship, not mine." The woman rose from her seat and headed to the door. She pulled it open and called out for Marcel.

"Get in here," she said.

Marcel entered the room sheepishly. His eyes glazed over as he met the look Alexis was giving him. Alexis was sitting upright in the bed, her back propped against a mountain of pillows. Her arms were folded across her chest and it was clear from her expression that she was feeling some kind of way. Her eyes widened when she saw Marcel. She extended her arms and gestured for him to come to her.

Wrapping her arms around him, she hugged him tightly. "I was so worried about you," she gushed. "No one could tell me anything and they wouldn't give me an update on Sabine."

"We're going to give you two a moment," Josiah said. "Come woman!" He extended his elbow and Claudia took his arm. The two made an exit, giving Alexis and Marcel a few minutes to themselves.

"Do you remember anything?" Marcel asked.

"Bits and pieces. I remember I heard Sabine crying and I found her in that box. I was trying to get her out when something hit me in the back of the head."

Marcel's head bobbed slightly as she continued.

"I think I passed out for a moment, but then I was focused on getting to the baby. That's when I saw Belinda. She was talking but it didn't make any sense." Alexis paused as she replayed the moment in her head. "There were gunshots!" Her eyes suddenly widened as her voice rose. "It was Felicia! She had the gun and was shooting at Belinda. I remember she ran past me when Belinda took off running."

Marcel said, "I thought it was her, but I wasn't certain. Neither one of them made it on a bus. We don't know where they are."

"What about the others?"

"Everyone's safe. The buses were stopped once they were clear of the storm. At the moment, the FBI has put everyone up in a hotel, pending questioning."

"Did they find Christiana?" Alexis asked, concern for Belinda's daughter furrowing her brow.

Marcel nodded. "Your father's people found her and her friends hitchhiking out on the highway. The older two are legally adults, so they couldn't be held. One decided to return to his family and your mother found shelter for the other. Legally, Christiana being underage, she was put into state custody. But again, your mom came to the rescue and found a really good home for her. An elderly friend who'd lost her granddaughter? She said you would know who she is. Miss Hattie Something-or-other."

Alexis smiled, thinking of the murder case that had introduced her sister Lenore to the police detective assigned to investigate the death of Hattie Jeffries's granddaughter. King Randolph turned out to be the love of her life. Mama Hattie was a wonderful choice for Christiana if she gave the old woman a chance. She made a mental note to pay them a visit the first chance she got. "What about the Prophet?" she questioned, turning back to the conversation.

"Agent Waters and his team raided the Midwest facility and the Dallas property. He personally slapped handcuffs on Amos."

"And the files in his office?"

"The roof caved in during the storm and most of the building is floating downriver. As soon as it's safe, we'll send people in to recover what might be left."

Alexis nodded. "There was a senior citizen on the first bus. Sister Hannah. She's holding on to a backpack for me. I told her someone would be coming for it."

"And what's in this backpack?"

Alexis shrugged, a smug smile pulling at her lips. "Evidence that isn't floating downstream."

Marcel shook his head, imagining the risk she'd taken to get evidence against the Prophet. He would ask later, he thought, not wanting what he didn't know to disrupt their moment.

The room was suddenly quiet as the couple stared at each other. Marcel was the first to speak. "I was scared to death," he said. "All I could think was that I was going to lose you before I had a chance to apologize for my bad behavior." His voice was barely a loud whisper.

Alexis smiled. "You saved me."

"And you found Sabine."

"Have you seen Sabine? Is the baby okay?"

Marcel shook his head. "They wouldn't let me see her. But Dr. Jackson says she's fine."

Alexis's face was flush with exasperation. "Something must be wrong! Why won't they let us see her?"

As if by magic, the room door swung open and a nurse entered, holding Sabine in her arms. It was as if Alexis calling the child's name had conjured her up. Alexis's smile widened. She extended her arms to reach for the baby. Sabine's gaze swept around the room and when it landed on Alexis's face she began to jump with joy.

With Sabine in her arms, Alexis seemed to glow, an aura of light like a halo around them. The baby giggled gleefully, pushing herself up on her chubby little legs as she danced in Alexis's lap. There was no denying the bond between them. In those few short days, Alexis had connected to his daughter in a way Marcel had only imagined. Their reunion brought immense comfort to him as he watched the two of them together. He wiped a tear from his eyes.

Alexis's parents had followed the nurse into the room. They stood beside him in awe. Marcel could see on their faces that even they were taken aback by the connection between the two.

"She's a beautiful baby, Marcel," Claudia said. She clasped her hands together and pressed her palms to her chest. "Just beautiful."

"Both my girls are," Marcel said, a canyon-wide grin spreading across his face. "They really are!"

Chapter 18

Holding his daughter in his arms was by far one of the greatest experiences Marcel had ever had. As he nuzzled his chin against the top of her tiny head, he realized just how much precious time had been stolen from them both. The Prophet had failed every child born during his reign. Marcel couldn't begin to fathom the emotional loss experienced by those mothers whose babies had been taken from them. He knew he needed to make things right, no matter how long it took. He also knew he needed to start with his own daughter and her biological mother, if she were alive. As a community, following the Prophet, the Saints of the Moral Order had failed every family there and no amount of apologizing would ever change that fact.

Sabine had fallen asleep in his arms and Marcel had no intentions of ever putting her down. He was obsessed with his baby girl, and he couldn't wait to share his thoughts with Alexis. She had been asleep for a few hours, exhaustion finally catching up with her. He could have used his own nap but there were still things he needed to do before he could rest well. Amos was successfully behind bars, but until they recovered her body, Belinda was somewhere out there, and he didn't trust that she would just go away to never be seen again.

* * *

When Marcel's cell phone rang, he jumped. It had been a few years since he last carried a cell phone on his person. He realized it was going to take him a minute to become used to it again. He answered the line quickly, not wanting the ringer to wake Alexis or Sabine.

"Hello?"

"Marcel! It's Matthew."

"Agent Waters! To what do I owe the honor?"

"I was checking to see if you're ready to get back out in the field?"

"Didn't you hear? I've handed in my resignation. I plan to go back to being a lowly detective on my local police force."

"Say it's not so! You do undercover so well, and I need help taking down a drug cartel."

"Sorry, guy! You're going to have to recruit someone else."

Waters laughed. "Well, I still need you to come in to be debriefed. We need your official statement."

"Will do," Marcel answered. "Just let me get my family home. Once I know they're safe, I will come in."

"How are Alexis and the baby?" Waters asked.

"Sleeping peacefully. They make me jealous."

"I'm sure you'll get over it."

"I don't know if I want to. I'm jealous, but I'm also happier than I have ever been."

"I'm happy to hear that, my friend."

"How are things going with you?"

"Thanks to all your hard work, closing out this case has been easier than I anticipated. And I owe Alexis my sincerest gratitude. Those documents she had delivered to us were the last nail in the Prophet's coffin. She gave us dates, times, names, numbers and bank info. We should have no problem getting a federal conviction against him. He'll do life without parole."

"He deserves the death penalty."

"He deserves a public stoning, but it's not for us to decide his punishment. He'll go before a jury of his peers. I plan to personally walk him into the courtroom on that day."

"Anything on Belinda?"

"Nothing. Either her body will wash ashore somewhere along the Gulf coast or show up on police radar in some other state. But I'll keep you posted."

"What about Felicia?"

"We don't have anything on her either."

Marcel sighed, unhappy with his answers. That both women had been involved in the altercation with Alexis and neither could be found made him nervous.

Agent Waters seemed to read his mind. "I don't want you to worry about anything. Take care of your family and yourself. I'll handle this."

"Just keep me in the loop," Marcel concluded.

Disconnecting the line, Marcel hugged his baby girl a little closer to his heart.

Chapter 19

"Da da da da da!" Sabine laughed, clapping her hands excitedly. Marcel was grinning from ear to ear, excited to be teaching his daughter how to say daddy. Alexis shook her head, laughing with the two of them. They were waiting for her discharge papers, the doctor finally agreeing to let her go home. With a little intervention from the FBI and her parents, Sabine had been released into her father's custody and the three of them were getting the first glimpse of what they would look like as a family.

Marcel hadn't left the hospital since their arrival. He'd slept in a chair in Alexis's room and had arranged for a crib for Sabine. Officially, the baby had been released the previous day, but he was determined that since they'd arrived together, they would leave together. Dr. Jackson had run interference with the hospital, maneuvering them around the few roadblocks that had arisen. Now, Alexis was past being ready to be back in her own home. Space that was familiar and comfortable.

"We'll need to set up a nursery for the baby," she said, lifting her gaze to meet Marcel's. "I think, for now, the sitting room off the bedroom would be ideal. And you'll need to move your stuff in."

"Slow down there, partner!" He gave her a bright smile. "You make it all sound so easy, but we do have some things to work through, Alexis."

She blew a heavy sign, rolling her eyes skyward. "And we will. But right now, I want us settled and happy. I've missed you and I want you in my life, Marcel. And I love Sabine as if she were my own. I can't imagine the three of us not being together. Can you?"

"Can you forgive me for everything I've done?"

"I forgave you the day you explained yourself and apologized. Forgetting is what I've struggled with and will probably continue to struggle with until I can replace those memories with other memories. With better memories. With moments we haven't had yet. It's going to be a process, but I'm willing to work on it if you are."

"I don't deserve you," Marcel said, his voice a raspy whisper.

Alexis gave him the slightest shrug. "You're stuck with me anyway," she said as she stepped into his arms and pressed her lips to his.

Kissing Alexis was his all-time favorite thing in the world to do, Marcel thought as her mouth danced sweetly against his. Her lips were the silkiest pillows, soft and plush, and delicate like the sweetest flowers. He found himself lost in her kisses, her touch mesmerizing. Alexis had always been intoxicating and, once addicted, he was forever wanting more of her. He couldn't imagine himself ever kissing any other woman the way he kissed Alexis. He wouldn't even want to give it any consideration, despite the temptation that was often tossed in his direction.

He eased her closer against his body, his tongue slipping past her lips and between the line of her teeth. He teased her, allowing himself to savor the intimacy, and then their daughter pulled them both from the moment.

Sabine screeched. Loudly. Making certain they were both aware that she wanted their attention. Reluctantly, he tugged himself from Alexis, the two of them laughing. Sabine had pulled herself up, holding tightly to the edge, as she bounced on her legs.

"Is this how it's going to be, little girl?" Marcel said as he lifted the baby from her crib. "You blocking your daddy?"

Sabine gurgled and cooed as if she were carrying on a conversation. The noises she uttered were nonsensical and cheery. She exuded happiness and the baby girl's joy was now their joy.

The room door suddenly swung open and a young nurse entered. She was as bright and bubbly as the baby as she pushed a wheelchair inside. "Is someone here ready for their discharge papers?" she said.

"So ready!" Alexis exclaimed. "But I really don't need a wheelchair. I can walk.

"It's hospital policy," the young woman said. She pushed the chair forward and gestured with her head for Alexis to take a seat. "What would we look like if something happened to you before we could get you safely out the door?"

Marcel laughed. "Like a lawsuit to me!"

"Exactly. Won't happen on my watch!"

Alexis took a seat and held out her arms for Sabine. Once she was seated comfortably, the baby cradled in her lap, the nurse pushed them out the door and toward the front of the building.

* * *

Alexis's father had sent a car to pick them up. The ride home was wrapped in excitement and laughter rang warmly from the back seat of the vehicle.

Sabine's innocent giggles and wide-eyed wonder at everything around them was a reminder that she'd spent most of her young life in a crib with little attention. There had been no outside adventures and just the feel of sunshine on her little face had seemed to tickle her spirit.

Watching her watch them, her bright eyes darting back and forth, was joy like neither had experienced before. Discovering the world through baby girl's eyes was already giving them new perspective about their own lives.

"I love you, Marcel," Alexis suddenly said aloud.

He smiled, leaning to kiss her forehead. "I love you, too."

"I want us to work, but…" She suddenly paused, taking a deep breath.

Marcel could feel the intensity of the word *but*. But what? he pondered. Why did there need to be a *but* hanging on to the edge of her comment, like something ready to crash and burn their dreams. He pressed his fingers gently to her face, lifting her chin until her eyes met his. "But…?" he said softly, prodding her to finish her sentence.

"But it's not about what we want anymore. Every decision we make has to be in Sabine's best interest."

He nodded and blew a soft sigh. "I agree. And I think having you as a mother is in her best interest. Seeing the two of us in a loving relationship will be in her best interest. We're on a new journey in our lives and choosing to travel this road together, no matter the hurdles, will teach our daughter much about life, and that will always be in her best interest."

A pregnant pause filled the air as Alexis reflected on his words. She released the breath she'd been holding past her lips. "If you walk out on me again, I will hurt you, Marcel," she said firmly. "And if you even think about walking out on Sabine, I will end you," she concluded.

Marcel smiled, bending to kiss her one more time. "I made that mistake once," he said. "I won't ever make it again."

Sabine suddenly let out a loud, piercing screech. Eyes wide, she laughed, the lilt like champagne bubbles and cotton candy.

"That's right," Alexis said, "you tell your daddy! We will not be putting up with any nonsense this go-round!"

From the cars parked in her driveway, Alexis knew the whole family was there to welcome them home. The front porch had been decorated with balloon arches in varying shades of pink. As the limo pulled in front of the home, her mother was the first to rush out onto the porch to welcome them. The matriarch gave them both a hug before pulling baby Sabine from Alexis's arms.

"Hello, precious!" Claudia cooed. "I am your Grand-mère! You and I will be great friends!"

Alexis shook her head, tossing Marcel a look. "I think I have just become chopped liver," she said with a laugh.

"Grandchildren will do that to you," Marcel said.

"Don't be jealous. It's very unbecoming," Claudia said as she led the way into the home. Alexis laughed as she and Marcel followed, hand in hand.

Inside, Sophie cheered excitedly at the sight of them. "It's the baby! I want to hold her!"

There was a mad rush as the Martin family welcomed them home with hugs and kisses. Sabine was passed from arm to arm, the little girl seeming to love all the attention. She finally landed in Josiah's arms, and the whole room fell silent, watching as the child and the patriarch eyed each other.

Alexis rested her back against Marcel's chest as he pulled her close, his arms wrapping around her torso. The moment felt surreal, the abundance of love exploding with a vengeance around them.

Josiah was still staring at Sabine when he finally spoke, the baby pulling at his hair. "Are we to understand that you two have reconciled?" Josiah questioned.

Alexis answered. "Yes, sir."

"And I'm to understand, Mr. Broussard, that you have made amends for the hurt you caused my daughter and that it will not happen again?"

"I have, Mr. Martin, as I will continue to do so until the day I die. I assure you that I am here for the duration. I love Alexis and I plan to spend the rest of my life making certain that she knows just how much."

Josiah pressed a kiss to Sabine's cheek. She wrapped her tiny little arms around his neck and hugged him tightly.

Alexis shook her head as she tossed Marcel a look. "That's it. We are both dirt from this point forward. Her grand-mère and grand-père have been wrapped around those little fingers."

Marcel laughed. "I think I feel some kind of way about that."

"You'll get over it!" Claudia chuckled. "It's the way of the world."

Laughter rang abundantly through the living space. Alexis's sisters had adorned the entire room for a baby shower and welcoming party for their newest family member. Sabine would never again not know the love of family or protection from those who loved her wholeheartedly.

There was an abundance of food as their mother's private chef dished up bowls of gumbo and plates of Maque choux, crawfish étouffée, shrimp creole with salad, beans, bread pudding and chocolate-pecan pie. Her father had brought champagne and bottles bubbled over.

Standing off to the side, Marcel found himself overwhelmed. He didn't know how much he had missed the family until that moment. Watching them lavish so much attention on Sabine reminded him of all the times he had been welcomed into the Martin family's inner circle. How experiencing the abundance of love they shared always felt like home. He had wanted his sister to know what that felt like, and it saddened him that her life had ended so tragically.

Josiah and another man stepping into his space interrupted the moment. Marcel looked up, the slightest smile on his face.

"Marcel," Josiah said, "allow me to officially introduce you both. This is King Randolph. King, this is Marcel Broussard."

King extended his hand. His complexion was Hershey's-chocolate dark, and he wore a full beard and mustache. "It's a pleasure to meet you. I'm Lenore's fiancé."

"The pleasure is mine." A wave of confusion crossed

Marcel's face. "Are you the same King Randolph I'm interviewing with tomorrow?"

King smiled. "That would be me. *Captain* King Randolph of the New Orleans Police Department. I'm glad we're able to meet under more casual circumstances. Especially considering who our women are."

Josiah laughed. "I'll leave you two to bemoan your lot in life together," he said as he walked away.

King chuckled. "Lenore tells me you were with the police department before you went undercover for the Feds."

"I'd been a detective for a few years. I'm looking forward to the opportunity to come back."

"You're not interested in staying with the FBI?"

Marcel shook his head. "This case was intense. I realize how easy it is to lose yourself when you go underground for as long as I did. I don't want to experience that ever again. Especially now that we have the baby and Alexis is willing to give me a second chance."

"I can understand that. I would sacrifice everything for Lenore and her people. Family is everything!"

"Exactly," Marcel agreed. "I love police work and I'm good at it. I'm hoping that if I can get back on the force and come home to my girls every night that it will be a win-win for all of us."

"Well, we can definitely use good men in the department. We've gone through a significant shakeup recently trying to weed out all the corruption."

"I read about what happened with the previous Captain, Juan Romero. He'd been great to work for during my tenure there. I never would have suspected him of any wrongdoing."

"It took everyone by surprise. I had actually just started with the department, working my first case when it all went south."

Marcel nodded. "Have you and Lenore set a date yet?"

King laughed. "I imagine if you know anything about the Martin sisters, that we do things on their time, not ours. Lenore likes being engaged, but she's not overly excited about taking it to the next step."

Marcel laughed with him. "They get that from their mother," he said.

"I've learned the hard way not to cross Claudia," King said. "They all get vicious! I thought one Martin woman gunning for you was bad enough, but when they all turn on you—" he tossed up his hands "—heaven help you!"

The two men laughed heartily. They punched fists. "I think we're going to be great friends," Marcel said.

"Me, too. At least now I'll have a brother who understands my pain!"

Celeste was holding her hands over Alexis's eyes as she and her sisters guided her down the hallway toward the bedrooms. Alexis couldn't begin to imagine what they wanted her to see that needed to be a surprise. They came to an abrupt pause in front of what she thought was her home office. She was trying to remember the condition she'd left the space in, thinking that they had done some house cleaning for her.

One of them pushed her as another pulled, until they had her positioned where they wanted her to stand. Then Celeste uncovered her eyes.

Alexis blinked once, then twice, and suddenly she

gasped, her hands gripping the sides of her face in complete surprise. "Oh, my!" she gushed as she took a step forward. She wasn't in her office, but instead stood in the space that had once been her guest bedroom. Her mother and sisters had transformed the bedroom into a nursery.

Just days earlier it had been a mélange of creams and caramels with a hint of green florals. Now it was the palest shade of lavender with white furniture, white drapes and hints of plum accents. There were stuffed animals and learning toys in a jeweled toy box, and an assortment of baby supplies and diapers tucked neatly on the shelves. The closet was filled with an assortment of baby clothes and shoes in varying sizes; it looked like her family had purchased an entire baby store to adorn the child in.

Her mother and Sabine sat in an oversized chair, the baby holding a bottle of warm milk between her tiny hands. Tears suddenly slipped past Alexis's lashes as Lenore wrapped her in a warm hug. "Congratulations," she whispered into Alexis's ear. "We hope you like it!"

"I picked the colors!" Sophie said.

"We all pitched in," Celeste said. "We knew there was a high probability Sabine and Marcel would be coming home with you and you would need to have things in place to make the transition smoother. We thought we could make things easier after everything you went through."

"I love you guys so much!" Alexis said, still on the verge of an ugly cry. She struggled not to sob.

She moved to where her mother was sitting, sliding into the oversized seat beside her. "I love this chair!" she cooed as Claudia eased the baby into her arms.

"I do, too. It will be a nice space for you and Marcel to

just sit and cuddle your daughter; maybe read her a book or tell her a story."

Alexis leaned her head against her mother's shoulder. "My daughter," she said softly. "I had never really thought what that might be like."

"It's a beautiful thing," her mother responded.

"Any news of her egg donor?" Sophie questioned. "I don't want you to get too attached only for some woman to come in and burst your bubble."

"Sophie! Really?" Lenore snapped.

Celeste shook her head. "There's a time and a place, little sister. A time and a place, and you always seem to get it wrong."

Sophie shrugged her narrow shoulders. "There's no point in beating around the bush. It's not like she hasn't considered it. Right, Alexis?"

Alexis rolled her eyes skyward. She huffed a heavy gust of warm breath past her lips, the sigh feeling as if a weight was being lifted off her shoulders. "The FBI was able to confirm who Sabine's biological mother was and that she indeed died during childbirth. Her name was Raquel and she'd only been nineteen. She'd been in the foster care system most of her life. We don't know how she found her way to the Moral Order."

She rested her gaze on the baby before continuing. "They did an autopsy on the body. They found that she suffered from preeclampsia. The physician at the compound made the decision to deliver Sabine early via C-section. Her mother bled out after delivery because they didn't have the resources to stabilize and save her."

"That is so sad," Sophie said, her face twisting as if she might cry, too.

"I will be the only mother Sabine will know," Alexis said. "And I really don't want to mess it up."

Her mother hugged her. "You will do just fine," Claudia said. "In fact, I look forward to seeing you and Lenore raise your babies together."

The sisters all turned toward Lenore, heads snapping in unison.

Lenore's eyes widened, shock wrinkling her brow. She stammered and Claudia laughed.

"You don't need to say anything. I recognize the signs. You've been glowing for weeks now, and I'd guess your weight is up five, maybe ten, pounds?"

Sophie squealed. "Are you pregnant, Lenore?"

"Hush," Lenore said. She crossed the carpeted floor, moving swiftly to close the room door. "I haven't told King yet. In fact, I haven't told anyone! Damn! I just found out myself!"

Claudia laughed. "You really didn't need to tell anyone. All they need to do is look at you."

"That's so weird," Sophie said. "I looked at her and I didn't see it."

Celeste nodded. "It's like some strange voodoo stuff."

Alexis grinned from ear to ear. "Congratulations! I can't wait for Sabine to have a cousin."

"Or maybe a sibling?" Claudia interjected, tossing Alexis a quick glance.

Alexis's eyes widened. "Marcel and I aren't there yet," she said, blushing ever so slightly. "But soon…maybe… I hope…"

Sophie tossed up her hands. "I can't believe you!"

"What?" Celeste asked.

"You haven't done him yet! Have you?"

Alexis rolled her eyes again. "Shut up, Sophie!"

"See, she still hasn't done him. I would have done him already."

"That's because you're easy," Celeste said.

"Am not!"

"Yes, you are," the sisters all chimed in unison.

Claudia shook her head, the women rolling with laughter. For almost an hour, the Martin women caught up with all that had happened since they were last together. Alexis told them about the commune in the swamps and the women she'd befriended. They tossed around ideas on how they might help them with their lives suddenly upended. She talked about Marcel and the dreams and aspirations the two had for their future. They commiserated over their struggles and their successes, and bonded like they always did when they were together.

"Come," Claudia said as she gestured for them to form a circle while holding hands. "I am very proud of you girls," she said. "You will each be wonderful role models for Sabine and for the new baby."

"And I'm proud of you, Alexis," Lenore said. "You dove headfirst into the unknown, showing no fear. You are going to make an excellent mother."

Alexis smiled. "We both will. We've had a great role model to emulate."

"I know that's right," Sophie chimed. "Mommy isn't going to let either of you get it wrong." She squeezed her mother's hand.

"To the sisterhood of Sorority Row," Celeste said, raising her half-empty glass of red wine.

"The sisterhood!" they all chimed.

Tossing her bottle aside, Sabine gurgled, as if adding in her own toast. "Da da da da da da da!"

Chapter 20

•

Their home was finally quiet, everyone gone about their business. Claudia had made sure the food was put away, their kitchen was clean, and nothing remained that might have hinted there had been a party. Sabine had fallen asleep in Alexis's arms, each of her family members pausing to kiss the little girl's chubby cheeks and forehead before saying their goodbyes.

Josiah had taken the baby from his daughter's arms, rocking her gently before settling her down in her new crib. He didn't need to say what Alexis and Marcel already knew. She was now a Martin and would forever have his protection, and his love. He wrapped his arms around Alexis and hugged her tightly before shaking Marcel's hand and making his exit. Her parents had been the last to leave, the couple leaving arm in arm and sharing a ride to her home, and his.

Alexis was standing over the crib when Marcel entered the room. Staring down at Sabine, both marveled how peaceful she looked, not a care in the world. The stood side by side for a good few minutes, listening to her breathe.

"Your mother said to call her in the morning when you

get up," Marcel finally whispered. "I'm having lunch with your father after my interview with the police department."

"I think my parents might be getting back together," Alexis said. "They really seem to be happy with each other."

"Would you be disappointed if that didn't happen?" Marcel asked.

Alexis paused, considering the question. "No, not really. I'd be happy for them if they did, but they've always been the best of friends and I don't think that'll ever change. Them being friends is more important to me than them being a couple."

"That's one of the things that I've always respected when it came to your parents. They've always been able to put their personal feelings aside for the greater good of the entire family. They love each other, but clearly love their family unit more. Their friendship has been the stronger bond that continues to hold us all together. They've willingly put their romantic relationship aside when it threatens the peace they've found with each other."

Alexis sighed softly. "I pray that Sabine grows up to know that kind of love. And that we, too, will be an example for her to follow."

Marcel slid his arm around her shoulder and kissed her cheek. "I need a shower," he said. "And you need to get some rest. You have to be exhausted by now."

"Actually, I feel really good."

"Still, it's been a long day."

"You don't have to tell me twice. We both need to get some rest in case baby girl doesn't sleep through the night. It might be a week or two before the three of us are on a schedule that works well."

Marcel chuckled. "Ah, the joys of parenthood!"

"Go grab your shower. I want to double-check all the locks and maybe grab one last cookie before I turn in!" She smiled.

"There were cookies left?" Marcel's eyes were wide at the thought of the decadent chocolate treats they'd enjoyed.

"I hid them. If you're good, I might share one with you."

Marcel laughed. He pressed his lips to hers and gave her a gentle kiss. He slid his cheek against her cheek then left the room. Alexis stood beside the crib for a few more minutes, amazed at how her entire life had changed so quickly. She was Sabine's mother now and, short of actually being Marcel's legal wife, she was all his, heart and soul. Despite all the "feel goods," Alexis couldn't help but wonder how long it would last before something else blew up in their faces. She gently brushed the curls from Sabine's face with her fingers, the baby snoring lightly. Then she headed out of the room, intent on eating at least three, maybe even four, more cookies.

Alexis had shared her cookies with Marcel before heading into the bathroom to take her own shower. He sat on the edge of the bed looking uncomfortable, his gaze questioning.

"What's wrong?" she asked.

He took a deep breath before speaking. "I didn't want to just assume you wanted me here in the bed with you. If you'd prefer, I can sleep in Sabine's room on that chair or in the living room on the sofa."

"Sleep where you'd be most comfortable," Alexis answered. "But if I didn't want you here, I would tell you."

He nodded, not sure why he was suddenly feeling nervous.

"I won't be long," Alexis said. "And if you would please just make sure the baby monitor is turned on. My sisters bought a fancy digital thingy with a camera. I couldn't get a picture, so I know I did something wrong."

"I'll definitely check it," Marcel said as he took the last bite of the one cookie she'd given him. "Any more of these in the kitchen?" he asked.

She laughed. "In the basket behind the coffee filters."

Marcel jumped from the bed like a six-year-old. His jubilance made her laugh harder as she headed into the bathroom and closed the door.

In the kitchen, he grabbed another two cookies, taking a bite from one as he triple-checked the door locks. Outside, it had begun to rain, the late-night shower unexpected. He opened the front door to look out, noting the patter of raindrops against the stone-tiled walkway. The wind had also picked up and the rocking chairs that decorated the front porch were gliding back and forth as if someone were sitting in them.

A flash of lightning suddenly lit up the nighttime sky. Surprised, Marcel caught a glimpse of a shadow that gave him pause. It looked as if someone was standing across the street, watching the house. He took a quick step out onto the porch, staring intently across the street. Squinting through the darkness, he waited. A second flash of light illuminated the large oak tree that sat in their neighbor's yard. He glanced left and then right, his gaze slowly skating over the landscape until nothing else gave him concern. Breathing a sigh of relief, Marcel stole one final look before stepping back inside. Closing and securing the door, he stared out the door's sidelights for a few more minutes just to be certain no one was there.

When Alexis stepped out of the bathroom, Marcel was lying on his side of the bed, sleep pulling him into a sweet dream. The sight of him made her smile. She hadn't believed he would ever grace her life again and yet here he was, wanting to see her comfortable and happy. She had debated whether to relegate him to the living room sofa, but knew if they were to truly reconcile, pushing him away was not going to make that easy. Besides, she wanted him nearby. Needed him close. She looked forward to falling asleep in his arms and waking up with him beside her.

After cutting off the lights, she eased into the bed, sliding beneath the cool sheets. Marcel had fixed the monitor, and the camera was pointing at the crib, giving her a perfect view of Sabine. The little girl was sound asleep, stirring just slightly against the mattress. The sight of her filled Alexis with joy she hadn't thought possible. Her entire being vibrated with happiness.

She lay watching the monitor for a good long while then she turned, pressing her body against Marcel's back. She wrapped her arms around his waist and eased herself as close to him as she could manage. She felt his breathing shift as he slid his hands atop hers, caressing the length of her fingers.

Marcel had gone to bed wearing navy-blue briefs and nothing else. His bare chest was chiseled, his muscles hardened. Alexis snaked her hands over his nipples, tracing her fingertips over the small chocolate buds until they were both rock-candy hard. A chill raced the length of her spine and she quivered with pleasure.

Easing her hand downward, she paused when she reached the waistband of his briefs. The nearness of her had lengthened every muscle below his waist and the protrusion of flesh pressed eagerly against the cotton fabric that afforded him a semblance of privacy. She trailed her fingertips up and down the length of his male member until his breathing labored and his skin heated with perspiration. She traced little circles up and down and when the sensations sweeping between his legs seemingly became too much, he turned, flipping her above him.

Alexis pressed the side of her face into his chest as he kissed the top of her head, nuzzling his face into her curls. His hands trailed up and down her back, kneading and caressing her. He lowered his palms until he could cup her buttocks, one in each hand, and he squeezed the round of tissue easily. Her eyes lifted to meet his and there was nothing else to do but kiss him.

Marcel kissed her back, her mouth soft and luscious. Soon their tongues were dueling and she suckled his ever so gently. It took an easy turn and a quick pull and Marcel had tugged off her clothes, tossing the nightgown she was wearing to the floor. He lay above her and she was naked, the curve of her breasts brushing easily against his chest as his mouth clung easily to hers.

Lengthy caresses and eager touches complimented the wealth of desire that wrapped around them like a winter blanket. Marcel kissed the line of her profile, licked that sweet spot beneath her chin and suckled each of her breasts, his tongue flicking rhythmically from one nipple to the other.

How he had missed the taste of her! Missed touching her! Missed the little purr she muttered when the pleasure became intense. His own desire was raging as he watched her squirm, gasping for air as he licked and kissed and suckled his way down past her belly button to the crevice between her legs.

"Let me," she suddenly whispered, pushing him from her and onto his back.

Marcel smiled as she straddled his middle, hovering above the length of his cock. He held himself as she slowly lowered her pelvis against him. She was drenched and when the tip of his member kissed the velvet lining of her sweet spot, devouring every inch of him, it took everything for him not to explode with pleasure.

Alexis did a slow grind against him, lifting herself up and down until he was buried to the hilt inside her. She wiggled and lifted and lowered herself in a slow rotation. Round and round she went, slowly and then building up speed and intensity. Marcel cried out as she rode him like he was a wild stallion needing to be tamed. Then she shifted into overdrive and he felt her exploding against his flesh, her orgasm sending him over the edge as they both fell into a state of sheer bliss.

They came together, blinded by the intensity of each other's touch. Alexis screamed, tears raining past her lashes and over her cheeks. Marcel called her name over and over again as if in prayer and then he kissed her one more time, his hands clutching her face, his fingers tangled sweetly in the length of her hair.

* * *

Their sensual connection had never been problematic. That first touch, first kiss, first intimate act, had reawakened what both had missed even more than either had realized. Marcel made love to her twice more, interrupted once by Sabine whimpering for attention. Sleep had only served to reinvigorate them both as they became reacquainted, remembering each other's proclivities. Being intimate with one another made riding a bicycle seem like the most difficult thing in the world to do. There was an ease between them that felt natural and necessary. A longing that only the other could fulfill.

They sat cross-legged on the living room floor. Outside, the rain had finally stopped and the sun was just beginning to rise. Alexis had heated up the leftovers and they held bowls of gumbo in their laps. Laughter danced like a sweet breeze between them.

"I forgot how well you do that thing with your tongue," Alexis said.

Marcel laughed. "I have no idea what you're talking about."

"And that's okay," she said, her smile sly. "As long as you remember when it's requested."

"I'll do whatever you want me to do, especially if you bite your lip the way you do when you orgasm."

"I don't bite my lip!"

"Yes, you do, and it makes me hot!" He bit his own bottom lip teasingly. "So hot!"

She laughed with him. Taking a spoonful of gumbo, she savored the taste of okra, shrimp, chicken and andouille sausage. Gumbo for breakfast was pure delight. Gumbo for breakfast after good morning sex was sheer perfection, she thought.

Marcel echoed her thoughts. "This is so good!" he muttered as he swallowed his own spoonful of stew. "I could start every day like this."

Alexis laughed again. "You really need to get a few hours of sleep before your interview. I'd hate to see you miss out on your dream job because you're exhausted."

"I'll have you know I feel like a new man. In fact..." He paused, leaning in to kiss her lips. His voice dropped an octave, the cadence low and seductive. "I could do that thing with my tongue, if you wanted."

A slow smiled pulled across Alexis's face. "So, now you remember?"

"Maybe, but if not, I'm always open to you showing me what I need to do."

Her laugh was buoyant, filling the air with an electrical energy that lit up the room. "Oh, I can show you," Alexis giggled. "I can definitely show you!"

Chapter 21

The FBI's main field office on Leon C. Simon Boulevard was the epitome of institutional with its concrete exterior, fenced perimeter and prisonlike esthetic. Alexis and Marcel had both been asked to come in for debriefing, the FBI wanting to get their official statements on the record. Neither had been happy about leaving Sabine, nor were they overly excited about entrusting her to the care of the nanny Alexis's parents had hired. Instead, her new Grandpapa Josiah welcomed her at his front door, kissing her little cheeks as he'd waved Alexis and Marcel goodbye. Her father's home was a fortress, so Alexis knew the little girl was in safe hands and that, once Claudia learned the baby was there, she wouldn't be too far behind. They would miss Sabine but there wouldn't be any reason for them to worry about her.

The agent who recorded her statement was a buxom woman with waist-length hair the color of black licorice. She had delicate facial features and the deep vocal tone of a contralto singer. She wasn't one for small talk and her personality was just shy of icy-cold. Her questions were straightforward—What was her connection to the Prophet and the Moral Order? How were she and Marcel acquainted?

What had she seen? Who had she spoken to? How had she come into possession of the documents she'd turned over to them? She'd prefaced the interrogation with a polite, "Please start at the beginning and don't leave out any details."

Alexis's answers were just as straightforward. She didn't begin to think that there was something they didn't already know. Or that they weren't just testing her responses to see if what she said jibed with what Marcel had told them. The process was tedious, not always necessary, but being thorough now prevented crap from being exposed later that could threaten the court convictions.

An hour or so later, the agent thanked her for her service and escorted her back to the reception area to wait for Marcel. Alexis used the time to call her father and check in on Sabine.

"Daddy, hey! It's me. How is everything going?"

"I'm trying to get your mother to leave so that Bean and I can enjoy our time together!"

Alexis could hear her mother in the background laughing. "Bean? You gave our baby a nickname?"

"Was there something you needed, Alexis? Is everything going okay, sweetheart?"

She chuckled. "Everything's fine. I just wanted to check with you to see if all was well on your end."

"Bean is perfectly fine, and I am okay. Besides your mother being a pain in my posterior, all is well."

"Then I'll let you and *Bean* get back to it. I'm not sure how much longer Marcel and I will be, but you call me if anything comes up."

"Love you, baby girl!"

"I love you, too, Daddy!"

* * *

Marcel sat at a table with Agent Waters, two of their superior officers and a legal team from the federal prosecutor's office. He'd given his deposition, his statement video-recorded. He was feeling slightly off kilter as they prodded him for additional information, most especially when the focus turned to Sabine and Alexis.

"You put a civilian in harm's way when you enlisted Ms. Martin's assistance. How can you justify your actions, Agent Broussard?"

The man asking was young. Younger than Marcel, with far less field experience.

Marcel took a deep breath and held it before responding. "Ms. Martin had personal knowledge of the Saints of the Moral Order and how they operated. Knowledge that was useful to me, and to the Bureau. Every precaution was taken to ensure her safety. As well, Ms. Martin is a highly trained private investigator. She's a skilled marksman and quite capable of holding her own."

"And how do you explain the risk she took gaining access to the documents she found?"

"It's not for me to explain. You'll need to ask Ms. Martin that question."

Carl Bergman, the Special Agent in Charge, cleared his throat, coughing slightly. He lifted his eyes to stare at Marcel. "It's our understanding that you impregnated one of the women being held hostage?"

"You understand incorrectly. But on the advice of my legal counsel, I'd prefer not to answer any questions about that situation without my lawyer present."

"Did you even consider that you could potentially be charged with sexual assault?" Bergman persisted.

"No," Marcel said emphatically. "Because I never physically assaulted anyone, most especially not a woman. Nor did I have any knowledge of the pregnancy, or my child's birth."

"But you do acknowledge your actions resulted in a pregnancy?"

"I acknowledge that the actions of others resulted in my daughter being conceived. And, if you'd like to discuss it in further detail, my attorney will need to be present."

Waters shifted forward in his seat. "Agent Broussard has been very forthcoming about all his decisions since taking this assignment. I've detailed every one of his actions in my reports. I can personally attest to his character and will put my own badge on the line to support him. He did everything by the book and acted judicially from start to finish."

There was a momentary pause as everyone in the room stopped to consider his partner's comments. The federal prosecutor, a woman who reminded him of the British actress Helen Mirren, suddenly rose from the table. She was long, lean, aged like fine wine, with green eyes, silvery-white hair, and a bright smile.

"I think we're good," she said as the rest of her legal team stood with her. "Nice work, gentlemen. With everything you've given us, Amos Lee and his associates will be incarcerated for the remainder of their lives. You were able to neutralize a major trafficking ring and that was no easy feat. And please don't think we don't know all the sacrifices you had to make, Agent Broussard, to do what you did. Our government thanks you for your service. Should we have any questions as we get closer to the trial date, we'll contact you."

Bergman jumped to his feet, moving to shake her hand as she extended the appendage toward him. "Thank you," he said.

She shook hands with Waters and then Marcel. "Good luck, Agent Broussard," she said. "You should be very proud of yourself."

With a nod of his head, Marcel thanked her. He appreciated her comment but wasn't sure he agreed with her assessment. He knew he'd done some good. But he would always question if he could have done more.

Waters walked him out of the conference room. The two men headed toward the bank of elevators at the end of the hallway, not speaking until they were inside the conveyor.

"Do I need to be worried?" Marcel questioned, tossing a quick glance in the other man's direction.

"No. They know the truth. That line of questioning was purely precautionary. The Bureau wants to avoid the look of any impropriety at all costs."

"They also want to throw any potential liability under a metaphoric bus if it's deemed necessary."

"We won't let that happen," Waters said. "You're a good agent and you did a damn good job. We hope you'll reconsider working for us and come back to the fold."

Marcel shook his head. "Not an ice cube's chance in hell will that happen any time soon," he said

"Just break my heart again and again," Waters said.

The two men shared a good laugh, putting the interrogation out of their minds.

Alexis was sitting comfortably when they walked into the lobby to join her. Marcel pressed a damp kiss to her lips.

"How'd it go?" Alexis asked.

Marcel shrugged. "You never know," he said.

She smiled. "Well, this should cheer you up. My father nicknamed the baby 'Bean.'"

"Bean?"

Alexis nodded. "Like in jelly…"

Marcel chuckled. "I guess Bean it is," he said, joy returning the light to his eyes.

Alexis laughed with him.

"It's good to see you both together," Agent Waters said.

"We'd love for you to come have dinner with us soon," Alexis said. "We'd love for our daughter to meet her godfather."

Waters's eyes widened. "Godfather?"

Marcel grinned. "You've been the closest thing to a best friend I've had since this all started. I've trusted you with my life and with my family. I can't imagine asking anyone else to be the godfather to our baby girl or trusting they'll be there to support her if anything happens to either of us."

The two men slapped palms and leaned in for a one-armed hug. Agent Waters nodded. "I'd be honored."

Marcel stole a quick glance down to his wristwatch. "I have an interview in thirty minutes, so we need to get moving."

"Good luck," Waters said. "But if that doesn't work out, there's always a job for you here."

Marcel guffawed. "Don't jinx me!"

Alexis shook her head. "Thank you for everything," she said as she and Marcel headed for the door. With one last glance over her shoulder, she gave Waters a bright smile and lifted her hand to wave goodbye.

After a very late lunch, the two grabbing shrimp po'boys from Johnny's Po-Boys on St. Louis Street, they took a slow stroll along the French Quarter River Walk. Taking time to decompress calmed them both as they chatted non-stop. Alexis loved a good debate, and when she and Marcel didn't see eye to eye on things, she was always ready to argue her point.

The Mississippi River was murky, looking like muddy soup, and the current was strong, flowing out to the Gulf of Mexico.

The River Walk was dotted with tourists, families and couples snapping photos and enjoying the crisp afternoon air. Alexis held out her own cell phone in front of them, the two tilting toward one another as she snapped selfies. Marcel laughed as he wrapped his arms around her shoulders and hugged her close.

"You will never get me to eat a banana sandwich with peanut butter," Marcel proclaimed.

"But you'll eat one with mayonnaise."

"Exactly! You want to complement the flavor of the banana, not mask it with the taste of peanut butter."

Alexis laughed. "And I imagine you only want to eat it on whole-wheat bread, too?"

"No. It's equally as good on white bread or raisin bread."

"Mayo on raisin bread?" Alexis winced.

"With banana. Yes!"

Her giggles were contagious as Marcel laughed with her. He pulled her close and kissed her, allowing his lips to linger sweetly against hers. "You make me so happy," he whispered softly, his breath warm against her cheek.

Alexis smiled, a wide grin pulling her lips upward. "Promise you won't ever let me go?" she said.

"I promise," Marcel said, his expression suddenly serious. "I am committed to loving and protecting you for as long as you will have me. And I would like to make it official."

Marcel suddenly dropped to one knee, the beginning of the evening's sunset decorating the backdrop. He pulled a small velvet box from his pants' pocket.

Alexis's eyes widened and she slapped her hand across her mouth. She gasped. "Marcel!"

"I would very much like to make our *marriage* official. Will you do me the honor of being my wife, Alexis Martin? Will you marry me?"

Tears suddenly misted Alexis's eyes. She nodded eagerly. "Yes! Yes! Yes!" she chimed, her excitement corporeal. Her hand trembled ever so slightly as Marcel slipped the most perfect engagement ring onto her finger. The round, two-carat diamond in a six-prong setting floated above a brilliant pavéd band. It was exquisite.

"It's absolutely stunning," Alexis gushed. As he rose back onto his feet, she pressed herself against him and kissed his mouth again.

Around them, a crowd had gathered to watch, and a round of cheers rang through the air.

"I want to adopt Sabine," Alexis said as they settled the little girl down in her crib. It had been on her mind since they'd left her father's house, the family celebrating the news of their engagement with champagne and cheesecake.

Sabine had been excited to see them return, practically throwing herself into Alexis's arms. She'd clung to them both, refusing to let go.

"I want to be legally responsible for her," she continued. "She's our baby. And I love her like she's mine."

Marcel brushed his hand against his daughter's rosy cheek. She slumbered sweetly, her breathing slow and easy. Her eyes fluttered behind her lids and he imagined that she might be dreaming. Sweet dreams, he thought as she smiled ever so slightly in her sleep.

"I want that, too," he said. "We can start the process right away, if it's really what you want to do."

"It is. As long as it's what you want, too!"

"Alexis, I can't imagine anyone else raising my children. I've always known you'd be an incredible mother. Obviously, the circumstances of Sabine's birth weren't what either of us would have chosen, but I know that she will always know a mother's love as long as she has you in her life. Whether you adopt her legally or not, you're her mother."

"Well, I definitely want us to do it legally."

Marcel nodded. "I do, too. Now, what about our getting married? If I remember correctly, you wanted a fairy-tale wedding with all the bells and whistles. Which means a long engagement for us to do all that planning. I just don't want us to wait too long."

Alexis smiled. "I don't want us to wait at all. I don't need fairy-tale. I just need you. I think a civil ceremony down at the courthouse will be just fine, and the sooner, the better."

"It's whatever your heart desires!"

"Then tomorrow it is!"

Marcel laughed. "Then tomorrow it is!"

Alexis was startled out of a deep sleep, the sound of glass breaking echoing from the other side of the house. She sat upright, casting a look toward Marcel. He was lost in the throes of a dream, completely oblivious to anything that might have been happening. She wasn't overly concerned, knowing that they had keyed in the code for the alarm, and both had checked the locks before retiring for the night. But just to make sure she had only been dreaming, she knew she needed to check.

Rising, she used her thumb to unlock the gun safe on the nightstand. She retrieved her revolver, checked that it was loaded, and then walked from the bedroom to the nursery to make certain Sabine was still sleeping soundly. Once she laid eyes on the baby, she methodically checked every room in the home. When she was certain they were safe, and no one had breached their home, she lowered her weapon and moved back toward the bedroom. Checking the front door one last time, she peered out the sidelights to the outside. It was dark, not even the streetlights affording her an easy view. But, for a split second, she thought she might have seen a shadow standing beside her car. She stared, squinting slightly, and when nothing moved, she chalked it up to an overly active imagination.

Heading back to bed, she resecured her weapon then slid beneath the covers. Marcel hadn't moved, barely flinching a muscle. His body had finally relaxed, allowing him to finally rest well. She didn't want to wake him, knowing that it had been ages since he'd last been able to sleep without worry.

Wide awake, Alexis reached for her cell phone sitting on the nightstand. She typed in the four-digit code to unlock the device. Scrolling, she saw that she had missed a text message from Lenore congratulating her on their engagement. She'd also missed a call from a number she didn't recognize, but since they hadn't left a message, she chalked it up to being a wrong number.

She thought about playing a game of Candy Crush, but instead she began to scroll through the photographs she'd taken of them earlier. They actually looked happy, Alexis thought as she took a moment to admire one of the images where she and Marcel were staring at each other.

She paused to study another image and then saw something that caught her attention. Zeroing in on a single area in the background, she used her two fingers to enlarge the photo. As she and Marcel had posed happily, smiling widely into the camera, there was someone standing behind them. Someone watching. As the image refocused, Alexis gasped. Belinda Lee was standing there in the distance and nothing about the Moral Mother screamed that she was happy to see them. Nothing at all.

Chapter 22

Marcel paced the hardwood floor, stomping from one side of the room to the other. He knew Alexis hadn't wanted to tell him about seeing Belinda in her photos but since she had, his anxiety level was at an all-time high. He also had attitude about her waiting a whole forty-eight hours before sharing the news.

"Stop!" Alexis said. She slid a pan of blueberry muffins from the oven, resting it on the stovetop. "You're going to drive us both crazy if you keep it up."

"Are you for real right now, Alexis? Don't you think I have good reason to worry?"

"No. I don't. We have more safety protocols in place than we will ever need. My father has his team watching the house, the office and any other place we feel inclined to show up. Belinda isn't going to get near us or Sabine. Not in this lifetime or in any other."

Marcel cursed. His brow furrowed with frustration. "It could only take one person, making one mistake, for all that security to go south and then you or the baby or both of you are put in harm's way. So don't expect me to be casual about it all. Not right now."

Alexis rounded the corner of the kitchen island. She

slipped the oven mitts off her hands and rested them against the quartzite countertop. She met Marcel toe to toe, easing her hands against his waist as she looked up at him. She didn't like what she saw in his eyes, a mingling of fear and anxiety holding hands with rage and fury. She understood what he was feeling, but she had nothing more she could say or do to ease his unrest. She was equally as worried but knew that she needed to hold it together for him, for herself, and for Sabine. He needed to work through his own emotions. She took a large inhale of air, holding it deep in her lungs before she spoke.

"I should have told you the same night I saw her in the photo. I didn't because you were finally resting and I refused to disturb that and upset the balance of things. We desperately needed balance. So, I apologize for that. I wasn't trying to exclude you or hurt you."

She took another breath, blowing it softly past her lips. "Now, we have tons of help. We aren't doing this alone. But, more importantly, we have each other. And together we will get through whatever gets thrown at us. I just need you to relax and believe in us as much as I do."

Marcel pulled her close, easing his arms around her shoulders. He pressed a kiss to the top of her head. "I do believe in us. And I know you did what you thought was best. But I can't help feeling like we're sitting ducks waiting to be slaughtered. Belinda is vicious and, knowing all we've learned about her past, she's capable of anything. I hate feeling like we might be blindsided. I don't like feeling this vulnerable."

Hugging him tightly, Alexis allowed herself to lean on him, the two holding each other up for support. She rested her face against his chest. "Neither do I, but I trust you have my back like I have yours. Belinda will not get the best of us."

Marcel was silent for a good long while. He heard her words and everything in him wanted to believe that she was right. But, truth be told, he thought, underestimating Belinda could potentially end them all. And that wasn't a risk he was willing to take.

That next afternoon when Cash barged into their home, Marcel and Alexis both knew something was wrong. Usually calm and even-keeled, Cash was wired on high, and that was never a good thing.

"What's wrong?" Alexis said as their friend paced back and forth in a tight line.

"Your stalker. Belinda Bradley. Belinda Lee. Belinda with nine other aliases is a straight-up psychopath."

The couple exchanged a quick look with each other.

"Maybe you should sit down and tell us what you know," Marcel said.

Cash shook her head. She continued to pace. "I was digging to see what I could come up with about this Mother Belinda and the daughter, Christiana. What I found is that Belinda Whatever-the-hell-her-name-is has been tied to multiple murders across seven different states. Nineteen, to be exact, and those are only the ones I know about. No one's ever tied them together because she disappears and changes her name before the bodies get cold."

Cash handed the legal-sized envelope she'd been holding to Marcel. "And just so we're clear, you can trust the information, but you don't know who gave it to you," she said definitively.

"He understands," Alexis said as she watched Marcel take a seat at their kitchen counter to review the documents Cash had given him.

Marcel flipped through page after page of police reports and crime scene photos. Cash had drawn them a timeline, connecting Belinda in each and every case. She'd been like a vulture picking off prey. Most of the commentary surmised that she'd been retaliating against people she'd felt had wronged her or her beloved son. Revenge killings. Serial murders.

Marcel suddenly realized that marriage to Prophet Amos had given her a place to hunt victims never tied directly to her. Or so she'd thought. Murders that Amos alone would be charged with. The Saints of the Moral Order had become her hunting ground, the Prophet the only one policing her actions, and he hadn't cared as long as he'd been able to do whatever he'd wanted. They were two of a kind, corrupt and evil, and it suddenly hurt his heart to know that so many had trusted and believed in them both. He slid the documents back into the envelope and resealed it.

Swiveling about in his seat, he looked from one woman to the other, both studying him intently. "Thank you," he said softly, meeting Cash's gaze.

She nodded her head in response. "I'm going to go hug that baby," she said, heading in the direction of the nursery.

Alexis gave her a smile. She turned back to Marcel, walking into his arms. When he hugged her, his body was stiff, tension flooding through his spirit. He didn't need to say what they both already knew. Belinda was coming for her.

* * *

Marcel wasn't surprised to discover that his first case, on his first day on his new job, was to search for Belinda Lee. He didn't bother to express his dismay to Captain Randolph. King knew how he felt, having heard him rant for hours at the most recent Martin family dinner. But his connection to the church and personal knowledge of Belinda was why the powers in charge thought he'd be best for the job. No one seemed bothered by his personal reasons for wanting the woman taken by any means necessary.

King sat in the police department's conference room with Marcel and Marcel's partner, another new detective named Allan Ford. Ford had been a decorated police officer in Shreveport, transferring to New Orleans when he'd passed the detective's exam. He stood well over six feet tall, with a slim build, wiry frame and a bald head. Large, dark eyes and a Tom Hardy beard and mustache complemented his alabaster complexion. The two men had hit it off immediately and Ford was as eager to get out in the field as Marcel was.

"The Martin family has hired a private security firm to keep an eye on the family," King was saying. "They understand that we have jurisdiction and are working in conjunction with the FBI. If either of you run into any problems with them, I want to know about it. Is that understood?"

"Yes, sir, boss," Ford said.

Marcel nodded his agreement.

"Whatever you need is yours. Just keep me in the loop," King said.

Marcel slid his sealed envelope across the table toward

King. "I was asked to share this with you. It's information that may help us with this case."

King shot him a look then picked up the mailer. He slid his thumb beneath the flap, breaking the seal. He peered inside, threw another look in Marcel's direction and then pulled the stack of papers from inside.

"What's up?" Ford questioned, curiosity seeping from his eyes.

"Well, it's not good," King said as he flipped through the documents and pass them one by one to the other man.

"Where did these come from?" Ford asked.

Marcel and King exchanged a look. Neither man said a word, not wanting to explain the complicated relationship they had with the employees of the Sorority Row Detective Agency.

Marcel simply shrugged his shoulders then changed the subject. "I hear congratulations are in order," he said, his smile wide. "Alexis is very excited for you and Lenore."

King grinned. "It was definitely a surprise, but I couldn't be happier."

Ford looked confused, his eyes darting from one to the other. "What did I miss?"

"My fiancée and I are expecting our first child," King said.

"Good for you," the other man replied. "Congratulations!"

"Do you have kids?" Marcel asked.

Ford shook his head. "My mother is still trying to find me a wife."

The men laughed.

"Good luck with that," Marcel said.

King moved onto his feet. "Make the world a safer place out there," he said. "Go find our serial killer."

The Pines Village neighborhood sat in the east end of New Orleans. One of the lowest lying areas in the city, it had been significantly devastated during Hurricane Katrina. With one local park, several churches and significant commercial and industrial developments, it had managed to rejuvenate itself as a small percentage of families who'd lost their homes had returned to the area.

Marcel and Ford knocked at the door of Mrs. Hattie Jeffries. Marcel had been warned that she was a friend of the Martin family's and had only granted him access as a favor to Claudia Martin. But it wasn't Mama Hattie they were interested in speaking with. It was her new foster child, Christiana Lee, Belinda's daughter.

The elderly woman who snatched open the door was clearly not interested in the interruption. Her personality was as robust as her thick figure. She moved unsteadily on legs that looked like tree trunks and the housecoat she wore was a tad tight around her midsection.

The home was a shrine to everything Mama Hattie loved. The walls were lined with photos of family and friends in dollar-store frames. Magazines were stacked on polished wood tables. The furniture was old and well worn, and the abundance of clutter was meticulously organized. The curtains were open and the space was surprisingly light and airy.

"I don't like strangers bothering my girl," Mrs. Jeffries said to Marcel after he'd introduced himself and his partner.

Marcel nodded. "I appreciate you permitting us to speak

with Christiana. I assure you it won't take long and she's in no trouble."

"I know she ain't in no trouble! The girl just got here! She's been a good girl since that first day. Hasn't given me an ounce of trouble!" The old woman's head bobbed emphatically. "Goes to school, comes home, helps out. She's been a blessing to me since I lost my grandbaby."

Marcel smiled. King had shared that one of his biggest cases was the disappearance of Mrs. Jeffries's granddaughter. Months earlier, Michael-Lynn Jeffries had been found hanging in a local swamp. There had been a connection to members of the Saints of the Moral Order, putting them squarely on law enforcement radar. It had not gone unnoticed that multiple young women bearing the same tattoo as Alexis had been murdered.

The old woman pointed them toward the back of the house. "Her door is on the right. It's time for my stories, so y'all don't take too long."

As the duo maneuvered along the narrow hallway, past the bathroom, to the bedroom on the right, Ford bent to whisper into Marcel's ear. "Stories?"

Marcel chuckled. "The only remaining soap operas still on television. *The Young and the Restless*, I think, and *General Hospital*."

He paused to knock on the bedroom door and waited until Christiana invited them inside. Her face lit up at the sight of him, welcoming his familiar face.

"Elder Marcel!" She'd been playing on a desktop computer and stopped to jump to her feet.

"Please, I'm not an Elder. Just call me Marcel."

"Aren't you the new Prophet?" she asked, the question brimming with curiosity.

Marcel shook his head. "I'm no longer affiliated with the church."

Christiana actually looked disappointed. "That's too bad," she said, "I think you would have been a really good Prophet. I might have come back if you had been chosen."

He took a deep breath. "Christiana, this is my partner, Detective Ford. We need to ask you some questions about Belinda."

Christiana shrugged, her expression painted with indifference. "The Moral Mother could drop dead for all I care."

"Have you seen her since you left?"

Christiana shook her head. "No. And I don't want to. I doubt she'll even come look for me. Mama Hattie is my mother now."

"Do you know where we might find her?"

"No, Elder. I would think she's wherever the Prophet is."

"Prophet Amos is in prison, awaiting trial."

"That's where Belinda should be. She's evil, you know. They both are."

Marcel took a deep breath. "Christiana, do you know Mark and Leslie Gooding? Are those names familiar to you?"

A pained expression crossed the young woman's face. She appeared to be searching her memories for something familiar. "I've heard the names before. But I can't say that I know who they are."

"Your mother mentioned them to you?"

Christiana shook her head. "No. She and Prophet were

arguing and one of them said the names. But this was years ago. Before we came here to New Orleans."

Marcel glanced down at the file in his hand. "How about Wendy Duncan? Do you know who she is?"

"She was a member of the flock, I think. She and my brother were supposed to marry but then she left the church. They never saw her again."

Ford interjected. "Your brother was Stefan Guidry, is that correct?

The girl nodded. "Half-brother actually. Same mother, different fathers, for all that's worth."

"What can you tell me about your brother?" Marcel asked.

"Nothing really. He was never around when I was coming up. I wasn't even born when he started with the Moral Order and was Prophet. I mostly heard stories about him from my mother. I can't even tell you what he looks like."

"What kind of stories?" Marcel asked.

"How he was her golden child. How he had a vision to save us sinners. But then he disappeared and that made her crazy! Personally, I think he left to get away from her. She believes someone is holding him hostage against his will, which is why he hasn't come back or tried to contact her. The Prophet just lies that he was traveling, doing missionary work for the Lord. They couldn't have anyone thinking he would abandon the church. Which is funny because, when he was in charge of the church, she could have cared less."

Marcel nodded. "I've spoken with your social worker, and I know they told you that Belinda is not your biological mother."

Christiana nodded her head. "They did. Some man from the FBI came to talk to me, too, and he said they would do everything they could to figure out who my real family is."

"We all will," Marcel added. "I just have one more question. Can you think of any place Belinda might be hiding? Or again, where you think we might be able to find her? It's very important that we track her down."

He watched as Christiana pondered the question, clearly giving serious consideration to her answer.

She finally shook her head.

"I honestly don't know," she said. "But please be careful. As long as she's running loose, no one is safe."

Chapter 23

Alexis's sister Sophie was doing what Sophie did best. She'd been dragging her and Sabine from one baby store to another, determined to purchase every pink outfit for Sabine that she could find.

"She's going to be a fashionista. There's no time like the present to get her started."

"She will never wear half the clothes you are buying," Alexis replied. "You're wasting good money."

"It's Daddy's money so I wouldn't worry. When I told him we were going shopping for Sabine, he gave me his platinum credit card."

"Even more reason why we need to put all of this back."

"You are no fun," Sophie said, feigning a pout. "It's a good thing you have your auntie Sophie!" She leaned down to peer into the stroller, putting her face close to Sabine's. She kissed the little girl's cheek and Sabine giggled with glee.

"Because we all need one crazy relative in the family," Alexis chimed.

"Ha...ha...ha...!" Sophie went back to searching the racks for pretty dresses. She suddenly bubbled with excitement as if she'd had a moment of clarity. "You two should do matching mother-daughter outfits!" She waved her hand at the saleswoman. "Excuse me! Do you have matching mother-daughter outfits?" Sophie questioned as she grabbed the baby stroller and pushed Sabine off toward the checkout counter.

Alexis shook her head. Despite her reservations, Sophie had convinced her to get out of the house for a few hours. They were shopping at a baby shop called Zuka-Baby, the location apparently at the top of Sophie's must-check-them-out list.

Outside, a security team was keeping watch over the store and everyone coming and going from it. As far as Alexis was concerned, it would take an act of nature for Belinda to get anywhere near them. Leaving Sophie to her own devices, Alexis made her way over to the other side of the store where the children's books were shelved. She had no concern for Sabine's fashion choices but was determined that her baby girl would be well read.

She had only just begun to pull titles from the shelf to drop into her basket when she felt someone standing beside her. Tilting her head to see, her eyes widened in surprise.

Felicia smiled as she tossed a quick glance over her shoulder. Strapped to her chest was the baby boy named Marcus, his eyes wide with wonder. It was in that very moment that Alexis noticed the resemblance between the two. She gasped.

"Marcus is *your* baby," she said, unable to hide the shock in her tone.

"He is," Felicia said softly. "And because of you and what you did, I was able to be reunited with him."

"I can't believe I didn't realize that until just now."

"That's because he wasn't the baby you were there to focus on. I see things have worked out for you and the Elder?" She nodded in Sabine's direction.

"We are making it work."

"I'm happy for you."

"What happened that day?" Alexis questioned. "Out in the swamp when you were chasing after Belinda? I remember seeing you with Marcel's gun."

Felicia chuckled. "Sorry about that. But I wasn't sure what would happen when we left. I needed some security."

"Why were you shooting at her?"

"She was really trying to kill you. I saw her hit you with that rock, and before she could swing a second time, I started firing and chasing after her."

Alexis closed her eyes. The memories suddenly flooded her mind and her heart had begun to race with anxiety. She remembered the blow to the back of her skull. She remembered falling forward, stunned and dizzy. She remembered Belinda's voice above her, the woman cursing her very existence. It suddenly dawned on her just how close to death she had been. Because she remembered Belinda blaming her for Prophet Symmetry's disappearance and her daughter running away.

You took my children and now I'm going to take yours, Belinda had shouted over the gust of wind blowing with a vengeance. *Your mother will suffer like I have!*

And Alexis remembered Felicia running past her, shouting that it was going to be all right.

"Why did you do it?" Alexis asked. "Why did you risk your life to save me?"

Felicia took a deep breath. "I'm a lot of things, but

mostly, I'm a survivor. I will do whatever I have to do to take care of myself and my son. But I'm not evil. You were fighting for your family, and I saw that. Marcel was why I was able to work in the nursery and because he made it possible for me to be close to my son, I had to tell him about Sabine and keep him close to his daughter. Had I become the Elder's wife, I would have pushed for a vote against Amos to unseat him and make Marcel the Prophet. I knew once he was seated, we could reunite all the babies and change things."

A tear rolled across Alexis's cheek. She wiped at it with the back of her hand as Felicia continued.

"Belinda killed my husband, Marcus's father. His name was Lawyer. John Lawyer. John was a devout follower. I'd been in and out of jail for petty crimes when we met. John convinced me to change my ways and follow him. When I became pregnant, we were both so excited. But John discovered they were selling the babies and he threatened to expose their operation. Belinda killed him and she threw his body in the swamp to the gators. They told me he'd left, but I was there that night. Hiding. I saw what happened. After that, I pretended to be a good sister and I followed the rules, waiting for the first opportunity to get both of us out of there. Then you came along, and…well…you know the rest."

"Have you given a statement to the FBI?"

"I told them I didn't know anything, if that's what you're asking."

"But they need to know about your husband and the circumstances of his death!"

Felicia shook her head. "Sorry. No can do! I saw too

much, and I've also seen how the Prophet and Belinda twist things to make it everyone else's fault. That's not a risk I'm willing to take. Marcus needs me and I need him. My baby is my priority, like Sabine is yours."

"I really wish you'd reconsider," Alexis persisted. "Your testimony could be invaluable."

Felicia shook her head. "Sorry."

"How'd you know I'd be here?" Alexis questioned.

"I didn't. I actually came to shop for Marcus when I saw you. He and I are staying with John's parents until I can get on my feet."

Reaching into her handbag, Alexis pulled out a business card and wrote a number across the back. She passed the card to Felicia. "Call. There's a ton of help for the women who were displaced."

"Thank you."

"I owe you. I won't ever forget what you did for me. And for Marcel and Sabine."

Felicia turned to leave, hesitating for a split second. "Be careful, Alexis," she said. "Belinda hated you. I don't know why, but from the moment you arrived, she was hell-bent on destroying you. That night you were attacked wasn't an accident. That you survived with only a black eye, made her even angrier. She never lets things go. Getting even is a mantra for her. I have no doubt that the minute she thinks she can get to you, she's coming for revenge."

"Thanks for the warning," Alexis said.

Felicia smiled. "When things quiet down, maybe we can do playdates with the kids? Of course, that's if Belinda hasn't turned you into fish food between now and then. I'm sure I can learn a lot about this mommy business from you."

"It's a date!" Alexis said, laughing. She waved goodbye and Felicia waved back at her.

Minutes later, she moved to the front of the store where Sophie was arranging to have all her selections for Sabine delivered to their home.

"I saw you making new friends back there. Is everything okay?" Sophie asked.

Alexis nodded. "Actually," she replied, "I was catching up with an old friend."

Winding down after a long day together had become a regularly scheduled event for Marcel and Alexis. They'd had dinner and dessert, and had given Sabine her bath before putting her down for the night. When the little girl finally slept, the two spent time catching up with each other.

Marcel sat at the end of the sofa. Alexis lay across the sofa, her legs extended and her size sevens in his lap as he gently massaged her feet. She was relaxed, her eyes closed, thinking about her encounter with Felicia. Something the woman had said kept vibrating on repeat through her mind... *The minute she thinks she can get to you, she's coming for revenge.* She suddenly sat upright, pulling her toes from Marcel's touch.

"I know how you can catch Belinda," she said.

His eyes narrowed as he looked at her curiously. "Was my foot massage that bad?" he asked, looking befuddled. "I'm trying to get you to relax and you're thinking about Belinda."

"Weren't you thinking about Belinda?"

"I was, but I was trying not to let it show."

She chuckled. "Clearly, neither of us was doing a good job."

"So, what's your idea? How do I catch Belinda?"

"We bait her!"

Marcel paused, his eyes blinking rapidly as he absorbed the comment. For the first few seconds, he wasn't certain he'd understood what she was saying. And then it hit him like a sledgehammer against a concrete wall.

"You're really asking me to purposely put you in danger? Did you fall down and bump your head today and not tell me?"

"No, I did not bump my head. Think about it. Belinda is all about vengeance and she wants to exact revenge against me for Symmetry not returning to her, and also for Christiana leaving her. She needs to blame someone, and I drew the short straw. If we give her an opportunity to come for me, she will. She won't be able to help herself. You'll be able to apprehend her then."

Marcel threw up his hands. "You can't be serious. That's way too dangerous."

"I'm very serious. And I need you to get on board with the idea so you can put a plan in place. I need to trust that you'll be right there to protect me when it goes down."

"This is not going to happen, Alexis."

"It has to, Marcel. It's the only way we will ever be able to have a normal life without always looking over our shoulder worrying about where she is and when she might show up. We can't live with a security detail following us forever. That's already gotten old and it's not how I want us to raise Sabine."

Marcel sighed. "Let me sleep on it. I'll discuss it with King in the morning and see what we come up with. Until then, please don't do anything rash."

"What could I do?"

"Promise me, Alexis." His tone was stern and commanding.

Alexis smiled. She held out her hands and then crossed her fingers. She slowly slid them behind her back. Marcel shook his head at her, his eyes rolling skyward.

"I promise!" she said.

Marcel sat in the captain's office, the two men sharing their morning coffee. He'd had a long night and was beginning to feel like the day might be even longer.

"That woman has my stomach in a tight knot. I don't know what she might be planning to do. I do know she won't do what I ask of her."

King laughed. "Welcome to my world!"

Marcel drew a large hand across his face. His head waved from side to side. "And what really irks me is that her idea's not half bad. But if I know her, she'll go rogue before we can put safety measures in place. Obedience is not her forte."

"Brother, do you hear yourself? Obedience! What woman are you involved with?"

"Don't ever tell her I said it, but there are a few things the Moral Order got right."

"Obedience being one of them?"

"Look, it's extreme, but what's wrong with a wife being submissive to her husband?"

"I'll let Claudia answer that question for you. How do you want our mother-in-love to reply? With two fists or with one?"

Marcel laughed. "Definitely don't tell them I said anything." He huffed out a heavy sigh. "I just don't want Alexis taking any unnecessary risk. I have a responsibility and duty to protect her. I love her. I want to keep her safe."

"Then I'd delete the words 'obedience' and 'submissive' from your vocabulary and any other misogynistic thoughts that crazy cult was preaching. Because I don't want to see *you* get hurt," King said with a hearty chuckle. He leaned forward, folding his hands together atop his desk. "Look. Off the record, it is a good idea. So, partner with the woman and work with her. You two can do this and have it work, and you'll have an entire team supporting you."

"So, you think I'm worrying for nothing."

"No. I think you have every right to worry. But you control the narrative. "Don't let Belinda, or Alexis, think they have the upper hand."

Marcel nodded as he gave the comment some thought. He reached across the desk for the phone.

"Who are you calling?" King asked.

Marcel smiled. "Josiah Martin."

Chapter 24

Alexis stood in the doorway of her home and waved as her parents whisked Sabine into the car. Josiah had insisted on taking the baby to lunch with them, wanting to show her off to their friends. She'd been invited, as well, but figured she'd let them go about their afternoon without her. Sabine was in good hands, and she trusted the baby would be safe.

As she closed the front door, she noted the black sedan parked across the street and the other resting down at the corner. She would not have been surprised if one of the agents was perched in a tree in her backyard. Her father had balked when she'd asked him to pull off his security team. She hadn't told him why and didn't think Marcel had either, but her father had been adamant that he had no intentions of releasing them from their responsibilities until *he* was certain no one from the Moral Order was a potential threat.

It had only been a week since suggesting she be bait for Marcel to capture Belinda. Marcel was still considering her idea, believing that they had plenty of time to act. The FBI had reported spotting Belinda in Texas near what was left of the ministry there. They dismissed the concerns that she might be coming for Alexis, promising to let them know if things changed with Belinda's location or if she was sighted elsewhere.

Baby-free for a few hours, Alexis had made plans to visit Christiana to catch up with her. She'd gotten a glowing report about the young woman's progress and thought she'd surprise her with a shopping spree. She also thought that if law enforcement was wrong about Belinda and she was lurking near, seeing Alexis with her daughter might push her to make a mistake and show herself.

Either way, Alexis reasoned, she would be more than ready to protect herself and those around her. If Belinda wanted a fight, Alexis would give her one. She double-checked the magazine on her gun and secured it in the holster beneath her blazer.

Law enforcement had been tracking Belinda for two straight days. Despite police efforts to apprehend her, she'd slipped out of their grasp twice. Marcel knew that given ample opportunity, it would only be a matter of time before she played her hand, and then he would play his. He had also predicted Alexis would take the first chance she could find to get in the game, determined to best them both. He would steal her thunder and apologize to her later, he thought, once Belinda was no longer a threat.

The surveillance van he and Detective Ford occupied was equipped with state-of-the-art gear that included high-resolution cameras, sensors, communication systems and recording devices. Two officers were manning the cameras and the van's interior had begun to smell like stale corn chips and grape soda. One of them had managed to buy a dinner plate of oxtails, peas and rice, and macaroni and cheese that also scented the small space. The close quarters were not forgiving.

Belinda had been located days earlier, standing outside of their home behind the massive oak tree in their neighbor's front yard. Josiah's team had picked up her trail and had been on her ever since. She had utilized her underground contacts to maneuver her way around town without being caught and, just like Marcel had suspected, the right lie in the wrong ear had put her right where the New Orleans Police Department wanted her.

"The suspect is moving into the building," one of the officers announced.

Marcel shifted his focus to the cameras, watching as Belinda entered through the front doors of the Hotel Monteleone on Royal Street. The extraordinary Hotel Monteleone was a New Orleans treasure with a rich, decadent history. It had been the stomping grounds for a lengthy list of distinguished Southern authors that included the likes of Ernest Hemingway, Anne Rice and John Grisham. It was also home to Josiah Martin.

Alexis's father had been drawn to the property for its Truman Capote connection, the American author of *Breakfast at Tiffany's* and *In Cold Blood*, a favorite of his. He'd been living in its penthouse suite since vacating the family house after his divorce. Most recently, Claudia had been frequenting Josiah's temporary home more often.

Marcel watched as Belinda sauntered through the hotel lobby as if she belonged there. Undercover agents with the police department and the FBI had been situated throughout the lobby, posing as desk clerks and hotel staff.

Marcel reached for a microphone. "Everyone stay calm,"

he commanded. "Our suspect is moving toward the elevators. Do not… I repeat…do not approach her. I don't want to see her spooked."

Belinda paused to have a conversation with one of the women from housekeeping. The two stood beside a large grandfather clock that sat room-center. He watched as she seemed to stare at it, drawn to the extraordinary detail in the olive ash burl overlays and decorative carved appliqué. It was a stunning piece of furniture and Belinda reached out her hand to drag it along the clock's front edge. When she did, the two women laughed as if they were old friends.

"Let's go get our killer," Marcel said to his partner.

Ford nodded. "Ready when you are!"

Jumping from the van, the two men hurried across the street and into the hotel lobby.

Marcel paused as one of the officers was feeding him intel through his earpiece "Our suspect is in the stairwell. I repeat…the suspect has entered the stairwell." Certain Belinda was headed to the penthouse floor, he and Ford raced to the bank of elevators, planning to be waiting for her when she arrived.

Alexis was on the phone with her sister Lenore. The two women had been gossiping together for a good half hour, Alexis catching up on Lenore's pregnancy woes.

"I'm retaining so much water, it's ridiculous! My feet look like puffed pastry spilling out of my shoes. And I'm relegated to flats. I can't even begin to imagine trying to slip on a high heel."

"What's your doctor say?" Alexis asked.

"That this is normal. That although each pregnancy is

different, that it's normal for the woman going through it. Personally, I don't agree, but he insists that it'll get better."

"What's Mom say?"

"She's put me on a cucumber and green juice regimen. Apparently, cucumber contain electrolytes that will help regulate my blood pressure levels. They're also a natural diuretic and will reduce my sodium levels so that my body can maintain fluid balance. At least that's what Mom says."

"I'd be the first to say Mom knows best."

"Maybe, but I'm starting to think I should have gone the movie star route and hired a surrogate. This is for the birds!"

Alexis laughed. "Maybe, but I can't wait to find out for myself."

"Are you and Marcel thinking about another baby already?"

"I am. I haven't discussed it with him yet, but I want our kids to be close in age. No more than two, maybe three, years between them."

"How many kids are we talking?"

"I think three is a good number."

"I used to think that, too, then I got pregnant. Now I'm reevaluating my options."

The sisters laughed. Lenore suddenly went quiet, the gesture so abrupt that it threw Alexis off balance.

"What's wrong?" she asked. "Are you okay?"

Lenore hushed her and the two paused, both listening. For what, only Lenore seemed to know. "Where are you?" Lenore suddenly asked.

"Down here in Pines Village, sitting in my car. I just

dropped Christiana back home to her foster mother. What's going on?"

"Something is going down at Dad's hotel. I'm heading in that direction."

"Something like what?" Alexis asked, a wave of anxiety sweeping over her.

"Police activity. I had turned on King's police scanner and it just came over the radio."

Alexis started the engine to her car. "I'll meet you there," she said as she hit the gas and pulled her vehicle into traffic.

The conveyor doors opened directly into Josiah's penthouse home. Ford stepped out first, sweeping left and then right. Marcel was close on his heels, the two clearing the way until they came to the dining area with the floor-to-ceiling windows that looked out over the city.

Inside, Josiah sat at the dining room table, looking completely perturbed. A firearm rested on a China dinner plate in front of him, and there was a half-full glass of whiskey beside it. Belinda stood beside him, a revolver pointed at the back of his head. She was ranting and his disinterest was painted all over his expression.

"Drop your weapon!" Marcel shouted.

Belinda bristled, clearly caught off guard. She took a visible breath, her chest rising and then falling. Her eyes darted back and forth as she strategized her exit.

"I will kill him," she snapped. "You drop your weapon!"

"That's not going to happen, Belinda. You're surrounded."

She laughed, a demonic chortle that sounded like nails against a chalkboard. "Elder Marcel," she said, spitting his name as if it was bitter against her tongue.

"That's *Detective* Broussard."

"I knew it was you. I knew it the whole time. But my dear Prophet trusted you."

"He didn't trust you, though, did he? He knew what you were capable of and how far you'd go to protect yourself."

She scoffed. "He knew nothing but what I wanted him to know."

"It's over, Belinda. You don't need to do this. Give yourself up and I'd be willing to put in a good word for you."

She mocked him. "You'd do that for me? Awww…isn't that sweet of you! You do know you'll never be the Prophet now, right? You betrayed the entire congregation. They will never seat you after this."

"I'm not interested in leading your cult. You can have it. Your leadership has turned out to be nothing more than a congregation of liars, cheats, con artists and killers."

She laughed again, her hand dropping ever so slightly beneath the weight of the firearm she held.

"Why are you here?" Marcel asked, his brow lifted curiously.

"This man and his demon spawn killed my son. I'm not going to let them get away with that. I plan to make this whole damn family pay. Including you. Then I plan to take that sweet baby away and raise her as my own. Or I may slit her throat, too, and make you watch!"

"Well, that's never going to happen," Marcel said snidely. "Not as long as I'm alive."

"I can grant that wish for you," Belinda replied. She suddenly aimed her gun at Marcel.

"I'm going to make them pay for what they did," she screamed, pointing the gun back at Josiah.

"What did he do?" Ford suddenly asked, interjecting as

he took a short step forward. He and Marcel exchanged a look, both moving cautiously.

The question seemed to startle her as she shifted her weapon back and forth between the three of them.

"It's okay," Ford said. "I want to know."

"My son was the original Prophet! He built this legacy, and many have tried to steal it from him. I should have been there, but I wasn't. I should have been there to support him when that Jezebel he's married to tried to take him down. But I was weak! And then he was gone. And I've done nothing but try to make sure the Moral Order is standing when he comes back to take his rightful place. And then I hear that he's dead. Killed by Alexis Martin and her father. He was a God and they tried to destroy him! So, I must destroy them. I must avenge him for what they did!"

A voice in his ear and in Ford's whispered softly, "We have her in our sights. We can take the shot. I repeat…we can take the shot on your command."

"You don't want to do this," Ford said. "You need to tell your son's story. People need to know what they did. If you harm him, the message will be lost in the commentary about what you did. They will shut the truth down. Drop your gun and let me help you."

His comment seemed to give her pause. Belinda seemed to waver for the briefest moment and then she shook her head. "No," she snarled venomously, and then she pulled the trigger.

Uniformed police officers had cordoned off the entrance into the hotel. When Alexis arrived, Lenore was pacing back and forth, arguing with one of them. As she crossed the street toward her sister, King exited the building and moved swiftly in her sister's direction. They both reached Lenore at the same time.

He snapped, clearly not happy with either one of them. "Why are you two here?"

"I heard it on the police scanner. What's going on?" Lenore asked, ignoring his tone.

"We're executing an arrest. Neither one of you has any jurisdiction here and you both need to go home!"

"Does this have to do with Belinda Lee?" Alexis asked.

"Where's our father?"

"Are Mom and the baby upstairs?"

"I heard it was a hostage situation. Who's the hostage?

"Where's Marcel? Is he here?"

The two were suddenly peppering the captain with questions faster than he could answer them. He shook his head. "Go home! Now! And that's an order!"

Both women bristled as he turned abruptly. He was walking away when his radio chattered, information echoing over the airwaves.

"Shots fired! Shots fired!"

King picked up the pace, running back toward the front door. Then someone else shouted into their radio, his words resounding through all their speakers.

"Officer down! I repeat...we have an officer down!"

Chapter 25

The fatal shooting of serial killer, Belinda Bradley Lee, made national news. Amos Lee had been indicted on fifty-six felony charges and what remained of his church was now under the leadership of a new Prophet. A documentary about the Saints of the Moral Order had been green-lit by a major movie studio; and Marcel and Alexis had both been tapped for the speaker circuit to talk about the culture and tactics of religious cult environments.

All of the Martin family stood off to the side watching as the City of New Orleans honored Detectives Marcel Broussard and Allan Ford for their service and Josiah Martin for his bravery. Detective Ford was still recovering from the gunshot that had wounded his shoulder, his arm stabilized in a sling.

Josiah Martin, who had walked away unscathed after being held hostage by the crazed maniac, stood with his first grandchild in his arms. Sabine Martin Broussard clutched him tightly around his neck, her eyes wide as she took in all the hoopla. Her bright smile was infectious and filled them all with hope and joy.

Thinking back to the day fear had held her in a viselike grip, Alexis felt her heart begin to pound and her stomach lurch. News of a police officer being shot had rippled through the fellow officers and the crowd that had been gathered. She and Lenore had both raced for the door but had been stopped from entering the hotel's lobby. Despite their best efforts to get inside, the officers followed King's command and barred them from entry.

She and Lenore had stood for almost an hour, waiting for news. They'd watched EMS being hustled up to the top floor and had repeatedly dialed their father's phone, their mother's and Marcel's. Not getting an immediate answer had driven them both crazy.

Claudia and Sabine were the first allowed out of the building. Both cleared by emergency personnel, Claudia had called for transportation back to Alexis's house. At the sight of her mother and daughter, tears streamed down Alexis's cheeks. She hugged her baby, kissing the child's cheeks, and her mother hugged her and Lenore, squeezing them both tightly.

"What happened?" Alexis questioned when she finally caught her breath.

Claudia shook her head. "I don't know. We were enjoying a sip of brandy and a great conversation when Josiah had to take an emergency phone call. The next thing I knew, he ordered me to take the baby to the safe room and secure ourselves inside. When he finally let us out, there was a dead woman on the dining room floor and most of NOPD crawling around your father's penthouse."

"Daddy's okay?" Lenore asked. "You said he let you two out?"

"Your father is fine. Annoyed, but that's normal for your

father. When I left, he was still giving a statement to the police."

"Did you see Marcel, Mommy? Was he there?"

Claudia shrugged. "I didn't see him, dear. But that doesn't mean he wasn't there. It only means that when they took us out the back door, I missed him. Have you called him?"

"He hasn't called me back and I'm worried. They said a police officer was shot."

"Do not panic," her mother admonished. "Not until you know something for certain."

Alexis released a soft sigh.

Claudia said, "We should go to your house to wait."

"I'm not leaving," Alexis proclaimed.

"Yes, you are. Your daughter needs to be put down for a nap. She also needs a warm bottle and her mother's lap. Lenore needs to put her feet up. Her ankles look like an elephant's, which is not a good sign. I need to make her some juice. So, let's go. Now. We'll order up some food for dinner."

"My car's parked over there," Alexis said.

"Leave it. Your father ordered a car for me and the baby. We'll all ride together. We can pick up our cars later. When things quiet down."

Things quieting down had taken some time. Back at Alexis's house, they'd turned on the television to the local station for the breaking news. It was almost midnight before the men finally found their way home.

When Marcel walked through the front door, Alexis threw herself into his arms, determined to never again let him go. Lenore clung to King, and even their parents had hugged, intent on finding balance with each other. They were a teary lot, everyone crying easily as hugs and kisses rounded the room.

Alexis suddenly punched Marcel in the chest, a wave of rage flooding through her. "You scared me to death. Don't ever do that again!"

Marcel chuckled as he rubbed his pectoral muscle, the rising bruise actually hurting. He leaned to kiss her cheek. "I'm sorry about that. Everything happened so fast."

Taking a seat, he detailed all that had happened, filling in the gaps of information that would be new to them. It had been his partner who'd been shot by Belinda, and Marcel who'd delivered Belinda her final blow.

"You used my father as bait!"

Josiah interjected. "He did not use me. I volunteered. And congratulations! I heard it was your idea. You should be proud to know that Marcel executed your plan brilliantly."

Alexis glared in Marcel's direction, icy daggers shooting from her eyes.

He laughed. "You knew I was not going to allow you to put yourself in danger. That wasn't ever going to happen."

"That wasn't your decision to make, Marcel!"

"Baby, I love your confidence and I have the highest respect for your abilities. What you've been able to accomplish is inspiring. But as the father to your future children and the man who will soon be your husband until death do we part, I will make whatever decision that ensures I get to wake up to your beautiful face every day for the rest of my life."

Josiah chuckled. "That's a good man you have there.

Both of you girls are blessed. You're mad right now and that's okay. You'll get over it."

Claudia cut in. "Or stay mad! Do what works for you. Just do it in love."

King lifted his glass. "To love," he said as he kissed Lenore, a large palm resting against her pregnant belly.

"To love," Marcel echoed.

Alexis rolled her eyes, the faintest smile pulling at her lips. Now, standing here with her mother and sisters, as the two men she loved most in her life would surely be honored, it was nothing but love that filled her heart, and the room.

Staring down into Sabine's crib, Alexis marveled at what a wonderful little girl she was. She'd been a joy all day and the family had loved her nonstop. Excitement was building for the new baby that would come and she and Marcel couldn't wait for Sabine to have a cousin who'd be more like a sibling. Alexis could already imagine the love they would have for each other.

Marcel peeked into the room, a smile lifting the exhaustion in his face. "Everything okay?"

She nodded, throwing him a quick glance over her shoulder. "I just like to watch her sleep," she whispered loudly.

He pointed down the hallway. "I'm going to head to bed. It's been a long day."

"It has. It's not often that you get the key to the city and a whole day named after you."

"I'm special!" he said teasingly.

She giggled. "That you are, Marcel Broussard!"

He smiled. "Come to bed, Mrs. Broussard, so I can love on you until you fall asleep."

Following behind him, Alexis slid beneath the freshly washed sheets, easing her body against his as he wrapped himself around her. Marcel planted damp kisses across her neck, trailing his tongue along the line of her ear and suckling at the lobe until her breathing became labored.

"I want more babies, Marcel," Alexis muttered.

He chuckled softly. "I will give you more babies."

"We'll need to find a church or go back to my mother's."

"We'll find a church," he gasped as she grabbed him with both hands.

Marcel palmed her breasts and pulling at her nipples until they were hardened buds beneath his fingers.

"I love you," Alexis moaned. "I love you, Marcel!"

Marcel lifted himself above her, peering down into her face as they locked eyes. "I love you, Alexis. I've always loved you!"

He kissed and teased her, his own excitement lengthening every muscle in his body. His hands were warm, his touch enigmatic, and when they were both damp with perspiration and eager for more, Marcel slowly found his way home as he captured her mouth beneath his own.

* * * * *